THE Madonna OF Las Vegas

Also by Gregory Blake Smith

The Devil in the Dooryard
The Divine Comedy of John Venner

Gregory Blake Smith

a novel

THE Madonna OF Las Vegas

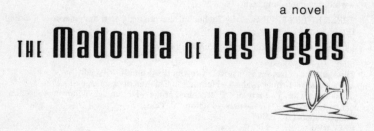

THREE RIVERS PRESS
NEW YORK

Published in the United States by Three Rivers Press, an imprint of the Crown
Publishing Group, a division of Random House, Inc., New York.

www.crownpublishing.com

THREE RIVERS PRESS and the Tugboat design are registered trademarks of Random
House, Inc.

Library of Congress Cataloging-in-Publication Data

Smith, Gregory Blake.
The Madonna of Las Vegas : a novel / Gregory Blake Smith.— 1st ed.
1. Waitresses—Crimes against—Fiction. 2. Children of criminals—Fiction.
3. Las Vegas (Nev.)—Fiction. 4. Organized crime—Fiction. 5. Widowers—Fiction.
6. Artists—Fiction. 7. Casinos—Fiction. I. Title.
PS3569.M5356P67 2005
813'.54—dc22
2004020974

ISBN 1-4000-8186-6

Printed in the United States of America

DESIGN BY ELINA D. NUDELMAN

10 9 8 7 6 5 4 3 2 1

First Edition

For Laura

Contents

Chapter 1

Standing in line to Jump Off the Golden Gate Bridge

At the party, he began setting women's hair on fire. It seemed the right thing to do, what with the Apocalypse on CNN and all. The first time had been an accident, the ash from his cigarette somehow finding its way into the office receptionist's hairdo, but now he was on his third victim, sitting in the office lounge with his arm draped over the back of a couch, nonchalantly nosing his Kool's smoldering tip into the black hair of one of the waitresses from the Golden Calf. He would quit in a minute, he told himself. He would pack up his moral destitution and go home.

His name was Cosmo Dust and that wasn't the worst of it. Just what the worst of it was changed from day to day, though a good candidate right now was the Apocalypse taking place on television: the FBI up in rural Montana with their klieg lights and armored vehicles, the Kenotic Messiah reading from Revelation to the eager cameras. On another day he might have listed his living in Las Vegas, painting the ceiling of the Sistine Chapel for a living, being 5'5" tall . . . oh! he could go on, but here he caught a whiff of acrid smoke from the cocktail waitress and rose to go before anyone else noticed.

Outside, he was dismayed to see he would have to stand in line to jump off the Golden Gate Bridge.

This was his friend Crazy Herman's millennium party, held at the offices of Amalgamated Illusion, the commercial art company responsible for most of the turrets and sphinxes of post-Sinatra Las Vegas. The offices were housed in the snack bar of the old Las Vegas Drive-In, the drive-in grounds themselves filled now with Quonset huts and windowless staging buildings in which every imaginable casino set could be designed and built. Cosmo himself had worked on the Versailles Palace and the Tomb of Tutankhamen. But just that morning, halfway through a three-year job of reproducing the Sistine ceiling for the Golden Calf casino, he had quit. Quit, just like that—*snap!*—right in the middle of painting God separating light from darkness, thirty feet above the blackjack tables. He had climbed down from the scaffolding, called Sane Herman with the news, and then driven headlong out into the desert where, with Lake Mead shimmering like a mirage in the distance, he had sat in his van in a state of euphoria eating CheezTwists and drinking Jolt and imagining a new life for himself. But the euphoria had slipped away, no new life had presented itself, and now he was back, not back on the job, exactly, but back at Amalgamated Illusion, setting people's hair on fire and looking for ways to destroy himself.

In the line ahead of him he could see his assistants, Betty and Veronica, holding hands and awaiting their turn. They liked to jump together.

Oh, there were moods when he wished it were the *real*

Golden Gate Bridge and not just Amalgamated Illusion's virtual-reality version, the Realer-Than-Real Experience that had won Crazy Herman fame and a bit of fortune from the virtually disaffected. Cosmo had already experienced it any number of times. You paid your five dollars and put on the usual VR gear—headpiece, gloves, body stocking—and at the press of a trigger found yourself standing on the edge of the Golden Gate Bridge, the sounds of traffic behind you, the cool ocean breeze at your back, ahead of you the lights of Alcatraz, and Berkeley in the deep distance if it wasn't virtually hazy. If you turned to your left you saw the dusky greenery of Marin, to your right the Presidio, and behind you the terrifying Pacific. But just look down and boy! it was enough to give you virtual vertigo: the gray, moonlit waters of San Francisco Bay; the tiny waves (you were up two hundred feet, after all); behind you a car horn; maybe a randomly generated voice crying "Jump!" At UCLA someone had done a statistical study of how many people actually did jump, bent their knees and lifted themselves off the floor and felt the sudden whoosh of air, the spinning lights, the uprushing water—3.8 seconds; that's how long it took a human body to travel the distance in both real and virtual worlds—and then . . . well, instead of the impact (how could you wire the body for *that*?), Crazy Herman's kicker: Just as the water grew life-sized, there was a flash of brilliant light and then the theatrical segue to one of twenty-four randomly selected afterlives ranging from the Buddha's Fire Sermon to the Hallelujah Chorus to a brief soliloquy by one of the suicides in the Eighth Circle. Among teenagers it was a status thing to collect all twenty-four.

Cosmo, an hour earlier, had awakened in the emergency

room with Dr. Kildare peering down at him and whispering that everything was going to be all right, son.

Thing was, it hadn't been so bad at first—painting the Sistine ceiling, that is. Cathy had been alive still, and he had been able to keep his real life separate from the fakery of the Strip: Cosmo Dust imitating Charlton Heston imitating Michelangelo Buonarroti. He'd even become something of a celebrity, the artist up on the scaffolding a must-see at the Golden Calf, with the local TV stations running stories about him, even a two-page article in *People*. But that was okay because at night, while their heads lay on adjacent pillows, he would talk to Cathy about the technical difficulties, about his battle to do the job right—real fresco, not some bogus Las Vegas job, but real lime, wet plaster, powdered pigments. There were the Tuscan colors to be matched, the laying out of full-sized cartoons. And then there was the problem of the building code requiring a sprinkler system in the ceiling: How to camouflage the sprinkler heads in the folds of God's robes, in the Ignuti, in the architectural trompe l'oeil? He had gone about it with a good heart, from time to time calling his old mentor back at the Restoration Lab of the Boston Museum of Fine Arts for advice and maybe to gloat a little. After all, how many modern-day artists got to paint the Sistine ceiling? Even if it was in a Las Vegas casino.

But then Cathy had died, and what had before been something that had kept him in touch with his old life, something he had shared with his art-professor wife, had turned into mockery, into caricature and plagiarism. Left on his own he began to feel overwhelmed by Las Vegas, blighted by the inauthenticity, driving up and down the

Strip because he didn't know what else to do in his grief, crippled by the sight of the Roman Forum, the Chrysler Building, the Eiffel Tower, for Pete's sake. The final straw was when the Venetian opened and he found replicated next door to the Golden Calf all the beauties of Venice: the Piazza San Marco and the Campanile, the Rialto Bridge and the Torre dell'Orologio with its carved Madonna and Child, its field of blue enamel and golden stars.

Because they had met in Venice, five years ago, before Cathy got her job at UNLV, when she was still a graduate student and Cosmo was on a one-year internship at the San Gregorio Restoration Lab. He had been part of a team working on the stabilization of the Carpaccio *Annunciation*, every morning crossing the Grand Canal at the Gritti *traghetto*, putting on his smock and dust mask and working on the rotting, fungus-blackened canvas. He had been at it for five months, loving it, making plans to stay in Venice by hook or by crook once his internship ran out, when one day a pretty American showed up with the Superintendency's permission to see the painting. She was doing her dissertation on altarpieces of the Veneto, she said, and had a theory about Carpaccio's. Had he ever noticed a higher than usual proportion of *terra verte* in the skin tones? She was dressed in turquoise capri pants, a scrunchy bending her hair into a jaunty question mark. Fifteen minutes of talking to her in front of the painting, with the magical city on the other side of the walls urging him on, and he'd asked her to marry him. She'd laughed, taken it as a compliment—no, no marriage, how about an afternoon coffee instead?—and had put her hand in his as they made their way through the slanting alleys.

Oh, how the memory of those days smote him! He had followed her from church to church, palace to palace, all over the watery city, so full of love it had leaked out his fingers and toes. In the evenings, as the sun began to set and the *calli* grew blue with shadow, they would close their guidebooks and let themselves get lost, turning down whatever alley presented itself, delighting in the ancient stonework and the tiny piazzas that opened unexpectedly. From time to time they would happen upon a niche with a salt-scarred Madonna and Child, and she would cross herself at the sight of it, the naïveté of the gesture making his heart ache. She was, he was amazed to learn, a practicing Catholic. A believer—no kidding—in Christ, redemption, miracles. Nor was faith the only quaint thing about her. She'd gotten her hands on an 1880s Baedeker and was putting herself through what she called her Henry James Grand Tour, reading the high-toned Victorian prose in front of the Ca' d'Oro or the Ponte dei Pugni and trying to see the city as Isabel Archer or Milly Theale would have seen it. An Irish girl from Boston with sea-green eyes and a love of Renaissance madonnas, annunciations, heartbreaking pietàs—he went to bed at night thinking of her, woke in the morning thinking of her, spent all day in front of Carpaccio's Virgin thinking of her.

When in the evenings after their explorations they settled on an outdoor restaurant—it was November, beginning to get cold, but they always took a table in the campo—they would share a liter of wine and some carpaccio, talk over the day's discoveries with their fingers and faces growing cold. He would tell her about his childhood, growing up in depressed Pawtucket, Rhode Island, his father gone, his mother a bookkeeper for a Bradlees department store. He'd get the teary violins in tune, trying to play for sympathy. When he couldn't help himself anymore he would reach under the table and with a drunken smile caress her leg. She would call him *buster* then—watch it, buster!—and tally all the reasons why she couldn't marry him. There was her dissertation to finish and a teaching job to be found. In a few months he would have no means of support. He was shorter than she was—yes, he *was*—and she was Irish, she was Catholic, marriage to her meant family.

For Cosmo it had never *ever* been like that before. He nearly fainted the first time he'd dared, while they kissed in an out-of-the-way *calle*, to lift his hand to her breast. She had let out a little gasp at his touch. And then she had held him and kissed him so deeply that for a moment—he couldn't explain it otherwise; there were a couple of missing seconds, an inexplicable haze—he actually *had* fainted.

He wanted to go on record as saying that he was not really shorter than she was, but almost. He looked—oh, the indignity of it!—like one of the Beach Boys, the little one, Cathy said, with the too-big guitar and the sandy hair swept across his forehead. But he had a sweet face that girls had always liked. And he was kind. And he loved things. And one day, standing in the cool, stony air of San Giorgio Maggiore, gazing at the Tintorettos, Cathy Cullen had told him she'd written home to let her parents know she was getting married.

It was (he realized, still standing there waiting to jump off the Golden Gate Bridge) the most beautiful time of his life. A time when the universe added up, when the planets moved in perfect circles around the Earth, around Venice, around the still point of Cathy's shining face. It took him three months to convert to Catholicism. When the priest catechized him, he answered that yes he believed that God was good and loving, that life was sacred, and when he was asked if he knew who his savior was, without missing a beat he said, "Cathy Cullen," and at the priest's abrupt alarm, smiled, touched the man lightly on the sleeve of his soutane, and said, *"Certo, padrone,"* his savior was Christ, Jesus Christ.

They were married the Saturday after Easter in Santa Maria dei Miracoli, Cathy's mother crying in the front pew, her father wondering how this runt had snared his brainy, lovely, talented daughter. For their honeymoon they rented a car and drove to Treviso, then up through the Dolomites and over to Rapallo. They stopped at every church along the way, checking out the altarpieces, the side chapels with their rude frescoes and marble saints.

In one tiny village, he remembered, they'd happened upon a lovely Mother and Child in terra-cotta, a mere fifteen or sixteen inches high. A second earlier, it seemed, the Madonna had been holding the infant Jesus in one of the usual Renaissance postures, but the sculptor had caught them at the moment when the naked baby had kicked himself upright, his fat feet wobbling on the Madonna's thighs, and on his laughing face—this was the stunner—the sheer joy of life at the brim. The Virgin had him by the waist, steadying him, smiling down at him with love and disapproval. Neither of them had ever seen anything like it. There was something reckless in the infant's posture, his arms thrown out in promiscuous embrace, his knees and elbows chunky with Renaissance fat, rude health, his curly hair in need of a haircut—

"It's beautiful," Cosmo had whispered.

"Isn't it?" Cathy shivered beside him.

They gazed at his little boy's penis.

"I could almost believe in a Christ like that," Cosmo had said. He went from penis to belly button to laughing lips.

"You *do* believe," came Cathy's quiet voice. And for a moment, with her lovely self beside him, and the baby laughing at him, and the wet, still air of the ancient church all around, he almost had.

Afterward they'd walked along a country road, a bottle of wine under Cosmo's arm, a loaf of peasant bread in a bag banging against Cathy's knee. On either side of them were olive groves, the contorted limbs climbing toward the sky and then clutching back at the earth as if they couldn't make up their minds which way to grow. They turned off the road, followed the double rut of a tractor path. The birds were singing. The sky was bright. There were wildflowers, and the smell of manure from somewhere. Halfway through their lunch, sitting under an olive tree, he couldn't help himself, started to paw his wife, who was trying to manage a too-big sandwich. And a year later, back in Boston, the sandwich would again be too big, spilling out the edges while Cathy laughed and tried to push a springstung Cosmo off her. It had been Easter then, too: the same birds, the same bright sky. They had even just come from church, from Mass if not from the Virgin with the Laughing Child, and on the way home had gotten sandwiches and dawdled in the fens. It didn't take long for them to see how they were repeating their honeymoon, the rank odor of the earth coming alive, the toy-store colors of tulips and crocuses like punch lines to a joke somebody somewhere was telling. They had picked their way through the rows of bikinied coeds forcing tans on the lawn and turned into the Victory Gardens, gone down this path, that path, whichever way would take them away from people, from the Red Sox fans streaming toward Fenway Park. When they found a dry plot, hidden from the path, they sat down to eat their sandwiches. By now they knew exactly what they were doing, what moment they were re-creating, and Cathy had hardly eaten two bites before Cosmo was on top of her. They laughed and kissed and groped and said "Don't!" to each other. He'd had to wrestle her underpants off. She'd undone his zipper. "Only for a minute," he'd whispered in her ear. Because, she'd whispered back (they had said the same thing in the olive grove), they hadn't engaged any of the devices forbidden by her—sometimes she'd admit—idiotic church, had they?

"Have we, darling?" her voice thundered in his ear.

Oh, their spring-cold faces buried in each other's hair! The cries from Fenway reflecting off the distant buildings as if the world were cheering them on! For the minute or two of that clumsy, reckless union, it seemed the universe reverted to an old self: not just their honeymoon come back to them, or even their time in Venice, but as if the world possessed again the clarity of classical mechanics—perfect motion, perfect love. When he tried to ease himself out Cathy wouldn't let him, kept her hand pressed behind him until he had finished. He had rolled off of her and seen overhead, against the blue blue of Heaven, a biplane trailing a banner urging Miracle-Gro on the fans at Fenway.

"Remember . . ." she had whispered beside him, out of breath, and didn't finish. Because of course he did remember: the pruned limbs of the olive trees against the Italian sky, the smell of manure, the sound of a child somewhere distant in the breeze that drifted across their half-naked bodies.

Afterward they had walked arm in arm—dazed with happiness, Cosmo's sperm already swimming toward Cathy's egg—back toward their apartment. Neither of them heard the servomotors turning, the tumblers falling.

Chapter 2

Among the love Assassins

This time when he virtually died, a triathlete who just happened to be passing by pulled him out of San Francisco Bay, administered mouth-to-mouth resuscitation, gave him a pep talk, smiled the smile of the healthy and fit, and sent him on his way.

Which was out of the booth and straight into Betty's and Veronica's arms.

"Cosmo!" they squealed. "Darling! We've been *waiting* for you!" And they each took him by an arm. This was their shtick: They liked to baby him, pet him—he was so little, so *cute*—never mind that he was technically their boss.

"Positively *waiting*!" Veronica cooed, and pecked him on the cheek. "You *have* to tell us what happened."

Their names weren't really Betty and Veronica, but they had the look: Betty with the blonde ponytail and the retro bobby socks; Veronica with that sleek, blue-black hair rolled under at the shoulders. He'd hired them straight out of the Rhode Island School of Design back when the Sistine ceiling was still in its planning stages. They had helped him grid out the ceiling, draw the cartoons. After Cathy died it had been they who had packed up her things and—so he wouldn't have to do it himself, they'd said (and oh! how his heart had broken when he came home and found her closet empty!)—trucked them over to the Clark County Women's Shelter.

"I quit," he said in answer to Veronica's questions. They were steering him toward the old drive-in snack bar where Crazy Herman had his lab.

"We know," Betty said. She put her hand on his chest, stroked him. They were lesbians, so this sort of thing was somehow okay. "But why?" And she sighed, laying her head on his shoulder: "Dear Cosmo!"

"You know why," he answered.

"Because it isn't the *real* Sistine ceiling?" Betty asked. This was an old conversation of theirs. "Because it's fake?"

"Just because it's fake," Veronica said, scolding him with a little tap on the shoulder, "doesn't mean it isn't real." And before he could object they hustled him into Crazy Herman's lab.

"Just in time," Crazy Herman called without looking up from his computer monitor. Cosmo stopped just inside the doorway and looked around. The room was full of love assassins. He tried to back out but Betty and Veronica steered him into an aluminum lawn chair, stood over him like handmaidens.

"We're getting new quarries," Betty whispered. "Round three. So pay attention." She patted him on the shoulder. "It'll be good for you," she said. He slumped where he sat.

This was his world now. Not just painting the Sistine ceiling in the Nevada desert (though he had quit that, hadn't he?), but cartoon lesbians and love assassins and Crazy Herman and his alternative self, Sane Herman. And there was Polly Sensoria, like a frieze along the walls: Polly Sensoria, the virtual-sex goddess Crazy Herman had spent the last five years trying to breathe binary life into, gazing down at him from a variety of concupiscent printouts.

Crazy Herman read a name off his computer screen, then the vital details: "Blackjack dealer, one-point-two Degree of Difficulty."

One of the assassins made a note of it. Cosmo groaned and tried to get up, but Betty leaned a heavy hand on his shoulder.

For a year now Love Assassin had been all the rage at Amalgamated Illusion. Cosmo had signed on a couple of months ago in a fit of despair and had regretted it ever since. Unlike regular Assassin, where quarries were simply hunted down with a water pistol and shot, in Love Assassin you had to seduce them first—real human beings, you understand—all the time keeping your intentions secret, your pistol hidden, with points being awarded for first base, second base, etc. What with the Degree of Difficulty based on beauty of face and figure, and the trickery, the counterfeit, the meanness—it was not a game for someone who was trying to hold on to the memory of his wife's turquoise capri pants.

"Forget it," he said now, when Crazy Herman started the program for the selection of Cosmo's next quarry. "I told you I'm not playing anymore."

"You have to play," said Veronica on his right. "It's life."

"I quit."

"You can't quit," said Betty on his left. "It's life. You have to play."

He gazed up at Polly Sensoria along the walls, her luscious lips, her teasing eyes, her breasts tipped up as if to ask what did he think he was doing quitting the Sistine ceiling like that, not to mention killing himself every chance he got, and being such a retard at Love Assassin, and looking like one of the Beach Boys. . . .

"I'm not alive," he said. "I just jumped off the Golden Gate Bridge. I'm dead."

"VR suicide doesn't count."

"Neither does VR love."

"Wow," put in Crazy Herman, dragging his fingers through his dreadlocks. He was staring at Cosmo's quarry on the screen.

"What?"

"Great quarry," he said, peering at Cosmo with a touch of awe. He angled the monitor so that Veronica could read it.

"Abort. Ignore," Cosmo said. "No one else is supposed to know."

"Six-point-eight Degree of Difficulty," Veronica read from the screen.

"Whoa! Time out!" one of the love assassins called. "Even Pharaoh was only four-point-six." Pharaoh being one of the ambience employees of the Golden Calf, a bodybuilder paid to dress up in a loincloth and breastplate and mix with the casino crowd.

"Six-point-eight?" Cosmo repeated. Crazy Herman turned the monitor his way. He saw there his own name, his handicap, his current score (zero), and, down below, his new quarry: Annunciata D'Angelo.

"Dudes and dudettes," Tim Munjoy, one of the programmers, said. "Six-point-eight Degree of Difficulty can mean only one biomorphic form at the Golden Calf: the Pope's daughter. Do you factor me?"

"Sure, tell everyone," said Cosmo.

"That chick is seriously hypostatic," he said. He spoke too loudly, from what Crazy Herman called Walkman's Disease, though in Munjoy's case it was a tiny TV w/earphones that he carried with him everywhere. "Have you scoped out those two goons she's always with?" he asked.

"Bodyguards," someone said.

"Strictly ambience," Veronica pooh-poohed.

"Ambience or no," Munjoy said, "she comes up to me the other day, and the goons are with her. I'm working on the Red Sea, running a last-minute check." He pulled the TV earphones out of his ears, as if for the moment real life was where you wanted to be. "I've got CNN on, the sound up, and she comes waltzing down the center of the Red Sea all Lana Turner–looking and stops in front of my TV and watches the Kenotic Nutcase for a minute, and then she goes something about how 'If only it were true.' 'If only what were true?' I go. 'If only it were true he was the Messiah,' she goes. At which point I look at the two goons to make sure they see that I am not abusing this nice girl in any way whatsoever. 'Then it'd all be over,' she says, and she makes a gesture at"—and he turned to the other assassins like maybe they saw, too—"at something, I don't know." And he hurried back inside his earphones.

The rest of them exchanged looks.

"At what?" someone said. "What did she—"

"What?" Munjoy said, plucking off the earphones.

"What did she mean?"

"I don't know, dude. That's the problem with reality, as I've indicated before. You can't rewind." And he snapped the earphones back on.

"Paging Cosmo Dust!" someone called suddenly from the hall. They all turned toward the door, where the office receptionist poked her head in. Cosmo thought her hair still smelled a bit scorched. "Somebody here to see you, Cosmo." And she made a face as if to warn him.

And then they were there. The goons, the bodyguards, the ambience employees, standing in the doorway with their dark suits, expensive shoes, graying temples. It was as though the computers Crazy Herman was using to create Polly Sensoria had been listening in on their talk and had wired together the Pope's daughter's bodyguards just for fun, for practice. To show off.

"Mr. Dust?" one of the goons said to the room in general. At the sound of his name, Cosmo had the thought that it was all a put-on—the Pope's daughter, the 6.8 Degree of Difficulty—all the love assassins' idea. But when he looked across at them—Munjoy with his mouth open, Crazy Herman with potato chip crumbs in his beard—something about their surprise made him feel a little ill.

"Maestro!" the goon said, recognizing Cosmo. At least the computer had enough taste not to give them sunglasses.

"What?" Cosmo managed to say. Munjoy recovered himself enough to pick up his little Sony and put it in front of his face. The other goon—he was a tad shorter, thicker—made a c'mon gesture with his fingers.

"What do you want?" Cosmo stalled.

"We want you should come with us," the taller one said; then, weirdly: "Out into the mythic landscape."

"Yeah, the mythic landscape," the shorter, tougher one said. "There's someone wants to see you."

At which Cosmo looked to the others for help, but each of them was stunned still, as if they'd jumped off the virtual Golden Gate Bridge only to discover that some hiccup in the program had made it the real bridge, with real water rushing up at their real bodies.

"What mythic landscape?"

They laughed, spread their palms like, who was this retard? then gestured at themselves, their hair, their tans, their sharp suits like, wasn't it evident?

"A piece of work," the taller one said; and then, like he was conjuring a world: "The Copa Room. The Chapel of Love. De Sotos cruisin' up and down the Strip."

"Now let's move," the shorter one finished, and—Jesus!—there it was: the suit elbowed aside to reveal a shoulder holster with a gun, a heater, a rod!

"*Benny,*" the taller one chided. He held up the palm of his hand as if to slow things down. "Forgive him," he said, and he made a chivalrous smile around the room. "What my brother means to illustrate"—and he indicated with a meditative gesture their different selves—"is that what we have here is text and commentary." He paused, as if to let that sink in.

"Cut the crap, Marco."

"Symbol and referent. The thing itself and its parody."

And he smiled, pleased with himself, surveyed the room to see if he'd smoothed things over.

"Throw the shrimp in the car and let's move. Mr. D'Angelo's waiting."

At which the taller one—Marco—inclined his head toward the shrimp, pursed his lips as if he wished he could go on, but—alas!—Benny had a point.

"Can't it wait?" Cosmo squeaked.

"It can never wait."

And with a bow he moved back so that the doorway was clear.

Chapter 3

The Pope of Las Vegas

It was a black Packard he was escorted to, a 1930s job with long sloping fenders, running boards, those massive headlights. "Nothing so nostalgic as the sinister," Marco remarked as he opened the rear door for Cosmo. They pulled out onto the Strip—Benny driving, Marco riding shotgun—headed north, past the Luxor and the Tropicana. There were mythic landscapes everywhere Cosmo looked: the skyline of New York, the Eiffel Tower, the pastel shades of Mandalay Bay. When he and Cathy had first arrived he had expected to find the Vegas of the fifties, if not bighearted whores and the ghost of Liberace, at least donut shops in the shape of coffee cups, burger joints ditto. But his first day in Vegas had been the day the Sands had been imploded, and he had watched with a dim apprehension that something important was happening. This was the *Sands* (Cathy had read to him from her *Discover America* guide), built in the early fifties by Joey Stacher and the Jersey mob, the casino where Sinatra and Sammy Davis, Jr., and the rest of the Rat Pack had hung out. Cosmo had had the thought that the whole thing should have been put in the Smithsonian. But it came down while the crowd sipped champagne in plastic glasses and the TV cameras got videotape, and for a month afterward the rubble was carted off by the truckload to who knew what landfill in the desert. In its metaphorical place there grew the architectural orgasms of what Crazy Herman called post-Sinatra Vegas: the Tinkerbell towers of Excalibur, the Piazza San Marco of the Venetian, Ellis Island here, the Eiffel Tower there, and now, thanks at least in part to Cosmo Dust, the retro-heresies of the Golden Calf.

Into which Benny turned.

They sped past the rows of Lebanon cypresses, glided to a stop under the massive porte cochere. The doorman came toward Cosmo with a smile for the VIP, opening the door for him and calling him "sir." There was the usual fanfare of pharaoh music coming out of woofers in the carport pylons, tweeters in the shrubbery. It was Marco who accompanied him inside, while Benny disappeared with the Packard into the underground garage. In the foyer rotunda they passed the famous statue of the golden calf, gilded with real gold leaf back in the fifties but now a bit antiquated in scale and conception. Inside the casino proper there was green felt everywhere, gold mirrors on the ceiling, chandeliers, mosaics, a hanging garden along one wall. The cocktail waitresses were dressed in Cleopatra chic, brass bangles framing their foreheads, a scarab descending into the cleavage of each. For the blackjack dealers it was your basic Mediterranean slave costume—short white chiton showing off the legs of male and female alike. Though it was nothing new to Cosmo—his job had familiarized him with the casino over the last year—the raw, massive, playful, blinding bad taste of it all was a little reassuring.

In the elevator, Marco took out a key and inserted it in a keyhole where the button for the fourteenth floor—the penthouse—should have been. The door closed and the elevator rose. Cosmo wanted to ask, among other things, how they had known where he was, but decided instead to keep his mouth shut. When the elevator stopped they stepped into a foyer enclosed on one side by a bulletproof glass door, behind which a ritzy hallway receded. At the sight of Marco, a guard stood up and buzzed the door open. When Cosmo made to step through, he said, "Excuse me, sir," and—no kidding—frisked him just like in the movies.

"Sorry," said Marco with a smile, "a residuum from earlier days."

They went about halfway down the hall, stopped at a door, knocked, and after a respectful pause, entered. What Cosmo expected was the eighty-something-year-old person of Angelo D'Angelo—white-haired, white-suited, manicured feminine fingers: the Pope of Las Vegas—seated, let's say, behind a mahogany desk on which the only object was an elegant lamp with a green baize shade, lamplight breaking across the furniture in moral chiaroscuro, concertina on the soundtrack, etc., etc. What he got was an empty room, lavishly appointed but empty all the same, and Marco telling him to wait here, please, and then disappearing behind a door at the far end of the room.

So he waited. The room had that penthouse look—wet bar with gold-plated plumbing, upholstery everywhere, one wall nothing but window and breathtaking view of the

Strip, all lit up in fairy-tale fashion. When Marco reappeared, he made a simple motion with his hand for Cosmo to come. There was the faint sound of something, a voice—no, a TV—coming from the other room. Cosmo crossed the plush carpet to where Marco was standing, looked to him for help or direction, and then stepped into the next room.

And there he was: the Pope of Las Vegas, sitting propped up in bed and watching CNN on a TV off to one side. He didn't look at Cosmo when he came in, but maybe that was just Mafia stagecraft. The room was identical to the one they'd just come through, with the same stupendous view, but this one a bedroom with the smell of ointments, medications, old age. The bed itself had the look of having been salvaged from some sixties renovation of the honeymoon suite: plush leatherette headboard, Louis XV canopy—Cosmo was enough of a pro in the bogus design line to wonder whose work it was. Over in the corner, like a hallucination, sat a priest reading a book.

"Is this him?" the Pope said when a commercial came on. He turned his head with some difficulty and eyed Marco. "Dust?"

"Right," said Cosmo.

"My painter?" he said, still to Marco.

"It's him, Mr. D'Angelo."

"The son of a bitch," he muttered, as if Cosmo weren't right there in front of him. He spoke with one half of his face, the other half drooping downward. In the light off the Strip, Cosmo thought he could see a rivulet of drool down the dead side of the man's chin.

"Mr. D'Angelo is upset," Marco said, crossing to the bed and adjusting the pillows behind the Pope. "He's heard you've decided to stop painting the Sistine ceiling. He's hoping that that's just a rumor."

"No rumor," said Cosmo.

"He's hoping," Marco repeated, straightening up and enunciating the words carefully, "that that's just a rumor."

On the TV the Norelco Santa Claus was skiing down a Claymation mountain on his rotary-head skis. He had skied down the same mountain every Christmas since Cosmo was a boy. You would think the Apocalypse would change a thing or two.

"No rumor," Cosmo repeated and shoved his hands in his pockets. "I quit." Behind him there came the sound of a door opening. After a moment Benny came into the room. He gave Cosmo the stink-eye.

"You can't quit," Marco said—hadn't Cosmo been told that once already tonight? "On the other hand," he went on, "if you're just tired—Michelangelo himself found the work a terrible strain—then perhaps we can help. What's your salary?" And when Cosmo didn't respond: "Whatever it is, we'll have Amalgamated Illusion double it, and when you're done, as a bonus, we'll send you on a vacation. Venice, Florence, the real Sistine Chapel. Wherever you want, our treat."

Still he didn't answer. On the TV the Kenotic Messiah was calmly explicating the first seal.

"Or is there something else we can help with? Artist's block? Inauthentic identity?" And when Cosmo threw him a look of surprise: "Ah! Why didn't you say so? Take a page from our book and be thankful you got an identity to imitate. And not just *any* identity: Michelangelo!" And he placed his hand on his heart in awe. Cosmo gritted his teeth and gazed out the window at the Strip, at the Mirage's volcano erupting across the way—bogus lava, phony steam, fake catastrophe.

"Michelangelo . . ."

He turned to see the Pope leaning forward in bed, staring at him, his eyes hollow, his mouth sagging. Somewhere underneath the melting skin, under the waste of age and stroke, was the man who had known Meyer Lansky, who had taken over the Golden Calf from Izzy Englestein in the fifties and run it with muscle and cunning, who had remade it in the age of corporate casinos into a mythic Mafia hangout, the sole family-owned casino left on the Strip. *Get Connected*, as the ads put it, Benny and Marco look-alikes on the posters, with sunglasses, dark suits, Sicilian tans.

"Michelangelo," the old man said again. He was patting the mattress for Cosmo to come sit beside him.

"What?" Cosmo said, not moving.

"Please," he began to say, but a fit of what looked like pantomime coughing gripped him. His chest seemed to collapse. Benny and Marco moved to him, helped him slip down until he lay flat, fussed over him until the silent coughing passed. He waved them off, turned his face away toward the wall. Cosmo, feeling a little sheepish, took a few solicitous steps toward the bed.

"I'm dying," the old man said to the wall. The skin on the side of his face looked translucent. Cosmo gazed away and saw—how had he not noticed before?—that over by the wet bar a little altar had been set up. Amid the gold-plated faucets and swan-necked tap he saw a crucifix, a statue of the Virgin Mary, and some candles.

"You got lots of life left, Mr. D'Angelo," came Benny's

voice from behind. The old man closed his eyes, waved the back of his hand listlessly in the air. Then he beckoned to Cosmo to come closer.

"You understand," the old man said to him.

Cosmo stood at his side, wondered what it was he understood.

"You understand loss."

And at that he felt himself drawing back. The fringe from the canopy touched the back of his head.

"Your wife," the old man said. He lifted his hand to his cheek, touched himself delicately, almost painfully, with his fingertips, and then looked past Cosmo. "It was him?" he managed to call to Benny and Marco. "Right?"

"It was him, Mr. D'Angelo."

On the TV the Kenotic Messiah was explaining the Greek word *kenosis*—empty, emptying, the empty.

"Your wife," the old man repeated. "Senseless. Horrible." He closed his eyes and shook his head from side to side. Cosmo twisted about where he stood, shot a look at the two men behind him like, what the hey?

"My own wife . . ." Again he made the godfatherly gesture, the back of his hand waving the empty air away, the pain, the absence. "The two of us, we understand."

Over in the corner, the priest had put down his book. In the half-light his soft eyes searched Cosmo's face. There seemed to be—strange trick of the light!—a smile on his face.

"I have to go," Cosmo muttered.

From under the covers the Pope reached out a hand, grabbed him by the wrist.

"My own wife," he said, "may Heaven forgive me, she

would have loved"—and he paused, caught his breath—"this ceiling. I know she looks down from Heaven." And he closed his eyes, some emotion having taken hold of him. A minute passed. "Your people," he said finally, and there came into his voice a phlegmy anger. "Amalgamated Illusion. They didn't want—" He had to stop, to shake his head to keep the coughing down.

"They didn't want to do it right," Marco took over. "The way Mrs. D'Angelo would have wanted it. They just wanted to put up a Sheetrock ceiling, paint it, pretend it was the Sistine ceiling. We had to insist."

"Yeah," said Benny, and he shot Cosmo a look of warning. "We insisted."

The Pope was nodding his head. "Real fresco," he managed to say. "Wet plaster. A real ceiling. A real Michelangelo." And he turned his yellow eyes on Cosmo. "You can't quit."

There was definitely a smile on the priest's face. It was not some trick of the light. He was smiling.

"My assistants," Cosmo said, "they can take over."

"The two lesbian broads?" said Benny. "Don't make me laugh!"

"Talented painters," he pressed on. "Graduates of the Rhode Island School of Design. They've been learning from me." And then, inspired: "After all, Michelangelo had his *garzoni.*"

"*Garzoni?*" said Benny. He looked around the room at some imaginary audience. "What's this crumb telling us?" He fixed his eyes on Cosmo. "You little shrimp, Michelangelo fired his *garzoni!* You think we don't know about the Sistine ceiling? Pope Julius? Who do you think you're dealing with?"

He took a threatening step forward. Marco had to hold out a restraining hand.

"Maestro . . . ," he said to Cosmo, musical, conciliatory. "*Now* we understand. Eh?" he said to Benny. He held the shorter man by the back of the neck, patted him on the belly. "Eh?" to the same imaginary audience. "The maestro understands better than we think. He knows his role. The difficult personality, right?" He nodded at Benny, made a this-guy's-okay gesture. "The *terribilità* Pope Julius complained of. On the job, off the job. Firing his helpers. Going off to Carrara to sulk. He understands." And then, to Cosmo: "Don't you, maestro?"

"No."

"He understands. He's giving us the Sistine Ceiling Experience. He's threatening to quit. He's a real Michelangelo."

The Pope was shaking his head, dismayed, depressed. "I expected humanity," he said under his breath. He let go of Cosmo's wrist. "Sympathy."

"He's a punk," said Benny.

"I expected him to understand."

"He *does* understand." This, from Marco, with a meaningful look. "Don't you, maestro?"

"His wife," the Pope repeated. "You said his wife was killed?"

"Never mind my wife," Cosmo muttered.

"I expected a man of feeling," the old man whispered painfully. He closed his eyes, drifting away. "Nothing but emptiness. Nothing but back talk."

And as if there'd been a signal Cosmo missed, Benny came forward and with unexpected grace sucker punched him so hard his gut seemed to explode. He dropped to his knees, curled over onto his side, and lay there hugging himself. Benny stood over him, his fists at his sides.

"Tomorrow morning," he said. "You're either up on that scaffolding, or you're dead in a Dumpster. Which is it going to be?"

Cosmo didn't answer, stared at the fibers in the carpet. The pain kept rippling through him, down his legs, his arms, out his fingers and toes.

"Doesn't have to be a Dumpster," Marco put in. "We got a variety of ways. We got the traditional. We got the mythic. We got ways that reference the culture. Ways that quote the historic."

"An ice pick through the ear is always good," Benny joined in.

Marco made an appreciative gesture. "Very classical."

"The lamp cord around the neck."

He tipped his head to one side in evaluation; then, dreamily: "Still . . . there's something about a bullet to the head." And he took a handgun from his shoulder holster, hefted it in his hand, appreciated it. "Simple. Elegant. What do you think, Michelangelo?"

"I don't care," Cosmo muttered into the carpet. He pulled his legs up under him, like a child.

"The gracefully classical? Or the edgy pathological?"

But before he could answer there came a groan from the bed.

"Mr. D'Angelo!" Benny cried.

The old man was fishing a hand through the air, his chest heaving, his eyes wild. When he caught hold of Benny's outstretched arm he held on to it as if he were drowning, then began to work his way out of bed. After a minute he managed to get to his feet, and then, with Benny's help, to shuffle around the foot of the bed toward the wet bar, where the little altar was. Cosmo stood up, his stomach still clenched, and looked to Marco for a sign, and then back at the old man as he lowered himself onto his knees before the wet bar.

"Hey," Benny was saying. The Pope's hand had just dropped from making some gesture. "He wants you."

"No," said Cosmo.

To which Benny jerked his thumb get-over-here. Cosmo threw a look at the priest—wasn't this his line?—and then went and stood at the kneeling man's side, waiting for the desperate grip that would urge him to his knees. But he was on the wrong side, the paralyzed side, so he crossed to the other side where, sure enough, the dying man's hand caught his wrist and pulled him down.

"Help me," came the whispered entreaty.

Cosmo stared straight ahead. Taiwan, Korea, Slovenia: Who manufactured madonnas nowadays?

"Michelangelo. Help me."

He gazed sideways at the ruined face, the transparent eyelids, lips the color of intestines. Forty years ago, how had it been? The Copa Room with a broad on each arm? Eisenhower in the White House and Sammy Davis, Jr., onstage, maybe a Havana cigar, the pulse of blood and passion and the story of Rubber Legs Larry to tell over and over?

"Holy Mother," the old man said. His voice was weak, entreating. "Beseech your Son to change this man's heart." He waited for his breath to return. "Help him finish this great work. Ah, Holy Mother! He's just a punk artist! But he's trying. He doesn't know anything, but he's trying."

Cosmo stared at the half-dead face beside him. When was the last time someone had prayed for him? he wondered. Had Cathy ever? In the privacy of her heart, or under the camouflage of Mass, had she ever gotten down on her knees and whispered to God about him?

For months after she died he had talked to her, muttering to himself in the casinos like a lunatic, eluding Betty and Veronica, Crazy Herman, and the others, sleeping in motel rooms because he couldn't bear to return to the apartment. And every morning—how the memory came back to him!—standing in the shower with the water beating on his head, unable to move, unable to lift the washcloth, to turn the shower off, to step back out into the world. Each day he had had to drive down the Strip to Amalgamated Illusion, and each day the sight of the Venetian coming to life where the Sands had once stood had been like a slow-motion horror: the beauties of Venice usurped one by one and erected in the Nevada desert. The Campanile, the Torre dell'Orologio, the winged lion of San Marco atop its column, the Rialto Bridge, where he and Cathy had given a tourist their camera to take a picture of them . . .

Damn his soul, but he could see them even now! Not in his mind's eye, but right out the window—*there!*—reflected in the mirrored façade of the Mirage across the way: the Piazza San Marco with its striped poles, gondolas, quatrefoils, and colored marble, his life with Cathy, his love, mocked and parodied in the middle of the Nevada desert. It made him, even now, sick, bitter, black inside.

He turned away, stared down at the dark carpet, closed his eyes. God help him, but he felt like weeping.

"Michelangelo . . ."

This was the world, then: parody, plagiarism, desecration.

". . . help me."

What a fool he had been to try to fight it!

"Holy Mother!" the old man whispered.

"Tomorrow morning," warned Benny.

Somewhere, inside him, there should have been Cathy's voice saying "no." But it was a world of Love Assassin, wasn't it? Of the Golden Gate Bridge. Of Polly Sensoria. Of Venice here in the American desert. Wasn't it?

Chapter 4

The Dark Gods

The next day, back up on the scaffolding, he was painting Satan in the wet plaster where God was supposed to be. He hadn't meant to do it, had resolved upon waking that morning to give the dying man what he wanted—was that not, in its own way, a gesture of sympathy?—but oh, a couple of bourbons while Betty and Veronica were preparing the plaster and now he couldn't help himself: Satan with big Renaissance muscles, *contrapposto* torso, stretching across the infinite reaches separating light from darkness. Off to the side, his assistants were sharing a cigarette, p.o.'ed about having to work the day before Christmas, not to mention about Satan.

"Cosmo, darling," Betty called to him, "let's not."

But he just sipped his bourbon, wet his brush, and while he worked on the devil's laughing lips, tortured himself with memories of Venice, of the Fenway, of the Laughing Child. And with the still-weird fact that for months after Cathy had died his phone had rung in the middle of the night, just one ring. In the stillness of the apartment, a sudden mad twitter, sometimes several nights running, sometimes with weeks in between. Every time he had lifted the receiver there had been nothing there, no dial tone, no voice, nothing but the feel of some empty presence at the other end of the line. He had told the police detective assigned to Cathy's case about it, and she had had the phone company look into it. There had been talk of telemetric glitches, echoes, shadows in the line: They could change his number if he liked. What he kept to himself was that he couldn't rid himself of two ideas. The first was that it was Him—oh, not Satan exactly, but some dark force, a cosmic imp, someone who had it in for Cosmo Dust, getting his kicks by calling him from somewhere outside the world. (He had been, he knew, a little out of his mind in those days.) The other was what kept him from changing his number: It was Cathy calling, Cathy from somewhere inhuman—inside the telephone line, caught in the relays, in the digital spectra—trying to reach him.

"Hey!" someone said. He startled and turned and saw one of the cocktail waitresses—he had a standing order for Wild Turkey—peering at him over the padded edge of the platform he was lying on. "Did you stick your cigarette in my hair the other night?"

He stared back at Satan overhead.

"I had to cut the burned spot out." And she stuffed her fingertips up under the black Cleopatra wig the Golden Calf made all the cocktail waitresses wear and tugged at the hair underneath. "It was really smelly."

"Yeah, that was me."

"Well, shoot!"

He started sketching a little assistant, a little dark god peering out from behind Satan. "I was just practicing."

"What? Being a creep?"

If he were going to do it right, paint his own personal dark god, he'd make him about four feet tall, give him horns and halos, both, the halos like wisps of luminous fog around the peaking horns. He'd stink, of course; maybe he'd have clumps of manure hanging from the shaggy hair on his hindquarters, but also manicured nails, well-groomed hooves, fresh breath, a cavity or two. What else?

"What else indeed?" the dark god said from behind Satan . . . But oh, no you don't, Cosmo thought and closed his eyes.

"I'm waiting," said the cocktail waitress. He kept his eyes closed, turned onto his side, and looked at her. CANDI, her name tag said.

"For what?"

"For what do you think? For an apology. You burned my hair!"

"I was drunk."

"You're drunk now."

"And *not* burning your hair," he said and reached over and took his bourbon from her tray. "Thanks."

"See?" she said and let her tray hang down at her side. "That's how things should go. You say thanks, I say you're welcome, and nobody gets their hair burned. Got it?"

"You're welcome," he said.

"It's a question of acting civilized. Otherwise, where would we be?"

"Where are we now?"

She screwed up her face. "Where we are," she enunciated carefully, "is alive. Civilized. Nobody's taking a gun out and shooting us just for the fun of it. There's no reason they shouldn't, but they don't."

He stared at her. Didn't she know?

"Nobody's shooting us?" he repeated.

"Right."

"Nobody's injecting cyanide in, say, candy at the local Jack-B-Nimble, even though they could. Is that your idea?"

"Right. Exactly."

He could tell by the open face, the hurt left there by something—love, life, the occasional trick—that she didn't know about Cathy. Where she was a year and a half ago when there were all the news reports, he didn't know. Where she was, for that matter, when people pointed him out when he crossed the casino floor, he didn't know, either—but this, this was genuine. He hoisted himself up on his elbow so his head was just inches from the Creation and smiled at her.

"I'll say thank you from now on," he said.

"Good," she answered, like maybe she believed him and maybe she didn't.

"And please. And you're welcome."

"That's the idea."

"Good manners are what the dark forces want from us," he said, tasting the idea. He looked to Satan and his helper for confirmation. "Could be. Why not?"

"And don't drink so much," she said.

"Okay. Starting tomorrow."

"And get rid of . . ." She wagged her index finger at the ceiling.

"Satan."

"Yeah, get rid of him. And the little guy behind him. It's not funny."

"Right. Thank you." And, unaccountably, he held out his hands for inspection like he used to do in kindergarten, palms up, palms down. But she misunderstood the gesture, put down her waitress tray, and grasped hold of his hands in a train-station farewell. She gave them a squeeze, then turned and started down the ladder, disappearing piece by piece: ankles, kneecaps, cleavage, collarbone. Then, with a final smile, face, head, hair. She kept her waitress tray poised the whole time.

"Degree of Difficulty somewhere in the negative numbers," Veronica called from her step stool. Betty was seated cross-legged on the scaffold below her. "Now let us scrape the plaster off while it's still wet. It's such a bitch when it dries."

"Haven't finished my dark god yet," he said.

"It's Christmas Eve, Cosmo. Come shoot craps with us."

"Gotta work," he said, and dismissed them with a wave of his brush. He stretched himself out flat under the vault of Heaven.

If there were a cosmic <<REWIND button, he'd aim his remote at that day in the Fenway and recall the precise instant when every particle in the universe had cried "Life!" and twenty-six-year-old Cosmo Dust and his wife Cathy had not yet said "No!" Rewind things just so he could do something, say something, zip his zipper up differently, so that the carom of his and Cathy's history would be altered by some few degrees, bringing them to a present that did not include Las Vegas and an abortion and a cyanide-laced

Easter egg and Cathy writhing on the living room couch, not to mention Michelangelo, Love Assassin, bourbon in the middle of the afternoon. Let some other present, some other world, take its place. Maybe he and Cathy in a quaint Cape Cod on the outskirts of Topeka, pink flamingos in the garden, Cosmo restoring a '63 Chevy Impala in the garage, and Cathy on a chaise lounge, pregnant with Baby No. 2. Heck, make it baby number three, four, five—

"Sorry, can't," said the dark god.

It was a curious thing, Cosmo thought, opening his eyes and turning to his other side, where the dark god squatted beside him on the platform, how the world mimics the forms in our heads. Because—wouldn't you know it—he had manure hanging from the hair on his hindquarters.

"It's what you wanted, isn't it?" said the dark god, a bit miffed. He consulted a clipboard. "Four feet tall, horns, halo, hooves, et cetera. I can change, if you like. Get a little more classical, a little less Hieronymous Bosch."

"Forget it."

"I do a good Goya."

"Forget it. Go away."

"Okay, but first, tell the audience about the abominable toddlers." And he pretended to hold a microphone out to Cosmo in his hoof, which was a hand now. Cosmo closed his eyes.

They came in his dreams—oversized babies, babies the size of linebackers, abominable toddlers with the lowering brow of the vengeful. They'd first appeared the very night of the day he had driven Cathy to the clinic and waited in the waiting room like a parody of an expectant father. They looked like accidents—the babies, he meant—like a malignant chromosome had moved them a link or two away from human. The dreams could take place anywhere, most horribly in the virid maze of the Fenway, but sometimes in the white hush of museums, on the broad water of the Grand Canal, and then for a year running in supermarkets, Cosmo wheeling a spavined cart through misted produce while a gigantic toddler trudged in pursuit, its face the color of pastry except for the angry red indentations around the temples. Overhead a fluorescent light flickered on and off. The babies followed him with menace, faith, hope, the neediness of the destroyed.

"We might," the dark god intoned in a scholarly voice, "at this point in our interrogation, our trial, our friendly chat, call to mind DANTE ALIGHIERI's concept of CONTRAPASSO."

"Get lost," said Cosmo, still with his eyes shut.

"It was the great Tuscan poet who developed the idea that the nature of one's punishment in the afterlife would be derived from the nature of one's sins in the earthly life. *Contra* meaning 'in return,' *passo* meaning 'suffering.' Thus, Count UGOLINO, famous for cannibalizing his sons, finds himself gnawing on an archbishop's brains in the IN-FERNO. Double-click on any of the hypertext entries for more information."

Oh, they had agonized over the decision, especially Catholic Cathy. She wanted kids—they both did—just not now, not yet. They were too young, too poor, too this, too that. There was Cathy's job at UNLV starting in the fall, the dissertation still not finished. They gestured at the ratty couch they were sitting on, at the empty space where a din-ing table should have been. Afterward, after they'd done it, they never talked of it again. They moved to Las Vegas to begin their new life, Cathy lecturing on Giotto to half-full classrooms and Cosmo helping to design the Tomb of Tutankhamen. More than once in their apartment on Paradise Road, as if in quiet acknowledgment of error, they had made love without protection, but it had never happened again.

"So?" said the dark god with a Yiddish accent. Cosmo opened his eyes. "You were expecting maybe a second miracle?"

He was wearing earlocks and a yarmulke now, a prayer shawl draped over his hairy shoulders. Cosmo drained his bourbon, turned on his side, and searched the floor below for some sign of Candi the cocktail waitress.

So was that it? he wondered. Had he gotten offered a miracle and turned it down, and now the universe had it in for him? This life of lost love, the mockery of mimicking the world's greatest artist: Was it a kind of penitential counterweight? And had he the other day upset the cosmic harmony by trying to put off the purgatorial flames, and so the dark forces—who knew, maybe they were the bright forces—had co-opted the Mafia to keep him engaged in his suffering?

"The Mafia," the dark god considered beside him. He ran a finger down his clipboard. "That was a decision made by our agents in the field."

Or was he just hopelessly in need of moral symmetry? Cosmo Dust jury-rigging a sin to match the suffering. All by way of preserving the security of moral cause and effect because guilt was an easier row to hoe than the blank of undeserved suffering.

Overhead, God stretched toward Adam; Adam stretched toward God. That was how it was. They never quite met.

"So what do I do?" he asked. The dark god seemed taken aback by the direct question. He morphed from imam to monk to maharishi.

"What do you do about what?"

"This," he said with a gesture at the ceiling above them, which somehow degenerated into including his own body. "The hurt in my heart."

"Oh, that," said the dark god.

"They killed my wife," he said, and for a second he thought he was going to burst out sobbing. "*You* did."

"Well . . . ," and he smiled apologetically.

"Look," Cosmo entreated, "just tell me if she's okay."

"She's not okay, kiddo. She's dead. She's a cosmic pixel on the face of the deep. She's zipping around at the speed of light."

And why the sudden vision of Cathy as a kind of quantum Tinkerbell should have been the thing that did him in, he didn't know, but he lost it, broke into sobs, a choking, drunken incontinence that he knew only too well though it'd been a couple of months since it'd happened to him last. She was *not*, of course, a pixel on the face of the deep; she was a rotting corpse two miles east of the city and oh! how the thought of that dear body decomposing could still drive him wild! It had been almost unbearable those first weeks—after the funeral, after her parents had come and gone, her friends, her colleagues from UNLV—the terrible loneliness of his Cathy under the ground. He had walked around the city in those days with a hatred so fierce he could have killed people just for breathing. For weeks he had tortured himself, looking for her, going from casino to casino, catching sight of her denim legs disappearing around a corner, her suede pumps under a blackjack table. In the shower every morning there was the sight of her shampoo bottle to be endured, at night her earrings where she'd left them on the nightstand. When Betty and Veronica and the rest of the love assassins had packed up her stuff and taken it to the Clark County Women's Shelter, he had tried calling the shelter to reclaim it. But they were wary at the sound of a male voice, had a policy about giving out the address over the phone. For days, weeks really, he couldn't rid himself of the feeling that there was a kind of salvific power in her clothes, in her scarves and her sweaters, and how—oh, how?—had he not found some way of getting them back?

"Are you all right?" said a voice next to him.

And now the dark gods were imitating her voice.

"Hey, you? Can I help?"

Somewhere inside the Laughing Child, a truth quark faked right and ran left.

Chapter 5

The Pope's Daughter

Somewhere in his swimming vision there was a woman. He had expected the cocktail waitress with another bourbon, but this was somehow Cathy, Cathy got up by the dark gods in one of her old sweaters, an off-the-shoulder, ooh-la-la sort of thing he remembered from some outing some other day in some other universe. He blinked his tears away while Cathy said, "You got it bad, huh?" in a voice that wasn't Cathy's, but wasn't quite the cocktail waitress's, either. He turned away, wiped his tears one last time. When he turned back, the sweater—along with the 6.8 Degree of Difficulty wearing it—was still there. He swung his legs over the edge of the platform, let them dangle there a moment while the world righted itself, and then lowered himself onto the scaffolding.

At the sight of his tear-streaked face the woman let out a low whistle. "Boy, they said you were a sad case."

As the universe would have it, she sort of looked not like Cathy, but like the cocktail waitress, Candi—same dark hair, same Cleopatra cut skimming along her jawbone. As to the sweater, after the first shock he tried to convince himself that he was just wobbly in the head, that it was only the same style, same knit, same slip of white collarbone dashing for cover.

"You can stop looking at my chest now," the Pope's daughter said. He looked up at her face, and then—damn his hide, he couldn't help it—down at her chest.

"I was looking at your sweater."

"Yeah, I'm sure."

He reached out, touched the ribbing on the cuff.

"Geez," she said and took a step back. "What's with the personal liberties? I don't even know you."

"I'm Cosmo Dust," he said. "Where'd you get the sweater?"

"What're you, retarded?"

"Drunk," he said, then: "Damned, doomed. Take your pick."

She drilled a quit-it frown at him and then, looking over the railing to where Benny leaned with his back against a craps table, made cuckoo circles around her ear, pointed at Cosmo.

Up close she wasn't quite the knockout she seemed from far away. Oh, sure, she had the high cheekbones, the gray eyes, the femme fatale look, but there was something a little crooked about her face, maybe the nose off-plumb, the eyebrows drizzling into her temples at imperfect angles.

"He's afraid of heights," she said with a little snicker, turning back. "Benny, I mean. That's how come I'm up here. Now if you'll quit with the weirdo act I'll give you some gum."

And she took a pack of Juicy Fruit out of her purse. He shook his head no. She shrugged, unwrapped a piece, and popped it in her mouth. The foil wrapper she wadded up and bombed at Benny.

"So the reason I'm up here," she said, picking a pill off her sweater's sleeve, "is because my father wants to comp you with a show and a suite for Christmas Eve. Benny was supposed to tell you, but like I say, he's afraid of heights. So I volunteered. It's boring being a princess, you know? And I'd sort of been wanting to meet the Michelangelo guy, anyway." She snapped her gum and looked him up and down. "What a dope, huh?" And she turned her back to him and began strolling around the scaffold.

So, okay, it wasn't the *same* sweater, but it was the same sweater. He watched her stop under the Creation, her purse banging lazily at her calves, and he had the momentary vision of his Cathy some spring day a few years back disappearing into one of the changing rooms at Macy's just as the Pope's daughter drifted over from Intimate Apparel, pausing at the clothes rack where Cathy had just been standing. He couldn't quite lose the feeling that it was someone's nasty practical joke.

"Ever wonder who this was?" she called to him after a minute, pointing at the female figure God clasps in one arm while He's stretching the other toward lifeless Adam.

"An angel," he muttered and began messing with his paints.

"Nope, it's Sophia," she said. "Wisdom. God's consort." And when he didn't respond: *"From the beginning was I present.* That's Sophia speaking. She's big with the Gnostics." She peered at him, then back at the figure on the ceiling. "Sort of a hobby of mine," she said by way of explanation.

The 6.8 Degree of Difficulty, the sweater, the coincidence

of it all. He found himself turning away, as if to deny complicity. Down on the casino floor Pharaoh was strolling past with his two handmaidens, golden asps snaking down their upper arms. Standing at a craps table off to the side, Betty and Veronica popped their pretend Instamatics. Benny kept his eyes turned upward.

"The Gnostics see the whole story of Genesis as a big con job got up by the dark powers," the Pope's daughter was going on. He turned to her: the dark powers? "Him," she said, pointing a finger at the figure overhead. "Not the true God, but just the Demiurge. He tells Adam and Eve not to eat of the Tree of Knowledge because He doesn't want them to find out what a fake He is." And she let out a laugh. "And get this: It's Sophia in the form of the serpent who tries to free humanity. Is that weird or what? But the Demiurge"—again with a nod at the God overhead—"he expels Adam and Eve from the Garden and we have this instead."

And she made a gesture at the casino, the world around. She looked for some response from Cosmo, then began walking to the far end of the platform.

"It all has to do with this world being a counterfeit of the true world," she said over her shoulder. "The Demiurge a counterfeit of the true God. Getting your spirit right so you can escape this world into the other—stop me if I'm being a bore."

This is what he would do: He would clean his brushes, put everything away, say Merry Christmas and good night to the Pope's daughter, to Betty and Veronica, to Crazy Herman and Tim Munjoy if they were still around, and then order himself a tidy dinner at some drive-thru window, go home, eat, evacuate waste, shoot himself.

"Schizophrenia, addiction, suicide: They're all attempts to cope with the dissonance, you know what I mean? The difference between what God says He is and what we see around us." She came back, stood in front of him, popped her gum. "Honestly, I didn't think you'd be such a dim bulb."

He tried to outstare her but she was too good at it and he had to turn away, occupy himself with searching for a cigarette—Betty and Veronica were always mooching his—resorting finally to his brush box, where he kept a stash. He found some matches, struck one with his thumbnail, lit his cigarette as carelessly as he could manage, threw the match on the floor. The Pope's daughter watched his little performance.

"This is a smoke-free casino," she said. "We thank you for not smoking."

He exhaled a balloon of smoke.

"Put it out or I'll have Benny come up and put it out for you."

"He can't. He's afraid of heights."

And he took another drag. The Pope's daughter eyed him a moment longer, then leaned over the railing, gestured to Benny. To Cosmo's surprise he headed straight for the ladder.

"I lied," she said.

He watched the burly shoulders come closer, rung by rung. From up above Cosmo could see that Nature, Fate—someone with a sense of humor, anyway—had given him a monk's tonsure.

"*Contessa?*" Benny said when he'd reached the top of the

ladder and planted himself on the platform. "Something wrong?" The Pope's daughter indicated Cosmo with a brief elevation of her chin.

"The shrimp's smoking."

At which Benny rested his eyes on Cosmo. "No smoking, douche bag." And he reached out, plucked the cigarette from between Cosmo's lips, and dropped it on the platform. He ground it out with the toe of his shoe. "Anything else?" he asked, turning again to the Pope's daughter.

"Thank you, Benny, no. I'll be down in a minute."

And sure enough, as if it were all choreographed, he cocked his leg over the edge of the platform and started down the ladder. They watched until he reached the casino floor again, took up his spot against the side of the craps table.

"Well," the Pope's daughter said, "anything else?" She lifted her brows in mock inquiry. "If not"—she took a key out of her purse—"suite eleven twenty-three. Bedroom, sitting room, cute little wet bar, a Jacuzzi in the bathroom. There's tickets for the Rat Pack show. A chit for some chips. Enjoy yourself. Invite some friends over."

She closed her purse and headed for the ladder.

"*Contessa?*" he muttered.

She didn't answer, adjusted the shoulders of her sweater one last time as though it were a motif that needed a final repeat, and then hiked a leg over the ladder. "I left a couple lines of coke on the wet bar for you. Maybe if I get hard up, I'll come visit."

And she smiled at him, bowed her head, and started down.

gregory blake smith

48

Chapter 6

Polly Sensoria on Her Divan of Diodes

For hours after leaving the Golden Calf he cruised up and down the Strip in his Amalgamated Illusion van. It was Christmas Eve and he had nowhere to go, no friends he could bear to visit or call, no family except his mother in her sad, two-room apartment back in Pawtucket. Cathy's parents were in Boston; their Christmas card sat alone and pained atop Cosmo's television set. He drove past Crazy Herman's apartment but all the windows were dark; ditto Betty and Veronica's. Was there a party he didn't know about? An antiparty somewhere? He used his cell phone to call his answering machine, but there was nothing, just a message from his grief counselor telling him that the holidays could be especially tough and that he was there for Cosmo should Cosmo need him.

So he drove, north and south on the Strip, into downtown Vegas, past the bail-bond bungalows and the wedding chapels, out Maryland Parkway to the cemetery where Cathy was buried, looped back through the UNLV campus. So intent on keeping moving was he that he barely noticed the green Jaguar following him, turning when he turned, letting a car or two come between them for a while, then reappearing in the rearview mirror with just the right film noir touch. But he was too lost in himself to make anything of it. Telling himself for the millionth time that he had to climb out of his grief, that he had to somehow come to understand Cathy's murder. Not solve it, of course—it was too freakish for that; there was no gumshoeing to be done, no address jotted on the inside of a B-movie matchbook—but understand what the world *meant* by it. Maybe then, instead of driving in circles, he could break free, head east, north, west, away—quit reliving that night, the explosion of horror in the living room, the grotesque joke. . . .

He drove toward his apartment complex, parked in the road across the way, and peered up at the dark windows of his apartment.

It had happened so fast. Three, four minutes, and it was over. He had been in the bedroom, fresh out of the shower, pulling on his pajamas while Cathy hid chocolate Easter eggs in the living room for him to find the next morning. He was just climbing into bed when he heard her call his name in a voice he would never forget. It had sounded—he told the ER staff later, and later still the police—like she was drowning. He rushed down the hall and found her gasping on the couch. And then she was vomiting, horribly. He called 911 but before the ambulance arrived she went into convulsions, then fell unconscious. In the ER he had lost control of himself and they'd had to sedate him. When he woke up, the world had changed.

Sometimes when he did this—sat outside his own

apartment—he imagined Cathy inside, alive. Sometimes he just imagined himself, in the dark, in the emptiness.

When he pulled away, back onto the road, he saw a car in the rearview mirror do the same. Hadn't he noticed it before? Those wide-apart headlights, the sleek hood when it passed under a streetlight? A Jaguar, right? For several blocks he kept an eye on it, making random turns, heading toward the artificial daylight of the Strip, where, sure enough, the Jag followed him in his lane changes, his turns. "What the hey?" he said to himself, but almost as soon as he said it, the Jaguar fell behind, put on its blinker, was replaced by a Jeep CJ, and then was lost altogether when Cosmo almost rear-ended a Suburban. At the next intersection he pulled a U-turn and, with one last look around for the Jag, headed for Amalgamated Illusion, where, surely, some of his co–lost souls were hanging out, mocking Christmas, Santa Claus, whatever was at hand.

On the radio a soprano kept insisting that her Redeemer liveth.

At AI the gate was unlocked, which meant someone was there somewhere. He parked and went inside, but the place seemed deserted—no cars, no trucks except for a row of company vans. He checked the snack bar, a couple of the staging buildings, the amargosa-overgrown playground out back. Oh, for a human being, he thought, unlocking Crazy Herman's lab, thinking maybe he was inside, but though the lights were on—computers, too—no one was around. On the walls Polly Sensoria peered down at him with that *ewig weibliche* look. She always seemed to be wanting something, asking for something, though what that something was—love, sex, a Tiparillo—remained unclear. She had begun life as a hacker handle back in Crazy Herman's Caltech days, then gotten incarnated as a programming toy, but now with the casinos backing the R & D with visions of franchising a chain of cyber-cathouses up and down the Strip, she was serious stuff, sure to make Amalgamated Illusion millions if only Crazy Herman and his team could figure out actual—that is, virtual—intercourse.

Not one to be left behind in his dehumanization, Cosmo had actually made out with her. All the love assassins had, for that matter, with Crazy Herman conducting exit interviews for likes, dislikes, suggestions. It involved putting on a full-body data suit and electronic goggles and stepping into a padded pod where you were fully isolated from any external stimuli (i.e., the real world) and where a woman's body, tweaked in the direction of the *Playboy* paradigm, existed in an electronic avatar that was like freebasing *Charlie's Angels*, as lovestruck Veronica had put it. You could have her dressed in a variety of fantasy costumes (bikini, bustier, nun's habit, analyst's pantsuit: your choice, Human), watch her undress if you wanted, watch her do this or that, depending on your cup of tea. But what Crazy Herman was working on, and what set Polly Sensoria apart from other VR programs, was tactile feedback. You not only could *see* Polly Sensoria and *hear* her whisper sweet porno nothings in your ear, you could *feel* her. You could reach out, as Cosmo had, and run your data glove over her hip, along her arm, across her stomach (this took some practice—if you miscalculated or moved too fast, you knocked the poor cyberdear for a loop), and feel the changing resistance of her skin. What particularly creeped Cosmo out was that her nipples felt cold when he first touched them, but that they warmed up the more he . . . well, you get the picture. The whole time he had had to keep reminding himself that there wasn't actually anybody there, that he was alone in a soundproof, lightproof pod, and that the flesh and the smile and the love in the eyes that looked deeply into his didn't actually exist. They were the product of writing biological reality into software, of algorithms and simgraphics and texture-mapping. His entire nervous system was the dupe of an electronic con job.

He was about to turn to leave when he had the thought that someone *was* there. Crazy Herman, Veronica, Tim Munjoy and his TV—someone was inside the pod with Polly Sensoria, and *that's* why the lights were on and the computers running. He crossed the room and—did one knock?—opened the door of the pod expecting to find a black-goggled, wet-suited humanoid groping the air, but no, there was only more emptiness, a data suit draped over a chair like someone's molted skin, and the black air, empty of Polly Sensoria. And yet—queer thought!—she was there somewhere, somewhere in the room, waiting like an electronic Madame Recamier, reclining on a divan of diodes. All he had to do was put on the data suit and the goggles and she would come to him, smiling, warm, ready. He remembered Crazy Herman trying to convince him a couple of months after Cathy had died to bring something of hers—some dress, a suit, a tight tank top—so that he could scan it in as an option, make Polly Sensoria available as Cathy Dust. He had meant it as a kindness—Crazy Herman didn't always understand the boundaries of the human—but Cosmo had demurred, shifted his weight, considered breaking into tears, excused himself. But now, standing there, he wondered why not. If the real had failed him, why not accept Polly Sensoria's virtual hand if it was the only hand being offered, the virtual heart, the virtual vagina, the virtual voice speaking. . . .

"Hey," he heard behind him.

No, he didn't. But he turned anyway, stared at the whispering air, the dust motes, the molecules he could almost see. In his pocket he fingered the key to suite 1123.

Back on the Strip he felt crazy and manic and like he was going down fast. A trip through the McDonald's drive-thru didn't help, nor did speeding up on the pedestrians in the crosswalks. Somewhere around midnight he could feel himself closing in on the convenience store where Cathy had bought the chocolate Easter egg that had killed her and where he went when it was particularly bad, sitting in the van in the parking lot drinking bourbon, beer, whatever was at hand, until the assistant manager came out to shoo him away. And he would have gone, too, except just as he was about to turn onto Desert Inn Road there it was again, the green Jaguar, its front grille a sleek smile in the rearview mirror. He slammed on the brakes right in the middle of the Strip and, without thinking what he was doing, swung the door open. A car swerved, a horn blatted at him. He ran back to the Jag, his fists ready and with such a shock of adrenaline in him that after the Jag had peeled out past him he stood in the middle of the Strip with the base of his skull pounding so badly he thought he was going to pass out. He had half-expected to find the Pope's daughter behind the wheel, but it'd been a man—Benny, Marco, some-one in a dark suit. After a minute he got back in the van, started the engine—it had stalled, stopping so fast—and with a whispered obscenity turned into the drive of the Golden Calf.

Chapter 7

The Dark Gods Choose a Jacuzzi

Inside he tried to get control of himself. He looked for Candi the cocktail waitress, for a free bourbon, asked one of the bartenders and learned that she was unavailable right now, sir. So he walked the casino floor trying to look relaxed and complete, like back in Amarillo he had a family of four and a swimming pool. Every once in a while he would hear the *pum-pum* of drums and Pharaoh would promenade past. At the Wheel of Fortune—the biggest sucker game in town, but not without its mystery—he sat and watched the wheel come up prime numbers more times in a row than he cared to admit. He took out all the money in his wallet and placed it on 19.

It came up 16.

Then 25, 9, 36 . . .

"You looking for me?" a voice said from behind him.

He turned in his seat. It was Candi, waitress tray palm-up, chiton cute as ever, but with a gaunt, edgy expression on her face. He tried to smile at her.

"I'm trying to recommit to humanity," he said; then, when she made a squirrelly face, "I'm lonely."

She arranged the dollar bills in her tip glass. "It's two hundred and fifty," she said.

"Not *that* kind of lonely," he said and tried to walk her away from the Wheel of Fortune, but she stayed where she was.

"It's two hundred and fifty," she repeated. "More if you want me to pretend I like you."

He showed her the hotel key in his pocket. "The holidays are the worst time," he said, quoting his grief counselor. "Take a break and come upstairs and we'll try being civilized together. We'll practice saying please and thank you."

At that she eyed him, then swore to herself, and—against the rules—plunked herself down in a seat at the Wheel of Fortune. "Have a little pity," she said into her waitress tray. "I'm trying to be hard-boiled."

"Why?"

"It's Christmas Eve, for Christ's sake," she said. "They're making me work a double shift. I'm tired. I'm strung out. I got this baby I had to go get when his day care closed. He's in the kitchen now. This can't go on."

The Wheel of Fortune operator cast his eyes at her, at Cosmo, then over at his pit boss.

"I can't take it anymore," she said. "I just want to be treated with a little respect."

He looked down at the wig where it mimicked growing in a whorl out of the crown of her head. "I respect you," he said. "At least you haven't been murdered by a maniac yet."

She gazed darkly at the turning wheel. "It's only a matter of time," she muttered and started fingering the bills in her tip glass again. The pit boss made like he wasn't watching. "Who knows, maybe you're him," she said and stood up. "If you are, do it quickly, when I'm not looking." And she stuffed a dollar bill in his shirt pocket like a tip and started to walk away.

"Suite eleven twenty-three," he called after her.

"Maybe if I get hard up enough," her voice sailed back to him, sounding strangely like the Pope's daughter.

Up on the eleventh floor he turned on the TV with the remote, surfed through the channels, watched Mr. Magoo as Ebenezer Scrooge for a minute, then Kermit as Bob Crachit, then another soprano maintaining that her Redeemer liveth (though she pronounced it "leaveth"), finally landing on CNN, where an FBI spokesman was explaining the idea behind psyops. The suite was pretty nifty, not unlike the Pope's bedroom three floors above, though scaled back a bit. He got out half a dozen ready-made daiquiris from the mini-fridge next to the wet bar, eyed the lines of cocaine, turned on the bedroom TV for more company, the bathroom TV, too. The three played Doppler patty-cake between the rooms. In the nightstand he found a Gideon's Bible and was turning to Revelation so he could follow along when the phone rang.

"Okay," Candi's voice said, "but if I come up I'm going to have to come back with some money. Understand?"

There was the sound of a baby somewhere. For a moment he thought it came from the psyops tape, but no, it was on the phone.

"Where are you calling from?"

"The kitchen. They're tired of looking after this baby. I'm going to get fired. Any other questions?"

"Look," he said, "the idea is for you to fake them out down there. Come upstairs, but instead of a trick you just relax, get in the Jacuzzi, have a strawberry daiquiri, whatever it takes."

"I still need money," she said. "They take a cut, you know."

"How much?"

She calculated, or maybe she was trying to decide how big a chump he was. "A hundred."

"Okay, we can get you a hundred."

On the TV someone had climbed out onto the roof of the compound in Montana, a dark figure, male or female you couldn't tell. The camera wavered.

"I don't want to do this anymore," Candi whispered into the phone, or maybe to someone standing next to her.

"What?"

"This," she said, as if it were self-evident.

You could see that the figure had a gun. He or she rested the butt on his or her thigh. The psyops tape had Nancy Sinatra singing "These Boots Are Made for Walkin'" dubbed over what sounded like a choir of Tibetan monks.

"I don't want to be me anymore. I don't want to be a cocktail waitress or a paid escort or a bogus mother. I want to go home to Wisconsin."

"Come up for a little human contact first," he answered. "I'm not engaging your services, but come up."

She swore softly into the phone. "I'm going to jump out of my skin," she said and hung up.

On one of the channels was an advertisement for a Dirt

Devil vacuum, on another an ad for an air freshener, then the First Alert Smoke Detector. Earth, air, fire, thought Cosmo, a bit spooked. He surfed back to the Apocalypse, Nancy Sinatra on an infinite loop, the figure on the roof gone. He got out of bed and went into the bathroom and started the Jacuzzi, cracked the door to the hall an inch, then fetched an armload of daiquiris—banana, raspberry, kiwi—and went back into the bathroom. He stripped and climbed into the whirlpool.

Half an hour went by. Candi didn't show. Neither did the Pope's daughter. He switched from CNN to MSNBC to Fox News, but they all had the same Apocalypse on. The daiquiris ran low, so he climbed out, got an armload of margaritas, and climbed back in. In another half hour he knew the precarious good mood he'd been managing was going to begin to wobble, and then he was going to fall and fall fast. He lay his head back on the tub's rim, closed his eyes. Was there any chance one could fall asleep, go unconscious, drown?

The phone rang.

Almost simultaneously there was a knock on the door, then a voice calling from the living room.

"Your phone's ringing."

It sounded like the Pope's daughter. He held his breath and slipped underwater; one of the jets pounded turbulence into his ear. But when he surfaced it was Candi who was standing over him. She really did have a baby, a dark-haired eight-month-old in a car seat. The phone was still ringing.

"It might be something important," she said.

"Everything important," he answered, wiping the water

from his eyes and pointing at the Apocalypse, "is on TV." At which the phone stopped. "Want a margarita?" And he started unscrewing one of the little bottles.

She looked different somehow. Same chiton, cleavage, brass bangles along her forehead, but there was something about her face, a look that was more assured. He slipped underwater again, blew bubbles until his breath ran out, and surfaced. She'd put the car seat on the vanity and was standing over against the sink, taking her outfit off.

"I don't give freebies," she said. Cosmo averted his eyes. "As long as we understand that." And she stepped into the Jacuzzi.

On the TV a night-vision camera was zooming in on a green patch inside the concertina wire the FBI had set up. If you didn't count Polly Sensoria, it'd been twenty months since he'd been with a naked woman.

"I don't want to get my makeup wet," Candi was saying. She held her head above the water so her collarbones were exposed. "It takes forever to do." And she gestured with her fingertips to the black lines that swept out at the wicks of her eyes. The courtesan look. "But the wig," she said, and lifted her hair from behind, took out a bobby pin, and dropped the wig on the floor. Strangely, bizarrely, she had the same haircut underneath, the same Egyptian-exotic page boy. Over in his car seat, the baby stared at Cosmo with furious concentration, as if he were trying to recognize him.

"What's his name?" Cosmo asked, to have something to say. She just shrugged.

"Strange kid," she said. "He never cries."

He wondered who the father was. Some trim hosiery

representative out of Tupelo, a midlevel manager from Phoenix? Candi watched him wonder, then stroked his shinbone with the tips of her toes.

"And what's *your* name, sailor?"

On the floor her clothes sprawled suggestively, her high heels spilled onto their sides, her panties in a cute puddle.

"Cosmo."

"And why do you want to recommit to humanity, Cosmo?"

Here was a woman. She had breasts, uterus, ovaries, all in working order. Why not give in? Carry her off to one of the wedding chapels, have babies and pink flamingos, say to hell with the dark forces—they couldn't get him twice, could they?

She was opening one of the little cocktail bottles, gargling a margarita. Her arms, he noticed, bore needle marks.

"So what's the deal with you and D'Angelo's daughter?" she asked after a minute; and then, when he didn't answer: "I saw her up on the scaffold with you today. Got a secret society going?"

He shrugged. "Sophia, the Demiurge, schizophrenia—"

"Huh?"

"—the Gnostics."

She let out a low whistle. "The chicks in the bathrobes."

It was his turn to say "Huh?" But before she could answer there was a knock on the door. She mimed an uh-oh look, like she was busted, then slipped down in the water. There was a second knock. Cosmo half-expected, on the model of when Benny and Marco had incarnated at the instant their names were mentioned, to see the Demiurge, maybe a Gnostic or two, materialize in the bathroom doorway. But when the door finally swung inward, it was the Pope's daughter.

"And here I thought we had a date."

She was no longer dressed in Cathy's sweater but in some sort of boudoir gown, a sheer, low-waisted thing that dropped in a silky rush to the floor. She glanced at the spilled chiton and inside-out stockings, then at the baby in his car seat, then back at the cocktail waitress in the Jacuzzi.

"So, who're you?" she asked.

"Just one of the girls, Miss D'Angelo."

"And you?" she said to Cosmo.

He didn't answer, looked instead from one Egyptian-exotic haircut to the other, then to the wig on the floor.

"If you'll excuse me," said Candi. She tucked her head in and started to stand up. "I gotta get back to work."

"You stay put," the Pope's daughter said. "I just need Michelangelo for a minute. You got some clothes?" she said to Cosmo.

"In the living room."

"Then I'll wait for you in the bedroom."

And she turned, the hem of her gown eddying around her ankles, and left.

"You got friends in high places," Candi whispered, and she whipped her fingers in hot-stuff fashion. Cosmo stood up in the tub, let the room steady itself, and then climbed out.

"You'll wait?" he asked.

She rubbed her thumb and middle finger together to indicate she still needed her hundred dollars. Over in his car seat the baby had given up on Cosmo and fallen asleep.

Chapter 8

The Contessa del Cancelliere

She was sitting in the dark, on the other side of the bed, next to the huge window that looked out onto the Strip.

"Shut the door," she said, and when he'd shut the door and was reaching for the wall switch, "Keep the lights off."

He just stood there, shirtless. Out the window he could see the ice-castle colors of the casinos, the butterscotch of the Mirage, the spumoni of Caesars. They flecked the darkness with motes of color.

"Has anyone contacted you?" she asked in a low, intent voice.

"What?" He tried to smile. What?

"Has anything happened?" And when he didn't respond: "After you were seen speaking to me?"

"Seen?" he wondered. "By whom?"

"I'm watched," was all she'd say.

What game, what diversion to keep a bored princess amused, was this? Had she gotten herself dressed up in the femme fatale outfit to play some part? Extravagant, pretty, pampered: Was amusing herself at the expense of dumb artists how she got her kicks?

"No one's contacted me."

She seemed oddly deflated.

"But this *contessa* business . . ."

She startled, threw him a look like, how did he know about that? He spread his palms in the colored air like, how else?

"Oh," she murmured and looked down into her lap. She seemed to have lost her place in the script. "They call me that sometimes."

"They?"

She didn't pick up the ball.

"Know anybody who owns a green Jaguar?"

"What?"

"Sure," he said, "play dumb."

She stared at him. He met her eyes. After all, he knew the dark powers, their agents and assigns.

"My mother," she explained finally, "was the Contessa del Cancelliere." And when he grimaced: "You can look her up. You can look *me* up."

He licked his index finger, made a gesture of paging through a nonexistent book.

"In the *Libro d'oro*. The book of the Italian aristocracy. But you have to get the 1975 supplement. The 1970 edition only lists my mother—I wasn't born yet. And the 1980 doesn't list either of us."

He didn't bite.

"We were disappeared."

"Sorry," said Cosmo. "I'm due back on Earth."

"They killed my mother when I was little."

"Good-bye."

"They *did.*"

"They?"

"I have newspaper clippings."

And I, thought Cosmo, have videotape. Courtesy of Tim Munjoy, who edited together a bunch of *Hard Copy* clips and KLVS footage. As a souvenir. It sat, unwatched, in one of Cosmo's closets.

"Why tell me?" he said after a moment. Did she tell every Tom, Dick, and Cosmo who came along?

"I have to tell someone."

"No, you don't."

She leaned forward, spread her fingers on the mattress next to her. "You don't know what my life is like. When my father dies . . . I don't know what will become of me."

I don't know what will become of me? Cosmo repeated in his head. He turned to see if there was a script girl he hadn't noticed somewhere in the room.

"I thought you of all people would understand."

He turned back. Something had come into her voice, some sympathy, or the mimic of sympathy.

"Your wife," she said in a gentle voice. She peered intently at him through the dark air.

"Let's leave my wife out of it."

"I only mean to say that we're alike. We have the same painful history. The world has treated us—" she searched for the word.

"Absurdly?" Cosmo supplied.

"We have the same wounds."

He didn't like that. This costume, this masquerade, whatever it was—femme fatale, gun moll, maiden in distress—

he would not accept the trespass of the false. Not in this one area, anyway, not if he could help it.

"Whatever you want from me," he found himself saying, "I haven't got it to give."

At which she looked at him, her face shadowed and mask-like in the dark. But she didn't speak.

"Look," he said after a minute; he wasn't going to be suckered. "Darker forces than you have messed with me. You are strictly bush league. Now, if you don't mind."

She eyed him—insulted, amused, he couldn't say. But she stayed where she was.

"Contessa?" he said with a touch of sarcasm. He moved slightly from where he was standing so that she had a clear path to the door. She cocked her shoulders from one side to the other, as if debating, then laughed a wet, trifling laugh. She stood up, letting the hem of her dressing gown drop in a sheer rush to the floor. She crossed and stood in front of him, and then, as if she'd been studying Grace Kelly in *To Catch a Thief*, took his chin in her fingertips, leaned into him, and kissed him on the lips.

"Ann," she said. "My name is Ann."

And without spending another look on him she headed toward the door. When she opened it CNN cascaded in, and then rushed back out when she closed it. Out the window the five-story Christmas wreath on the façade of Treasure Island blinked on and off. The Campanile wavered in the Mirage. He could see his own reflection suspended in the dark air, ten feet out on the other side of the window, as if he—and the unlit floor lamp next to him—were spirits on the outside looking in.

He heard the hall door open and shut.

When he went back into the living room the first thing he saw—what the hey?—was a gun. An honest-to-god, expensive-looking, small, black gun with some kind of long barrel lying picturesquely on the glass coffee table next to a complimentary dish of ribbon candy. It looked arranged, like a photo from the Neiman Marcus catalog. It stopped him dead in his tracks. The world shifted a little.

Had it been there before, when he'd gotten dressed, and he just hadn't seen it? Had she come in with a gun and left it there? As a joke? As part of the film noir shtick or something?

He crossed to the coffee table and picked the thing up. It was muzzle-heavy, with a smell of burned oil. He wondered if it was loaded, if there was a safety catch or something, and then realized that the gun itself was short-barreled and that there was—for Pete's sake!—a silencer screwed on the end. He twisted the steel barrel and felt the gritty slide of machined threads. The metal itself was warm to the touch.

"Hey!" he called to Candi. She didn't answer. The bathroom TV was still on.

Had he ever even held a gun before? He tried to think back. Maybe in his childhood some friend's pellet gun, but nothing else that he could remember. He took aim, pretend-firing first at the ribbon candy, then at the TV screen, then out the window at Vegas, the world, the universe.

"Hey!" he called again and started for the bathroom. "You didn't put this here, did you?"

He kicked the door to the bathroom open and Jesus H. Christ!

She was lying just as he'd left her, her head pillowed on

the rim of the tub, the ends of her hair reaching into the water, but her face was covered with blood. It came from her forehead, in three places, three rivulets of red, pooling in her eye sockets before running off in muttonchops down either side of her jaw. The water had turned pink.

"Candi?" he said.

"Apocalyptic fervor," the TV answered back, *"is a response to cultural crisis, to a sense of loss that results from the passing of an old worldview—"*

Did he feel ill? Did he feel like fainting? Did he feel perverted pleasure or any of the other reactions he'd seen in movies and books? He looked at the gun in his hand—fingerprints galore—and with the instinct of all those other innocents framed by the machinations of the B movie, dropped the thing. It had the good taste to forgo firing into the ceiling.

"Jesus!" he whispered and backed through the doorway, into the living room.

How could she have done it? Not how could she have done it in some moral sense, but how could she, in the bare half-minute between her kissing him and the hall doorway closing—he'd *heard* it, he was sure—how could she have picked up the gun from wherever she had hidden it, gone into the bathroom, shot Candi three times, put the gun on the coffee table, and left?

"—similar to the collective paranoia of the Crusades," the TV was saying, *"of pogroms and witch hunts—"*

What had just happened? It was like he had moved from a world governed at least nominally by the logic of real numbers to the wonderland of the irreal, the daffy equations of irrational numbers somehow erupting into the simple plus and minus of Cosmo Dust's sad life. Who would shoot Candi? And why? Because for all his antics, his making out with Polly Sensoria and the other attempts to deal with the stunningly meaningless, nincompoopish death of his wife, he had thought that when you came right down to it that it was him—some malignant, cosmic mark of Cain branding him—and him alone who was the object of the universe's humor and scorn. Was he now to understand that the dark forces' displeasure with him extended to the obliteration of casual acquaintances?

He went and stood in the doorway again as if he couldn't trust his senses. He said her name again—could it be a joke, some staged laugher, the point of which was beyond him?—and then crossed to the tub and with a dash of vertigo reached out and touched her, touched the blood in her eye sockets. It was real. The world was real. For the second time in his life he was alone with a woman whose death, if the rules had been followed, should have been somewhere off in the interstellar black at the end of a probability curve.

He picked up the phone—what else?—and dialed 911. Once before he had done it, in terror. This time he was calmer, in a kind of stupor almost, imagining the tape machine on the other end of the line slowly coiling while he spoke, his foggy, low-fidelity voice being played back a year from now on *Emergency 911*, the words scrolling along the bottom of the screen like subtitles.

"—*characterized by an erosion of structures,*" said the TV now, "*psychic, social, and personal*—"

Chapter 9

Aquinas in the Interrogation Room

"Thing is," Orel Sloan said, looking at himself in the mirror, "Richard Widmark has got this great sado-masochistic face. It's what my mug wants to be, but it can't quite get there."

They were in the IR, a soundproofed room with no windows, no clock, no doorknob on the door, no furniture except for a table and two government-issue chairs, irritating light, a tape recorder, a surveillance camera up in one corner, and a two-way mirror along one wall. They'd been going at it for what Cosmo figured was four or five hours now. And this after a couple of hours of being tested for blood alcohol, trace-metal tested, his pubic hair combed, his underwear confiscated, his hands nuked for barium and antimony. Exhausted, confused, hungover, he wondered if the Laughing Child was still laughing.

"Now your face," Orel Sloan said, turning back from the mirror, appraising Cosmo; he was casting the movie, "we gotta get someone angelic. Sweet-natured. And short." He snapped his fingers, like he had it. "Mickey Rooney!"

Just after he had dialed 911, he had tried to call the Pope's daughter, but the switchboard operator wouldn't put him through, wouldn't even acknowledge that there was an Ann D'Angelo living at the hotel, but yes, would take a message for her should someone of that name inquire at the desk. Then he tried Crazy Herman, but Crazy Herman's answering machine said he was spending Christmas on the planet Lux. He had felt very alone, sitting on the couch, wondering—among other things, God knows—how it was that the cocaine that had been on the wet bar had disappeared. There had been thoughts of wiping his prints off the gun and putting it back on the coffee table, but some instinct told him that the stupider his story sounded the more plausible it would be. When the blue uniforms arrived, he showed them to the body, let them use the phone to call Homicide, or the medical examiner, or whoever it was they called. By the time he was escorted out of the room and to the elevator, there were reporters in the hallway. For the second time in his life he had felt the heat of a minicam's light on the side of his face.

"So, soldier, this countess you claim gave you the come on—"

He had admitted to picking up the gun, so why they had to do a trace-metal test he didn't know, but he had let them aerosol his hands with some chemical and hold them under ultraviolet light. When his right hand showed the outline of the little .17-caliber gun and his left hand the imprint of the silencer, this detective, Orel Sloan—the first thing he had said when he'd arrived at the scene of the crime had been how he wanted to be played by Richard Widmark when they made a movie of all this—had asked him how it was that a revolver with a suppressor had come to be in his room and why, what with a dead prostitute and all in the bathroom, he had picked it up. When Cosmo started in on his story about coming out of the bedroom, etc., Orel Sloan had fixed him with suspicious eyes and asked did Cosmo even know who Richard Widmark was?

"Kiss of Death," Cosmo non sequitured now. He had given up being a cooperative witness about two hours ago. *"The Street with No Name."*

"—which *leaves* me," the detective repeated; he was on about the gun now: "trying to figure out whether you pulled the dumb play because you think we wouldn't expect you to pull the dumb play, or whether you really *are* dumb."

He didn't look at all like Richard Widmark, none of the gaunt face or lurking sneer. He was beefy about the shoulders, blunt-headed, his neck on leave of absence. Cosmo wondered if he treated every investigation this way, meaning was this his personal mythic landscape—hard-boiled lingo, crime-thriller leitmotifs—or had the universe had the foresight fifty years ago to breed and then coach him in the assumption of this particular persona, so that this moment in Cosmo's life would possess the *claritas* of a work of art?

"So you pop the broad, leave your prints all over that expensive little squib, and make like the innocent citizen when the coppers show—"

"Please . . ."

"—so dumb you'd pick up a gun with a gosh-honey-look-what-I-found, and then drop it right next to the murder victim."

At what point did the universe call "Cut!" At what point did the horrors of his life wipe off the greasepaint, step out of costume, and relax backstage with a cigarette and a bottle of mineral water?

"It doesn't look good, soldier."

"I want to go home."

"You're a material witness. You can't go home."

"Then I want to make my one phone call."

"Why don't you just spill and save us both a lot of headache?"

"Richard Widmark is dead," he said, and he closed his eyes, lay his head down on the metal table. He heard a *pfft* of contempt.

"Shows how much you know," came the detective's voice. "What we're talkin' about here is we're talkin' about the ideal. Casting. Sets. Costumes. The perfect film of this caper irregardless of time, place, other limiting factors. We'll never get anywhere, Dust, if you don't understand the paradigms."

He heard the tape recorder being shut off, then footsteps, the door opening and closing, and then just the buzz of the fluorescent lights.

So this was the drill. Wear him down. Twist him around until whatever self-destruction was latent in him burst forth in a confession. He had told them about the Pope's daughter, told them about the green Jaguar, reminded them of just who it was who owned the Golden Calf—the silencer and the three neat bullets to the head: Did that look like the sort of thing an ersatz Michelangelo was capable of? Where did one buy a silencer, anyway?

The door opened. This time it was a different step, a different presence. Heels. Perfume. He thought instantly of the Pope's daughter, but she was halfway to New York, Rome, Timbuktu by now. He neither sat up nor turned his head. Whoever it was pulled back one of the chairs and sat down. The tape recorder started again, but it was a good minute before anyone spoke.

"Women don't seem to have much luck around you, Mr. Dust."

He opened his eyes and stared straight into the metal tabletop. He recognized the voice, felt somewhere down in his heart the bruise of an old hurt.

"Have you been behind the mirror?" he asked. "Have you been listening the whole time?"

He remembered her name, mostly because she had the same name as the dead woman who haunts Kim Novak in *Vertigo*. Carlotta. Carlotta Valdez—parental joke or cosmic coincidence, he'd never learned. She'd been the primary investigator on what *Hard Copy* had called the "Las Vegas Cyanide Easter Egg Hunt." He had spent time with her, answering questions, being consoled.

"So who do you want to play *you* when they make a movie of this?" he asked after a minute, and he sat up and peered at her. She didn't look at all like Kim Novak. She looked, in fact—Cosmo had thought so even a year and a half ago—like a drawing of Thomas Aquinas that Cathy had had hanging on the wall of her UNLV office, delicate and homely, with a too-big nose and a stunned intelligence around the eyes.

"Got any new leads on my wife's death?" he asked. She considered him with Aquinas's thin lips and unwrinkled brow.

"Just an interesting new development."

That would be it, wouldn't it? Now they were going to suspect him of Cathy's murder. The new scenario: Husband injects cyanide into an Easter egg, which wife has just bought at the Jack-B-Nimble, then rushes *post facto* to the store and syringes two or three others, an unlucky kid from the Mayflower Apartments buying one in the couple of hours between plan and act.

"It's a frame job," he said. He didn't care what he sounded like.

"A frame job?"

"Right."

"And who's framing you?"

"The universe."

She kept an even composure. "Why would the universe want to do that?"

"Spite, boredom, envy, you name it."

He spun out of his chair and walked to the mirror. Who was behind it? Orel Sloan, eating a donut? Or a medley of Fate's forces, dressed in comic-book costume, each awaiting its chance to flame on?

"Let me understand your story," Carlotta was saying. Cosmo kept his back turned to her, his face still to the mirror. He needed a shave. "You were staying at the Golden Calf at the request of this—um—countess. What's her name again?"

"Annunciata D'Angelo. The Pope's daughter. You know who she is."

"We've phoned the hotel. They say there's no one staying there by that name."

Natch.

"But be that as it may. . . . You say she gave you her room key?"

That wasn't what he had said, but he didn't correct her.

"For what reason? Fun and games?"

"Are you aware," he said abruptly, "that you have the same name as the dead woman in *Vertigo*?"

It seemed to take her aback. "What?"

"Carlotta Valdez. The suicide who Kim Novak thinks is taking over her body. Have you lived your whole life and no one's told you that?"

She crossed her legs, looked thoughtfully at her hands, pushed back a cuticle. "Why did she invite you up?"

"She didn't invite me up," he sighed. He walked back to the table, sat down. "The Pope of Las Vegas owed me a favor. She was just delivering a message. I went because—" Because why?

"Because she was your quarry in Love Assassin?"

Oy, Jesus, he thought. How had she found that out? He rolled his eyes, began to explain, but the whole time he could see her making the easy leap to Candi as a kind of one-upmanship among the virtually murderous. He reminded her that it was the Pope's daughter who was his quarry, not Candi.

"Susan," she said. "Let's call her by her real name."

"Right," he said. He'd learned this bit of news two or three hours ago. "Anyway, I wasn't going to go, but I changed my mind, got drunk, saw Candi—Susan—who I knew very casually, and invited her up to my room where we undressed and sat in the Jacuzzi and watched the Apocalypse on TV. Case closed."

"How'd she get the three bullets in her head?"

"I don't know. The Pope's daughter was the only other person in the suite. The Crimestoppers Textbook says it has to be one of the three of us."

"Three?"

"Candi, too."

She shook her head. "Suicide is out. One bullet to the brain, maybe. Three bullets would require an unlikely level of concentration, don't you think?"

"Okay," he conceded. "The Pope's daughter or me. One of us is a murderer. Murderess."

"Unless . . ."

"Unless what?"

She let him say it.

"Unless someone came into the suite while the Pope's daughter and I were in the bedroom?" He gave her a doubtful look.

"How long were you in there?"

"Ten minutes," he said. "Max."

"That's enough time."

It wasn't like he hadn't already thought of it. But it would require such precise timing on the part of whomever. Did this detective really think such a scenario was possible? Or was this what they called the "out"? Give the suspect a phony way of taking himself off the hook, then maneuver him into contradiction and error, and finally into implicating himself?

"Did you have sex with her?"

He kept what he hoped was a dignified silence.

"We'll find out in any case. There'll be semen. Failing that, some of your pubic hair."

"No, there won't." He'd always figured there had to be an upside to celibacy.

"And with this countess. Did you have sex with her?"

He looked her in the eye. A year and a half ago she had held his hand. She had passed him Kleenexes. She had—how the memory came rushing back!—she had held his forehead when, overcome with nerves and grief, he had retched into the wastebasket under her desk.

"I didn't kill her," he said now, simply. And when she kept a noncommittal look: "I think I need to see a lawyer."

"Okay," she said, "but if you do, then we can't help you."

"Help me?"

"Once lawyers get into it, it becomes adversarial. Right now what we're trying to do is simply listen to you, get at the truth, you know?"

How big a chump did they take him for?

"It's just that there's a few things that don't add up."

He felt like crying. "Have you checked with the hotel? About who reserved my room? Who paid for it?"

She looked puzzled, or seemed to look puzzled. "*You* paid for it."

"What?"

"With cash. The clerk said you came in off the street, asked for a suite, paid cash, signed the register. Is that supposed to prove something?"

He closed his eyes, got himself under control. When he opened them again, he reached out, touched Detective Valdez deliberately on the wrist.

"I didn't pay for the room," he said. He enunciated his words as if precision would convey honesty. "It was a favor from Angelo D'Angelo, communicated to me by Ann D'Angelo. She lives on the top floor of the Golden Calf. She gets driven around town in a white limo. She's the daughter, or the adopted daughter, of Angelo D'Angelo. Look me in the eye and tell me you don't know who she is."

She lifted his fingers from her wrist. "The Golden Calf doesn't know who she is. Nor does the Department of Health and Human Services. She's got no social security number."

"And she's not listed with Immigration," Orel Sloan's voice barked over the intercom.

Cosmo shot a look at the mirrored wall, then let his head bang back onto the table. "Then I must have done it."

"Is that a confession?"

"If *you're* satisfied, *I'm* satisfied."

"There's no other explanation?"

"Only the fanciful, the insane, the paranoid."

And he put wrist to wrist. But she didn't move. The expectant hush of the intercom came on again, but no voice followed, and the hush faded. He took his wrists out of their imaginary cuffs. After a minute the door opened and Orel Sloan came back in.

"I sent one of the buttons for some breakfast."

"I've got nothing more to say," Cosmo muttered. "Arrest me or let me go."

"Oh, we're just getting started, sailor."

"Soldier."

"Right. Soldier."

He thought he caught, in Carlotta Valdez's eyes, a brief acknowledgment of sham and imposture. He answered her with a look of stumbling helplessness, but whatever glimmer of sympathy he had seen was gone. He stood up and moved to look at his tired face in the mirror.

"I miss my wife," he said, making the mirror cloud over with his breath. There was no answer from behind him. He wondered what he looked like from inside the mirrored room. Defeated? Remorseful? Guilty?

"The interrogation room can be cathartic," Orel Sloan said. "I got a wallful of criminal psychology dissertations on it. So, confess. You'll feel better."

"I confess," said Cosmo.

"See?"

"I confess to having loved another human being without irony or reserve." He banged his forehead against the mirror.

"Let's not get maudlin," said Carlotta Valdez.

"It's a crime the dark forces are swift in their punishment of." He banged his head again; the mirror trembled.

"Feel cleansed?" Orel Sloan asked.

"No."

"Did killing Candi cleanse you?"

"No." And then, snubbing Detective Sloan for Detective Valdez: "Aquinas"—Valdez blinked in such a way that for a moment he wondered whether she knew she resembled the great saint—"Aquinas maintained that to love another human being was to commit the sin of pride. Pride, because the heart is opened not to God but to another person. Which, from a cosmic perspective, is simply another version of yourself."

The two detectives exchanged a look.

"In other words, God punishes us for loving one another."

Carlotta crossed herself.

"Hence, a poisoned Easter egg."

"You're a fruit salad, pal."

He turned back to the mirror, addressed his unshaven face. "Easter, the Resurrection, salvation, nyuk-nyuk: Get it?"

"A cuckoo clock," said Orel Sloan. "And here's what I think. I think you zotzed both your wife and this Candi dame. I think you did it, and you don't even know you did it because you're a friggin' loony tune."

"You did it in a dissociated state," Carlotta Valdez put in.

"Yeah, a dissociated state."

"It's in a dissociated state," Cosmo said, "that Kim Novak jumps into San Francisco Bay. When she thinks she's Carlotta Valdez."

They stared at him.

"Of course, she's faking it. She doesn't really think she's Carlotta Valdez. It's an imposture."

"Listen, *gabacho*," Carlotta said suddenly, "let's cut the crap. You killed your wife and you killed this *puta* and who knows who else—we'll be checking our cold cases—and you did it in a mental state that makes you believe you don't know anything about it. You dropped the gun and you don't even remember dropping it. Or you put it on the coffee table and a second later, you come out of your nutzoid state and you see it there and wonder where the heck this gun came from."

He stared at her. And for a second, he wondered if what she said could be true. Had he been killing people for years now and just didn't know it?

"You're crazy," he whispered.

"It's happened to you, though, hasn't it? There are unexplained lapses in your life. Periods of time you can't account for. What the hell else would you be doing in the Golden Calf? Why would you—you, Cosmo Dust—rent a suite there? For what? And this countess—I mean, give me a break."

No, it wasn't true. He could account for the *what* and the *where* and the *how* of things in his life. Maybe not the *why*; he could no longer account for the *why*. But that, for once, was not the issue.

"The lapses, the missing periods, the eruptions of odd facts, of things that don't fit, things that aren't you. You've been dogged by the unexplainable for years. It frightens you. You know something's wrong but you can't figure it."

"No," he said, and he stared at his face in the mirror. "There are no lapses. I know who I am."

"You can't figure it because you're missing the crucial fact. This other Cosmo Dust, who knows about seventeen-caliber Bianchis. This other Cosmo Dust, who makes dates with whores."

"This is the face my wife used to kiss. This is the face she used to make fun of."

"And you killed her."

He shook his head no. And what he felt was a little explosion of relief at knowing at least that one thing to be certain, rational, a fact.

The door opened and a desk cop dressed as Santa Claus came in with a McDonald's bag. Orel Sloan took it from him and then indicated Cosmo with a nod.

"Get him outta my sight, Santa."

Chapter 10

The Gospel According to Mary of Magdala

They put him in a cell, regulation stuff: two bunks, stainless steel sink and toilet, fluorescent light, drab tile, narrow window. Exhausted, confused, scared, he fell into a sleep packed with dream-menace. At some point the cell door opened and someone came in. He tried to wake up enough to see who it was but somehow found himself back in his hometown, on the playground, where the tough kids had him down on the ground and were punching him in the bicep telling him to name ten cigarettes and when Cosmo got stuck on Tareyton, shouting at him to say *Uncle, did he give, say Uncle!*

"Say Uncle," someone in the cell said now. Cosmo writhed, drowned, fell over a cliff, murmured "Lucky Strikes," woke up.

"Say you give."

Someone was in the bunk above him.

"Say Uncle. *Then* we'll let up."

And over the edge of the bunk two legs dangled, hooves, hair, the smell of manure. Cosmo groaned and scurried back into his dreams, where he found Cathy, alive and in a tattered sundress she used to wear around the house. Only they were in Venice, in luminous Venice, and she had Candi's baby in her lap, the two of them sitting on a low parapet beside a canal, sunlight dancing on their faces. The baby was talking, adult, assured, and even though Cosmo could not understand him—it was some language just over the edge of his comprehension—he could tell that everything was getting straightened out. It had all been a mistake. Steps were being taken. Because there was the radiant city, the ellipses of light quivering on the baby's face, and the incandescent sky, and the salt air, and the sound of a door, somewhere nearby, a metal door clanging open—

"Hey, soldier, you're famous."

And a newspaper landed on top of him. He startled, blinked. Cathy and the baby and Venice evaporated. The cell door clanked shut and footsteps echoed away down the hall.

He lay on his side for a long time, staring at the gray concrete wall a foot away, then turned over and stared at the gray concrete wall on the other side of the cell. Diagonally across, on a little table, was a plastic vase filled with plastic forsythia.

He stood up, went to the window, and—why was it so high?—grabbed the bars and hoisted himself up to look out at the world. Except it wasn't the world. It was an interior hallway, more cinder block, fluorescent lights. He felt a quaver of claustrophobia and lowered himself back to his feet.

His watch said six o'clock. Was that morning or night?

He sat back down on his bunk and picked up the paper. The banner headline read "Tidings of Comfort and Joy!" and there was a story about Santa Claus, including interviews with the usual kids who'd heard the usual reindeer hooves on the roof. Below the fold—right next to the latest on the Kenotic Messiah—was the story of a murder at the Golden Calf. It was sparse in details, didn't name Candi except as an employee of the casino, said that a suspect had been taken into custody, even had a photo of Cosmo with his handcuffed hands before his face, but no name, no mention of the Sistine ceiling. He read it over as if there might be something between the lines that would begin to explain, but there was nothing.

Someone—a woman officer, backed up by another woman officer in the hall—came in with a Styrofoam takeout plate of turkey and stuffing and mashed potatoes, said "Merry Christmas" to Cosmo, and left. So it was evening.

He tried to eat, to drink, to read the paper to keep his mind numbed: the comics, the personals, then a section devoted to the holidays—an article on Kwanzaa, on the first synagogue in Las Vegas, on false messiahs throughout history (photo, of course, of the Kenotic Messiah), then—how weird was this?—a story about the New Gnostic Church. It made him sit up on his bunk.

Bay Area Group Says Messiah Is Here and She's a Woman

Berkeley—Ever heard of the Gospel of Mary Magdalene? Or the Testament of the Archons? These are just two of the Gnostic Gospels, religious texts of the Gnostic Christians, who flourished in the first centuries after

Christ. Persecuted by the Roman Church, these mystical Christians largely died out. Their beliefs and teachings remained conjectural until the discovery in Egypt in 1945 of a large cache of heretical texts.

Now the New Gnostic Church says one of the prophecies of those texts is about to come true.

According to the church's leader, Sophia, the Gospel of Mary Magdalene maintains that when the Messiah returns, he will return as a woman. Moreover, says the Magdalene Gospel, she will be the daughter of the rock, which scholars interpret as being a reference to Peter.

How can a contemporary messiah be a daughter of one of the twelve apostles? Sophia—she uses no last name—says the riddle is easily solved if one considers that by apostolic succession, the Roman Catholic Pope is commonly referred to as Peter.

"The Messiah," she says, "is among us. And she is the daughter of a twentieth-century Pope. But because she lives—as we all do—in the Demiurge's world, her existence is disguised by parody and deception."

He stopped reading, blinked, went back to the beginning and started again. The article continued:

Members of the New Gnostic Church, which claims a worldwide membership, live ascetically, dress in homespun robes, and practice mortification of the flesh.

They believe that the world as we know it is evil. It was made by the Old Testament God, whom they call the Demiurge. They believe that the serpent in the Garden of Eden was sent by the true God to help Adam and Eve achieve gnosis, or knowledge. The expulsion from the garden was the result of the Demiurge's desire to keep humanity ignorant.

The result is that humanity is in a condition of bondage. The material world is a forgery. Personality, emotion, relationships are all counterfeit, mere shadows of their originals in the spiritual realm.

"Because this world is a counterfeit of the true world," Sophia explains, "the messiah appears as a counterfeit of the true Messiah. And the daughter of the Pope as a counterfeit Pope's daughter."

Members of the New Gnostic Church believe that there is no moral law that governs them here. They reject the Ten Commandments as being the laws of the Demiurge.

"The New Gnostic Church represents a liberation from a deceptive and oppressive construction of the Christ," Sophia maintains. "With advances in DNA identification, the orthodox church knows we are a threat."

Because of that perceived threat, the New Gnostic Church is keeping secret the identity of their messiah. They believe that just as in the first centuries of Christianity, the Catholic Church is again committed to the Gnostics' destruction.

"Even now the Vatican is watching our movements. They have tried to place informers in our membership. But this time we will not let them pervert the Savior and what she means."

Was someone putting him on? Okay, so there was nothing in the article—he read it a second, a third time—nothing that began to explain the mess he was in, but surely there was something there—a counterfeit Pope's daughter?— some clue, even if it was only visible in parodic nods and winks, cosmic leg-pulling. That business about the home-spun robes—were these the chicks in bathrobes Candi had mentioned? Heck, he had seen them himself from atop his scaffolding, monky-looking women lurking on the casino floor. What on earth were they doing there? And the Pope's daughter herself, with her paranoia, her being followed, her had-anyone-contacted-Cosmo? Boy, had someone contacted Cosmo!

He tore the story out of the paper, folded the clipping, and was putting it in his pocket when a distant door opened and the sounds of footsteps came down the hall.

"Hey, soldier. Confession weighing on your soul yet?"

And Orel Sloan, accompanied by a uniform, appeared on the other side of the bars. He had a cell phone in his hand.

"Where's my lie-detector test?" Cosmo asked, arms folded across his chest.

"It's Christmas Day," Orel Sloan said. "We can't muster the necessary personnel. You wanna try the phone again?"

And he handed Cosmo the cell phone between the bars. He'd tried once before, Betty and Veronica in lieu of Crazy Herman, who was presumably still on the planet Lux, but no one had been home.

"Who you gonna call?"

There was no one. Betty, Veronica, Crazy Herman, Tim Munjoy, his grief counselor, the other love assassins: Who could help him? There was his mother back in Pawtucket, Cathy's parents in Boston, but really . . . Still, he had to tell someone. Someone had to know where he was. He dialed

Amalgamated Illusion, then the extension for the lab, hoping one of the programmers would be there.

It was Polly Sensoria who answered.

"Can I have some privacy?" Cosmo said through the bars to Orel Sloan, and when the detective had mugged a look and moved off down the hall: "Crazy Herman? Munjoy? Is somebody there?"

"I'm here for you," came the low, sexy voice of Polly Sensoria. This was Crazy Herman's little joke. Instead of an answering machine, callers got Polly Sensoria in secretarial mode, her verbal databanks engaged, searching their speech for key words and responding with appropriately seductive remarks.

"Somebody? If you're there, pick up the phone."

"Oh, I love it over the phone. I love to hear—"

In spite of himself, he could see her: legs crossed, short skirt hiked up her thighs, prim eyeglasses, hair held up with a No. 2 pencil in a precarious bun just waiting for you to reach out and let its digital luxuriance tumble down.

"Hello? Help! Hello?"

"Hello," Polly Sensoria keyed, *"I'm so glad you've—"* but there was a raspy click, an interruption, a space, and then a voice, doubtful, a little irritated.

"Dude. Is that you?"

It was Munjoy.

"Tim," Cosmo said. He was surprised at the urgency, the relief, in his own voice.

"Like, what are you doing? What is *happening* to you?"

"Have you seen the newspaper?"

"Newspaper?" Munjoy repeated. "That is, like, too Gutenberg for me. I saw it all on TV."

"I need help," Cosmo said. "I need a lawyer."

"Lawyers and I don't mix, man."

"Tim, you're my one phone call."

A hesitant silence came through the line. Then it seemed like there was a change in the tone of the silence, as if Munjoy had put his hand over the receiver, was conferring with someone. Cosmo looked between the bars, down the hall to where Detective Sloan and the police officer were having a confab, pretending not to listen.

"We could ask Sane Herman," Munjoy said finally. "He's into lawyers."

Sane Herman was one of the project managers. Cosmo hardly knew him, but he was better than nobody.

"Okay," said Cosmo. "Can you call him?"

"Dude, it's Christmas."

"I'm in jail, Tim."

"I'm totally aware of that, man. I'm tuned in to the master plot. The wrongfully accused. David Janssen in *The Fugitive*."

"Call Sane Herman. See if he knows a lawyer. A *criminal* lawyer, not corporate. You understand?"

"Barry Morse as Lieutenant Gerard."

"Is Crazy Herman there?"

"Got to find the one-armed man. Clear your name. I will relay this all to Sane Herman. He'll know what to do."

"Right," Cosmo sighed.

Then, as if Munjoy were suffering an atavistic slippage into the human: "Are you, like, okay?"

"I'm okay."

A silence hung on the line; then: "Later, dude."

And that was it. Orel Sloan was moseying back down the

hall. The fluorescent light made his skin green. He held out his hand for the cell phone.

"Lie-detector test, psychological examination, further interrogation. You got a big day tomorrow, soldier."

"You can't just keep me here."

"Sure we can," he said. "You're in custody." And he smiled like the phrase legitimized things, then turned around and headed back toward the doorway and the waiting officer at the end of the hall.

For how many hours he lay there, gazing up at the underside of the bunk above him, he didn't know. He tried climbing up onto the upper bunk and gazing at the concrete ceiling, but that wasn't any better. From time to time, he heard sounds from somewhere in the building, a distant cell door opening, closing, a shout, curses, someone weeping. He finally slipped into a horrible pattern of falling asleep and jerking awake, half-dreaming he was inside the elevators at the Golden Calf, going up, up, impossibly up, the faux hieroglyphs painted on the elevator doors a gibbering of eyes and faces, cats and cow horns. He kept trying to read them, coming up almost to consciousness and then plunging back into the riddle. He woke fully enough once to find himself back down on the lower bunk, tried to get up, then tumbled back into feverish sleep. This time he was in a ghost town, trudging across the stony rubble, only instead of the bleak abandon of the place there was a sinister presence, a bodied shadowy thing that with the vigor of dream-peril seemed to be infused everywhere. When he turned to look for Cathy she was always just gone, just turned a corner or stepped into a derelict building, and in her place was the menacing presence, consciousness in a stairway stringer that climbed to nowhere, eyesight in the very atmosphere. When he woke—after how many hours?—he was drenched in sweat. Someone was standing in the cell's doorway.

"Got friends in high places, Dust?"

He raised himself up on his elbow. It was morning. He didn't know how he could tell, but he could.

"What?"

"Get lost."

It was Orel Sloan, holding the cell door open. There was a uniform behind him.

"What?" he said again. He sat up, looked around.

"Scram."

He swung his legs over the edge of the bunk and stood up, shook himself free of his dreams. "What? What's happened?"

"Beat it."

"I'm not under arrest?"

"You never *were* under arrest. Who ever arrested you?"

He started down the hall. Cosmo pulled at his sticky clothes, hurried after him.

"I thought you wanted to hold me for psychological evaluation," he said, aware that in some bizarre, edgy way he was irritated at not being under arrest. "Didn't you say you were going to hold me for psychological evaluation?"

"Maybe we will, maybe we won't. Right now, you're free to take the air. The word came down."

The word?

"But don't leave town. Understand?"

They went down a flight of stairs, along a hallway, into the noise and hubbub of a squad room. In a glassed-in office he caught sight of Carlotta Valdez and someone else, a suit with a tan, sunglasses, an FBI chin.

"Mr. Dust?" the suit said when Cosmo walked in. He took off his sunglasses and shook Cosmo's hand. "I'm Joseph Sorvillo. I'm your lawyer. They treating you okay?"

He had it wrong. The chin was FBI, but the tie tack, the cuff links, the diamond stud in the right earlobe, they were something else.

"Did Sane Herman call you?" he asked.

"Sane Herman?" The lawyer smiled curiously, handsomely. "I've been retained by a friend of yours. But"—and he made a self-evident gesture—"we'll talk elsewhere."

Cosmo looked at Detective Valdez, then to Detective Sloan, as if for help.

"We'll be calling you, soldier," Orel Sloan said. "Don't lose hope. You might be under arrest yet."

"Don't count on it," Sorvillo said; then, to Cosmo: "But you *do* need a shave. Change of shirt. Freshly ironed slacks." And, with a wink and a tug at his own starched white cuffs, he said, "Nothing like a knife-edge crease to take the sting out of suspicion of murder." He smiled like an older brother, put his hand on Cosmo's shoulder, picked up his briefcase, and started toward the door.

"Wait," Cosmo said, confused. He turned back to where Orel Sloan had hiked his rear end up onto the desktop. There'd been something he'd been wanting to ask. What was it?

"Yeah?"

"The baby," he said after a moment. "Whatever happened to the baby?"

"What baby?"

"Candi's baby. The baby in the bathroom. The baby in the car seat."

The two detectives exchanged looks.

"What the hell are you talking about?" Orel Sloan snapped.

"The baby. I'm talking about the baby!"

He fixed Cosmo with a look bred-in-the-bone cold. "There was no baby." Then, quietly, almost to himself: "You really *are* a fruitcake."

Chapter 11

A Chance Card on the Roof of the Golden Calf

Outside it was the same old world, though there was new snow up on the Muddy Mountains. They got into Sorvillo's car—a yellow Cadillac—and drove down Paradise Road, the lawyer making small talk along the way: Did Cosmo want a bite to eat? Coffee? How about that change of clothes? What Cosmo wanted was to be taken to the parking garage of the Golden Calf, where his van was, and allowed to just, you know, go home.

"Can't," Sorvillo said. "Someone's waiting for us."

And he reached out, patted Cosmo on the knee.

At the Golden Calf they turned the Cadillac over to a valet and went into the casino, over to the bank of elevators, where a spooked Cosmo eyed the hieroglyphs on the elevator doors. Inside, Sorvillo inserted a key and the elevator lifted upward. But when they stopped, instead of the same dark hallway as three days before, there was a cold, windy brightness—the rooftop, it had to be—and trees and shrubs and the shimmering blue of a swimming pool, no less. Sorvillo guided him across the Astroturf toward the edge of the roof where, in between potted palms, Cosmo caught sight of the Pope sitting in a wheelchair, in a parka, with his eye to a telescope. Around him were several easy chairs and a television, a Persian carpet spread on the Astroturf. In one of the chairs was a priest, a different one from the other night. They drew up to the edge of the carpet and waited. At the other end of the roof Benny was practicing six-footers on a putting green.

"Is this him again?" the Pope asked after a minute, pulling his eye away from the telescope and squinting at Cosmo. He seemed stronger than he had the other night. "Michelangelo?"

"Right," said Cosmo.

The Pope grimaced and spat onto the phony grass, and then went back to looking through the telescope. It was aimed not at the sky but earthward, at downtown Vegas. "Whatta dump," the Pope said after another minute had passed. He laughed, coughed, put his eye back to the telescope, sighed. "Did we stick this guy or what?"

From down one of the paths that led through the rooftop garden Marco appeared—wingtips, double-knit slacks, a pleasant smile for Cosmo. Over on the putting green Benny had put up his putter and was coming toward them, too. They gathered around, waited patiently. After another minute, the Pope pulled away from the telescope and sank back into his wheelchair. He slipped his fingers under the afghan that covered his lap and gazed at Cosmo for a long minute.

"So, Michelangelo," he said finally, "you didn't like the way she gave head or what?"

And there leaked from the alive side of his face a

sibilance Cosmo figured was a laugh. Sorvillo and the others smiled.

"A seventeen-caliber Bianchi," the Pope said. "That's a girl's gun. Eh, Marco?"

"A pussy's gun," said Benny.

"This guy, this guest of my hotel, who I'm thanking for painting a religious subject on my ceiling, this Michelangelo, don't like the way one of my girls gives head, so he whacks her in my bathtub with a pussy's gun. I don't know what's the bigger insult here." And he looked around the circle of faces. "One, he don't like the way one of my girls does him. Two, he messes up one of my rooms, which is my hospitality to him. Three, he don't have the respect for me to do it with a man's gun."

"He's an artist," said Marco, "like, whatta ya expect?"

"An artist," the Pope said, and he turned his good hand palm-up in a parody of a Mafia don evaluating the situation. Or maybe it wasn't a parody, and Cosmo just couldn't tell the difference anymore. "Tell me, Michelangelo, what did I ever do to you that you should treat me this way?"

To which Cosmo kept his mouth shut.

"What insult, what disrespect? Tell me and let me make it up to you. Tell me what I did that you should come into my home and with a pussy gun whack one of my girls and mess up my bathtub and"—here he leaned forward, dragged his left side forward—"and try to freaking blame it all on my daughter!"

This last he said with such barely controlled rage that Benny had to step forward to make sure he didn't tumble out of the wheelchair. Cosmo stared at him, at the collapsed face and the blighted skin, and wondered just where the postmodern left off and the real began. He looked first at Marco for help, then behind at Sorvillo, but it was no go.

"Your daughter?"

"Don't play dumb! You think I don't know you've been trying to stick it to my daughter? You and half the other economy cuts in Vegas!"

At which Cosmo blanched but had the good sense to keep quiet.

"You think I don't know you been squealing to the cops? You think the cops come looking for her, asking questions, and I don't know?" He made a fist of his bad hand with his good, took a moment to catch his breath. "If she squibbed this bitch, what business is it of yours? Who are you that you think you can squeal on me and mine?"

"I never said—"

"Who the freak said you could speak? Did someone ask you a question that you should be speaking? If she squibbed this bitch and wants you to take the freaking fall, then you take the freaking fall. Understand?"

He nodded.

"Understand?"

"Yes."

With his good hand, D'Angelo pushed the dead side of his face up as if it might stay in place. "What I'm doing right now is restraining myself, Michelangelo. I'm restraining myself from asking Benny to take you to obedience school. You *capish*, asshole?"

"I *capish*," said Cosmo.

"Because if you don't, we got ways to instruct you."

"I *capish*."

"All right," he said. He was out of breath again. He leaned

back in the wheelchair, adjusted his bad arm on the arm-rest. "Jesus, Mary, and Joseph," he said, like Cosmo was such a sorry case. He tried to turn in his seat to look at Benny. "Can you believe this guy? He calls 911." And again there was the leaky hiss of his laugh. "What kind of a punk calls 911?"

"An artist punk," said Benny.

"He finds a dead body in his room, so what's he do?" And here the laughter almost choked him.

"He calls 911!"

They all four laughed. The priest, too.

Cosmo shifted his weight, wondered where she was now. Downstairs with one of her economy cuts? Rome? Or maybe just a few feet away, behind one of the trees in the rooftop garden, eavesdropping, gun in hand.

"Okay. Joey," the Pope said to the lawyer, "ask your client the questions." And he let his head rest, closed his eyes.

"Mr. Dust," Sorvillo said, coming forward. He put finger to chin, thoughtful. "We're a little worried. No one's seen Mr. D'Angelo's daughter since the night of the murder. We're hoping you can shed some light on where she might be."

Cosmo looked from one to another, from the lawyer to Benny to Marco to the Pope slumped in his wheelchair.

Sorvillo smiled, made an indulgent gesture. "Ann's a headstrong girl. It's not unusual for her to"—he paused, searching for the words—"go on a vacation. But we like to know what's what. As much as we can. Understand?"

Cosmo nodded.

"Okay." Sorvillo paused to get his ducks in a row. "First. Did you kill the cocktail waitress?"

"No."

He held an index finger in the air, cocked his head for warning. "Truth," he said. "We need the truth here." Then he smiled, gestured with his fingertips between Cosmo's breast and his own. "Attorney-client privilege."

"I didn't kill her."

"Any idea who did?"

Should he tell them the Pope's daughter? Was there anything to be gained by it?

"No. No idea. I didn't even know her."

"You mentioned a baby. At the police station. She had a baby?"

"Yes."

"In the bathroom with you?"

"Yes."

Sorvillo exchanged a look with Benny and Marco. Then, changing tack: "When Miss D'Angelo came to see you, what did you talk about?"

Cosmo shrugged. "Weird stuff," he said, and he screwed his face into a question. Sorvillo made a wavering gesture with his hand.

"She's had an unusual life," he offered. "She lives under unusual pressures."

At which the Pope muttered something, but kept his eyes closed, his head lolled to the side.

"What weird stuff, exactly?" Sorvillo asked.

Cosmo shrugged. Did he tell them about the Gnostics, the Demiurge? "She said her mother had been an Italian *contessa*. That she had been killed. She said she was being watched."

They took this in calmly; nothing new here. Cosmo felt

bold enough to ask was that all true, but Sorvillo let it be known by smile and gesture that *he* was asking the questions.

"You haven't been approached by anyone? Because of your relationship with Ann?"

"I don't have a relationship with Ann," he felt chafed enough to say.

The lawyer allowed the point. "No one's contacted you? Nothing out of the ordinary?"

"Any Jews?" Benny threw in.

"What?" Cosmo asked, turning to him in wonder.

"You know, Jews." Hiking his shoulders like, what's wrong with this guy? Sorvillo stepped in.

"There are people in the world who don't wish Ann well, Mr. Dust. Factions. Competitors. Men of influence like Mr. D'Angelo, they make enemies over the years. They attract problem cases."

"These problem cases, do they drive a green Jaguar?"

At which, strangely, the priest looked up.

"What?" said Sorvillo.

"A green Jaguar. I was being followed by a green Jaguar that night."

Sorvillo looked from Benny to Marco, who in turn looked at one another, came up empty-handed.

"You're sure?"

"It could have been coincidence," he allowed.

"Ever been followed by a blue van?" Benny asked.

"What?"

"Whatta you, deaf? A van. A blue van."

Cosmo shook his head no.

"Has anything else out of the ordinary happened?" Sorvillo asked.

"Out of the ordinary?" He couldn't hold back. "You mean other than Candi being killed, my being under suspicion of murder, and the Mafia coming out of the Smithsonian long enough to interrogate me? Other than that, you mean?"

"Don't be a smart-ass," Benny put in.

"The baby," Sorvillo said again. "You say she had a baby with her, but when you went back into the bathroom, it was gone?"

"All I said was she had a baby with her. Look, fellas." He spread his hands before him. "I don't even know this Ann. Fifteen minutes up on the scaffolding, and then that night for five, maybe ten minutes. She tries to involve me in conversation about her murdered mother, and when I don't bite, she gets up and kisses me. Then she walks away all la-di-da—"

Marco was flashing a hand signal at him—nix, nix—but the damage was already done.

"She kissed him?" D'Angelo said, opening his eyes. He lifted his head, blinked at the world, and then leaned forward in his wheelchair. The others had gone a little rigid. Cosmo wondered what the heck was the big deal.

"Yes."

"On the lips?"

"Yes."

The old man closed his eyes as if this—hadn't he said so all along?—this was what the world was declining into, this trespass, this violation of the hierarchy. He turned away and gazed over the edge of the roof, down at the Strip, or maybe at a Vegas only the museum of his memory held, with Studebakers and two-seater Thunderbirds going past, with headliner signs for Sinatra and Joey Bishop, Esso gasoline, drive-ins in the shape of burgers, wieners, cups of coffee.

"Did you hear that?" D'Angelo whispered to Benny, to Marco. "He kissed her."

"No," Cosmo corrected, "she kissed me."

"I must be dead," D'Angelo said. "I'm not here."

Marco and Benny exchanged looks.

"Michelangelo, you think I'm here? You think you see me?"

Michelangelo just stared at him.

"Come on, Mr. D'Angelo," said Benny, softly.

"If I was still alive, you think midgets would come into my house and whack one of my girls? Then feel up my daughter right under my nose?"

"I'm not a midget," Cosmo found himself objecting. The others turned to him as if grateful.

"You're a midget if Mr. D'Angelo says you're a midget," said Benny.

"He could have you whacked like that," Marco said with a snap of his fingers.

"Like *that!*"

"You remember Larry the Fish?"

"You remember Clarinet Joe? The way he had him pick out 'Taps' on the piano just before he stuck him?"

"Sure."

They grinned at each other, stage grins, the sort you see in the movies when the raw recruit's buddies are telling him, *You're gonna make it, kid, it's only a flesh wound.* Between them, Angelo D'Angelo had let his head sink onto his breast.

And for the first time it occurred to Cosmo that this whole thing was being got up for D'Angelo's sake, a diversion to make the old man feel like he still mattered, Cosmo and who knew how many others strong-armed onto a stage decorated with the props of mob nostalgia. He even wondered whether they might have killed Candi themselves, scripted her death as a kind of Chance card for D'Angelo to draw, the act open to conjecture along whatever lines would bring the dying man comfort—revolt in the ranks, old scores to be settled—and by simple bad luck, Cosmo had gotten himself plotted as a point along one of those lines.

"Uncle," he said. Benny, who had been reciting for D'Angelo a litany of reassuring crimes—look what they'd done to Englestein!—straightened up and eye-fucked Cosmo for interrupting him.

"Uncle," he said again anyway.

"Englestein!" Marco cried, picking up the ball. "We shoulda finished him off when we had the chance!"

But what really chilled him was the thought that the mob was just as clueless as he was, that this mummery of muscle and intimidation was only their way of reassuring themselves, trying to make sense of the senseless in terms they understood. And that they couldn't see that it was *they* who had wandered behind the proscenium, found themselves in the turbulence, unable to tell the difference between their own stage business and the extravaganza the dark gods had scripted for Cosmo.

"Uncle!"

Chapter 12

The Trial in the Desert

Back in his apartment he lost count of the number of times he climbed in and out of bed, turned the television on and off, put his work clothes on, took them off, ran cold water over his head, stared in the mirror, cracked the blinds an inch to see if the world was still there. He tried to calm himself by assuming a relaxation position his grief counselor had taught him, and then when that didn't work, by getting out everything of Cathy's he still had—her notes for her book on altarpieces in the Veneto, including the sketches he'd done for her that winter, their scraps of maps, floorplans, altar arrangements. But none of it worked. He opened a new bottle of bourbon and tried watching Edmond O'Brien in *The Barefoot Contessa*, then when that got to be too much, Edmond O'Brien in *The Girl Can't Help It*, then at midnight, four in the morning, noon the next day, Edmond O'Brien in *D.O.A.*, until the plot became all scrambled in his head, dead or alive, dying or living, he couldn't say.

In the gas fireplace, like tiny Salomes, the blue flames waved their bellies at him.

In the end he packed a suitcase with everything he valued in the apartment (how little there was!), grabbed his passport and his little stash of cash, and marched outside toward the Amalgamated Illusion van with a hell-or-high-water step meant to intimidate any reporters who might be lurking about. He threw his stuff onto the passenger seat, got in, pulled out past the Pair-o'-Dice Arms sign (Adam and Eve rolling a pair of dice), and headed for the Strip, then onto Highway 95, north out of the city. He kept an eye on the rearview mirror for Carlotta Valdez, Orel Sloan, a TV van, a green Jaguar. Was what he was doing suspicious, illegal? He didn't care, didn't know even where he was going, but going he was, driving into the cold desert, the mountains on either side of him with a pasting of snow, the alkali and mesquite waste all around, amargosa like pills of lint on the ribbed weave of the Indian Springs Gunnery Range.

Why not head east? Why not back to Boston, where he'd spent one beautiful year with Cathy? New England, where they at least had trees. Rain. A history of moral character, not this griddle of alkali, this blast of salt. He had friends there still, artist friends who maybe still had their souls in hand. Was it too late for him? No kidding now, he wasn't kidding. Couldn't he be scoured by some simple return? To Boston, to his old job at the Restoration Lab? He tried to feel the movement of the van—he was going eighty—as if it were taking him away in a whirlwind of retrocession, the spinning tires eating up the highway like some B-movie motif of return, the calendar leaves falling away, the spiraling tunnel of time. Oh, he didn't mean to go back to a world where the Laughing Child laughed—no, he would have to get out of the business of imagining Cathy come back, alive, suitcase in hand, as if it'd all been a bookkeeping mistake, sorry!—but back somehow to a future that evaded Las Vegas, a future that branched from the point where he had met Cathy, as if there were two Cosmos and this one, this anti-Cosmo, hadn't been in the Restoration Lab that day when the pretty American grad student had shown up, but had ducked out for an espresso and had never seen Nevada, the Pair-o'-Dice Arms, the Sistine ceiling in the desert.

On the roadside were highway signs warning him to look out for wild burros. He looked to the right, to the left. There were no wild burros.

Could escape be this easy? Could he do what he had never been able to do before, leave Cathy in the desert and go? Or was there something in the world itself, some force or quality of things-as-they-are that bound him to his life, something you could name and put a frame around: *What Killed Cosmo Dust, 1999, chocolate and cyanide assemblage, Collection of the Artist*? Worse, was that something inside him? Cyanide simply the extrusion of an interior state, the *pum-pum* of his heartbeat reified in the shape of Candi bleeding in the bathtub, Cathy convulsed on the couch? Did he trail death the way some people trailed perfume, a ponytail, bad luck?

Damn, but he kept seeing burros behind the rocky outcrops, behind the bushes, on the ridge in the distance. They weren't there when you looked straight at them—it was a speck of amargosa, a rustle of shadow—but look away and they came back, ugly little burro heads and burro bodies peering from behind the sagebrush, tramping across your brain.

In the near distance the mountainsides were scarred with horizontal striations, the remnants of old rhyolite and mercury and cyanide mines. But behind them the real mountains seemed to rise into the heavens, snow-peaked, pearly, shimmering with aerial perspective. He felt a deep impulse to drive toward them, to find whatever rutted road or burro path would bring him to the foot of those peaks, and when he couldn't drive any further, to get out and climb, up, up toward the cold and the snow and the bright, rare air. At times it even seemed like the highway was headed toward them, but the miles would roll by, the near mountains would loom and pass, the road would straighten, and the mountains in the distance would levitate away. By the time the sprinkle of shacks and trailers outlying Beatty came into view, the mountains seemed farther away than ever.

He stopped for gas in the tiny desert town, took a leak, bought some Hostess SnoBalls. It was the first day of his new life, his life as anti-Cosmo. What to do? Where to go? There was an old Ben Franklin variety store across the way with a WELCOME TO BEATTY—GATEWAY TO DEATH VALLEY sign on it. OPEN CHRISTMAS DAY, it said. It looked like it hadn't sold anything since the Ford administration. He crossed the road and went inside, found a pair of overalls in the boys' section (the indignity of it!) and a cowboy shirt his size— not the sort of thing Cosmo would have been caught dead in, but anti-Cosmo? One corner of the store was given over to antiques and collectibles, another to a beauty parlor, empty except for the beautician, seated in one of her own waiting chairs and reading a magazine. Cosmo went in and sat next to her. She looked at him. He smiled.

"You need a cut?"

"Maybe."

"What do you mean, maybe?"

"I'm thinking about it."

She grimaced and went back to her magazine. On the coffee table in front of him was a *People* magazine, the one with nonagenarian Katharine Hepburn on the cover. He covered it with a different issue and then—what the heck—picked it up, turned to pages 38–39 where, gosh, there was a story about some fellow painting the ceiling of the Sistine Chapel in Las Vegas. There were pictures of it and everything, God reaching out to Adam, an inset photo of the painter, kind of a handsome fellow but poor devil to have a job like that—

"Hey," said the beautician next to him; she was leaning toward him, her neck craned. "That's you."

"No, it isn't."

She looked at him straight on, then back at the magazine. "Sure it is."

"Nope."

She eyed the paint stains on his pants, his shirt inside his jacket, and squinted at his hair. "You don't need no cut," she said.

"Yes, I do."

"No, you don't. Anyway, I'm closed."

He looked at her pink smock, her scissors peeking out. "No, you're not."

"It's five o'clock. I'm closed. Ain't we closed?" she called to the variety store cashier.

"Nope," a voice answered from somewhere in the shelving.

"We're closed," said the beautician.

Back outside he kicked a clod of dry sod. He had always assumed that if he had an opposite his opposite was happy, healthy, living it up in Palm Springs or someplace, painting what *The New York Times* would call "the *Demoiselles d'Avignon* of his generation," and at day's end, by the poolside, enjoying a margarita brought by his wife, Kathy, babe at her breast, another in the oven. Whoever would have thought that anti-Cosmo was a vagrant, an Ishmael, the sort of fellow who made people ill at ease? He climbed into the back of the van and shut the door, and in the dim light, surrounded by fresco cartoons of God and angels—Sophia, to hear the Pope's daughter tell it—changed into his overalls and cowboy shirt. His work clothes he threw into an empty bucket.

It was only a few more miles before the sign welcoming him to Death Valley National Monument came into view. He passed it in full-blown despair. He ate a SnoBall, sipped from a bottle of bourbon he'd found in the back of the van. How was it that his grand flight—which might or might not be illegal, but which in any case ought to have been toward what he had once cherished, even if what he had once cherished was only available to him in outline, memory, gesture—had delivered him to a government road going downhill into heat and sterility and death? He gazed at the vast sink below him, the salty gray-white of the playa looking fantastically like a dusting of snow. Well, he'd always been an admirer of the proper background; where better to expire than Death Valley? He took the van out of gear, let it coast, turned on the air conditioner when it grew stuffy. His ears popped as he lost altitude. The mountains grew higher, the sun lower.

What a sight it was! Miles of chemical flats, borax marshes, the sludge of the heavens drained into the rocky defiles and baked into poison. And yet he couldn't rid himself of the feeling that it was snow down there. On the radio he managed to find one lost half-voice quivering in electronic limbo. He listened to it, nonsensical but at least human, until it, too, faded.

So, okay, if it wasn't snow, what was it, that whiteness out there? Was it salt, alkali, saleratus? Hard like concrete, or powdery like talc? He pulled the van over to the side of the road and got out, stood beside the fender looking out over the vast waste. The silence was spooky, and the utter absence of smell. Somewhere around here was the lowest point in the western hemisphere. He wondered, did they have it marked? Or was it anonymous in its significance, its palpable metaphor? The engine ticked beside him, cooling. He looked for bird, bug, bee. But there was only him, Cosmo Dust. The painter.

From off the passenger seat he took the bottle of bourbon and the remaining SnoBall. He left the keys in the ignition—if someone wanted to steal the van, let them—left his passport on the seat. That way, when they found his body . . . ha-ha. What the gallery-goer sees in this picture is the artist setting off across the trackless waste of Death Valley, the sun setting with the usual archetypal associations behind the distant mountains, note the desperate brushstrokes. Where he was going, he wasn't exactly sure. To check on the whiteness first, sure, maybe make it to the mountains. How far could they be? Fifteen miles? He could walk that far, couldn't he? But what then? Up to the snow? Even if he could make it, what then?

Maybe the trick to life was to forget about "what then," to forget about content and simply concentrate on composition, the crimson blood of Christ's wounds a chromatic counter to that red incision in the sky, tra-la-la, nothing more. If he ever got out of this mess maybe he could start a series of paintings drawn from his life, *Solipsism #1* through, say, *Solipsism #33*, reduce the horror to a question of composition—that triangle of baby, Jacuzzi, and crumpled chiton repeating the pyramid motif of bullet holes in the odalisque's head, note the detached brushstrokes.

Funny, the more he walked the more the whiteness receded. He kept thinking he would get there, that the next flat was where the real whiteness was, but when he got there, the ground was just the same, a dirty, gray, nondescript nothing. He bent over, scraped some of the grayness up, and put it in his mouth. Nothing. He turned and looked back at the van, an improbable metal rectangle a mile away. In another half hour it would be dark. What then?

"Non si può praticar con lui," Pope Leo X had famously complained about Michelangelo. Well, there was no getting along with Cosmo Dust, either. He had his own *terribilità*, thank you very much, and right now his *terribilità* took a swig of bourbon and told him to keep going, to put one foot in front of the other as if each were an insult to God. Surely Death Valley was as good as the Golden Gate Bridge, though he wasn't so sure what the etiquette was here. The

Golden Gate Bridge he had down pat: bad form to scream or unpleasantly contort the body. You wanted that solitary, exquisite cut through the somber air, facing the bay, never the ocean. The desert was quite different. Though in a pinch, he supposed, one could assume the comic-book default: clothes ragged, body stretched out, index finger pointing in the direction where one had last hallucinated water.

The air was turning purple, darkening by the minute. All that was left of the sun was a stripe of gold along the peaks of the eastern mountains. Time to go back to the van, okay? He was getting tired. For two days now his sleep had come in fits and starts, dream-riddled, a touch insane. And it was sure to get cold out here. Back home there was his remote-control fire. But he kept going, ate his SnoBall, drank his bourbon, zipped up his jacket. From time to time he thought he saw lights out in the darkness, headlights, perhaps, moving along the narrow road—four, five, six miles distant. They looked like spirits, wavering, uncertain. He thought of all who had died here, the mule skinners and the swampers, the Chinese borax workers, the forty-niners who had gotten lost on their way west, their burros left to fend for themselves, skeletons bleaching in the sun.

Could he just keep walking? All the way across the playa, up and over the mountains, snow for drink, food to be had from the occasional hermit on the other side. Could he walk to Palm Springs, where Kathy-with-a-K was waiting for him with a cappuccino and a new life? Christ had done it. Moses, too. Baked themselves in the desert and come out new men.

gregory blake smith

He looked around in the darkness for a good spot to pee, but it was the desert, so they were all good spots. His water pattered noisily. Straight ahead was his mountain, the moon rising, misshapen, over its shoulder. Maybe he'd find a place to lie down, take a little nap. Dream of green oases, glittering water, fragrant winds.

Okay, so he was drunk now. Tired, too. Lost. Thirsty. It wasn't everybody in this, our postmodern world, who got to play Jesus in the desert. Any minute now Satan was going to show up and start offering him stuff.

And yet, how beautiful it was! The deep velvet of the night, the stars like God had borrowed a handful of Tinkerbell's dust. He remembered looking at the midnight sky as a boy and feeling a shiver in his soul. It was as if the sky had been aware of him: distant, unimaginably vast, and yet cognizant of little Cosmo Dust lying on the grass in his backyard. What had happened? How had the stars gone from being sentient and caring, whispering his name in the past-his-bedtime breeze, to being the cold witness to his and his century's brutalization? Oh, even to ask such questions showed how lost he was, how far he was from anything that could save him.

He needed to sit down, lie down, maybe take a little nap before continuing. He gazed around at the invisible grimness. Which way, exactly, was the van? Could he find his way back if he wanted to? He lay down, put the bourbon bottle under the nape of his neck for a pillow, and gazed up at the stars.

Who knew, anyway? Maybe the world had miscounted over the course of two thousand years—a day here, a day there, in the small hours of the Dark Ages an April morning lost, a December midnight—and the millennium was not in four days, but tonight, in a few hours.

He tried to get comfortable. Turned this way, that way. Closed his eyes.

When they first came home from Venice, he and Cathy used to play a kind of game. They would lie on their bed, eyes closed, and place themselves somewhere in Venice. It didn't matter where: in some piazza they used to sit in, or some shop where they'd once bought a bottle of Chianti. And then they would start walking. In their minds' eyes, still lying on their bed, they would leave wherever they were and start to move through the city, picturing it, naming each building as they passed—did she remember this? did he remember that?—the color of the stone, the canals, the shops' signs. . . .

Now he tried the same game, only with Cathy instead of Venice, with her face, her hair, the way she used to sit on the edge of the bed and pull her socks on. He had done something like this those first weeks after she had died, nearly every night, drifting toward sleep, almost hypnotizing himself until he could not tell whether he was awake or asleep, only that Cathy was there, lying beside him, leaning over him, about to kiss him.

"Cosmo," he heard now.

He lifted himself onto his elbow, looked around, but there was nothing, just a scribble of sagebrush a few feet off. Had he fallen asleep?

He let himself lie back, closed his eyes, let the desert disappear. Cathy was standing in one sock in front of her closet, trying to decide what to wear. She had her hair in a ponytail, so it had to be a weekend—she never wore a ponytail when she taught—and she had on these plastic hula-hoop earrings that dangled down to her collarbone. He watched her cycle through a half-dozen summer dresses, standing in her underwear, holding prints, paisleys, polka dots pressed to her front and asking what did he think, and then taking them down, standing on her tiptoes to reach a hanger, turning her lovely rear to him, as if daring him. . . .

"Cosmo Dust."

In a moment he would lift his head and see who was there. In a minute he would let go of Cathy's culottes and open his eyes and see who was talking to him. As soon as he could he would lift himself onto his elbow, look around again at the stars, the black mountains, the purple air. . . .

Except that this time, off to his left, there were *two* scribbles of sagebrush. One of them had burro ears.

"You found us," the voice said.

Oh, sure, he thought.

"We've been waiting for you."

What he would do is he would lie still and quiet for five minutes, not thinking. He would lie still and quiet for five minutes trying to not think. He would lie still and quiet for five minutes wondering why it was you couldn't make your mind not think.

"It's the season of miracles," said the burro. "Time to review conventional motifs of rebirth."

And he clopped a step closer. Cosmo muttered something into the alkali earth.

"*Número uno*, of course, is baptism, immersion in water.

Then there's blinding light in the Saul/Paul line. Sickness, fever, the trial in the desert . . ."

Could you dream while you were dreaming? Like those Vermeer paintings hanging on the walls inside a Vermeer painting, could you dream inside a dream? If so, he voted for golden vistas, harmonious architecture, fauns and faunlets—not a dark god talking to him at midnight in Death Valley, California, while his dead wife pulled on her capri pants.

"The season of miracles," the burro repeated. "Time to reflect on messiahs who have been put to death."

He'd be four years old. And Cathy would be alive. They'd be home in bed, the three of them.

"Desert, sickness, fever . . ."

Again he muttered something into the dirt.

"What? I can't hear you?"

Help, he tried to say; then: *"Help!"*

And at the sound of his own voice he woke and stared at the sky. It swam muddy and remote in his vision. He raised himself on his elbow, looked around. There was nothing there. No burro, no person, and yet somewhere on the other side of the darkness, he could *feel* her, Cathy and the baby! If he got up, if he walked over there into the darkness, he would find them . . . if he could just get his eyes to clear, if he could just calm his heaving chest!

Chapter 13

A Miracle at the Pair-o'-Dice Arms

In the morning when he woke he was so thirsty his tongue felt like a sock someone had stuffed in his mouth. He sat up with difficulty, cold, aching, breathing as if he were just back from the dead. In the distance—how could it be?—there were palm trees, buildings, sprinklers pinwheeling in the morning sun. And grass: a golf course. A golf course in the middle of Death Valley.

He turned away, blinked, spent a minute looking out over the salty playa, back toward where the van must be. Then, down at the empty bourbon bottle at his feet. One, two, three, okay: *Turn.*

The little red flags above the greens waved as if they were expecting him.

So he stood up, stiff, solid, brutally thirsty. And with barely a glance at the mountains that had so beckoned him the night before, he began to trudge toward the greenery. There'd be water there, maybe a snack machine, other necessities of life. Over at the third hole a greenskeeper was staring as if he, Cosmo, were the hallucination. Behind him a rainbow shimmered in the whirling sprinkler. Cosmo waved; the greenskeeper waved back.

In the compound he found a restaurant, went into the men's room, and put his head under a faucet. He could smell bacon and home fries. Out the window were a parking lot, cars and RVs, a sign—THE INN AT FURNACE CREEK: WORLD'S LOWEST GOLF COURSE. In the mirror he caught sight of himself, or rather of anti-Cosmo, in his cowboy shirt and overalls. He looked for signs of rebirth.

He got himself a coffee to go. A couple of donuts, too.

Outside there were golf carts, a whole row of them. He moseyed over to one, coffee in hand, and thought, Why not? It was either that or tell someone the whole sob story while asking for a ride back to the van. He climbed in, switched the ignition. The electric motor whirred to life. He stepped on a sort of gas pedal and the cart lurched forward. He took a sip of coffee and almost ran over a little boy in a Spider-man outfit.

Out on the narrow highway he half-expected someone to call out, a pickup truck to overtake him. But no, he sailed along with impunity. After a mile a motorcycle passed him, coming the other way. The cyclist waved; it was more of a salute, really, brothers in arms. The coffee tasted wonderful. The donuts, too.

But he wasn't half an hour back in the van—heading south, whether back to Las Vegas or not he wasn't sure— when the cell phone rang.

"Hey, soldier," came the familiar voice; the signal was weak, cutting in and out. "Where you been? We thought you'd given us the big razoo."

He sat up straight, put his seat belt on.

"Thought you might like to know the baby checks out."

"What baby?"

A low whistle came through the phone. "Had another blackout, eh?"

"You found the baby?"

"I didn't say we found him. I said he checks out. The deceased had a baby. Though we might be a little puzzled about just who the deceased is."

What did that mean? Cosmo wondered. But instead he said: "Find the baby, and you find your murderer."

Or at least he thought he said it; the signal began to break up, then came back.

"You're aware, Dust, that we asked you not to leave town, right?"

"Right."

"So what's with the weak signal? Where are you?"

He was at the lowest point in the western hemisphere, according to the sign at the side of the road.

"I'm right here," he said; then, before Orel Sloan could follow up: "What do you mean you might be a little puzzled about who the deceased is?"

Something like a shrug came over the phone. Or maybe calculated misdirection. "She was a cocktail waitress, Dust. A pro skirt. Candi, Susan, who knows."

"*You're* supposed to know."

"We do."

"Then who was she?"

But here—and he wouldn't put it past the dark gods to be engineering this—the signal began to cut out again. He caught something about Ann D'Angelo, then nothing. He waited a minute, but the signal didn't clear. He hung up, threw the phone onto the passenger seat. It didn't ring again.

So three hours later when he opened his apartment door and saw the baby—the baby, for Chrissakes!—after the first hitch of disbelief, he figured it was Orel Sloan's doing: Candi's baby over on the coffee table, still in his car seat, his eyes open, a faint smile on his face as if he were glad to see Cosmo again. "Very funny," he said to the apartment. "Find the baby and you find the murderer. Ha-ha. You can come out now." But there was no answer. He went into the kitchen, opened the broom closet, then the bathroom—hello? He checked the shower stall, looked under his bed. There was no one there.

Back in the living room he stood in a corner and stared at the baby. Then he squatted and stared. Put his hand over his mouth in a pantomime of disbelief and stared. The impossible was happening again. For the second time in three days he could hear the hush of servomotors turning, the dark machinations.

There was only one explanation. If you weren't going to resort to paranoia or metaphysics, there was only one explanation. It was *her*. However crazy it seemed, *she* had killed Candi, taken the baby, and now, out of some twisted resolve or calculated checkmate, had hung him with the evidence. And even though his thoughts whirred with *why*, another part of him knew it didn't matter. *Why* was in her head, unavailable to him. It was the *what* he had to worry about.

He closed the drapes so that no one could see in and then crossed to the car seat. Just as he had with the baby's dead mother, he tested reality with his fingertips. How soft! He reached down and, keeping up a running deception of smiles and coos, lifted the baby onto his knee. Amazingly, the baby seemed not to mind. He looked about the apartment, at the blank TV screen, at a photo of Cathy and Cosmo on the Rialto Bridge. Was he hungry? Cosmo wondered. Wet? Thirsty? There was some half-and-half in the fridge, he knew. This baby was old enough to drink without a bottle, wasn't he?

"You want some half-'n'-half?" he asked.

And just as he did, there was a knock on the door. He froze, squatting there, waited breathlessly for whoever it was to go away. But instead he heard a scratching in the lock. He sprang up, put the baby back in the car seat, and hustled him into the bedroom. He had just enough time to land the car seat on the floor beside the bed—if it was the police with the apartment manager, they needed a search warrant, didn't they?—and toss a blanket over it, half-assed, before he heard the door open. He hurried back into the living room.

"Maestro!"

It was Marco. He was fitting a bobby pin, a nutpick, a locksmith's tool—whatever it was—into a little case, tucking the case inside his suit jacket. Benny came in behind him, carrying a laptop. He dropped it on the sofa and, with a stink-eye for Cosmo, went off to search the apartment: kitchen, bedroom, bathroom. Cosmo heard his shower stall door open, shut.

"Okay," Benny said, coming back. "Where is she?"

"Who?" Cosmo answered.

"Who do you think?"

"Miss D'Angelo's still missing," Marco put in. "We need to find her."

Cosmo looked from one to the other. Had *they* dropped the baby off? Gone out for a burger until he showed in the van, and now this?

"She's not here," he said with a shrug. "Why would she be here?"

"Because you got her mixed up in your lousy life," said Benny, "and now she's upset."

"We're investigating," Marco said, "trying to determine exactly who killed whom. And to that end," he said with a smile, stepping over to where Benny had dumped the laptop, "come have a look." And he popped the laptop open, turned it on.

"What?"

"A little state-of-the-art intimidation," he said and tapped some keys. Benny disappeared into the kitchen.

"I've already been intimidated."

"Old school," he said with a dismissive gesture. He swung the laptop around for Cosmo to see. On the display was a picture of a man slumped in a porch swing, his face bloodied and, strangely, like a joke, a pair of Mickey Mouse ears on his head. From the kitchen there came the sound of the silverware drawer opening.

"This greaseball," Marco said, "he was one of ours, but he was running poker games out of his room in the hotel. Las Vegas and you gotta run an illegal poker game? We asked him nicely to stop. But some guys."

"We gave him a serious headache," said Benny. He came out of the kitchen carrying the silverware drawer, sat down on the sofa next to Marco.

"But the ears," Marco sniffed critically. "It was our edgy period."

And he went to the next photo, a close-up of the bullet hole in the head.

"You took pictures?" Cosmo couldn't help saying.

"Nah," said Marco. "Not then. We were innocent like everybody else. These are police shots I got from a detective friend downtown. I got a whole collection. I'm writing a book."

At which Benny took up one of Cosmo's forks and bent it as if it were a Gumby figure. At what point, Cosmo wondered, was the baby going to add his bit?

"Thing is," Marco mused, "you don't get that feeling of transgression in Vegas anymore. The mob, it was part of what attracted tourists. I think that's what it was with the illegal poker games. Not just for Myron"—he indicated the dead man—"but the guys playing, too. They wanted that feeling of trespass." And he gazed wistfully at the laptop. "Nowadays, it's getting harder and harder to feel like you're doing something wrong."

"We could beat the shit out of this punk," Benny said, jabbing a fork toward Cosmo. Marco shook his head.

"My heart wouldn't be in it, Benny."

And he changed the picture.

"Ah," he sighed, "a fedora."

On the screen was another dead body, this one with its head toward the camera, feet splayed, a pool of blood forming along the curb. It looked like Brooklyn or Little Italy or someplace. In a semicircle around the body, standing with their hands in their pockets, fedoras covering their heads, was a squad of Sam Spade types. One of them was holding a heavy-duty Rayovac flashlight. Stenciled on the brick wall behind them was an ad for H. Litsky

Cream & Eggs. Cream and eggs? Cosmo wondered. It was all before his time.

"That's our Pop," Marco said.

"Our Pop," Benny agreed softly. "He was a stand-up guy."

A wistful minute passed.

"This picture here," said Marco, "what I wouldn't give to be in this picture here. You got your dead body and you got your cops. You got your blood. These things you can assign values to. Offscreen somewhere you got your enforcer. He's drinking a whiskey. Cleaning his gun. These things have their values, too."

Cosmo had edged backward, and he glanced into the bedroom to where he could see the edge of the car seat peering out from under the bedclothes. Maybe the baby *was* strange, like Candi had said. Slept, ate, evacuated waste. That was it.

"Look at the black and white," Marco was saying. He clicked through the next several pictures, all of the same scene. "I tell you, the world began to go wrong with the invention of Kodacolor, Technicolor. Things got all complicated—red, yellow, blue. You can't tell what's what."

"The *world* is red, yellow, blue," Cosmo ventured.

"Precisely," said Marco.

"Precisely what?"

"You got to *process*, son."

"Nineteen fifty-nine," Benny said. He'd stopped bending silverware. "We was kids. There were FBI guys at the funeral, taking notes."

"*My* book," Marco said, "is only gonna have black-and-white photos, black print, white pages. It's gonna have value—"

The phone rang. Cosmo startled, then looked at Marco, as if for permission to answer it. He crossed to where the phone was, picked it up, said hello.

"It's me," a familiar voice said. For a wild instant he thought it was Cathy. But then he knew.

"I can't talk now," he answered in as even a voice as he could muster.

"Someone's there? The police?"

"Yes. No."

There was a pause, then a whisper: "The Carousel Bar in an hour. Don't betray me."

And just like that, she hung up.

Red, yellow, blue, Cosmo thought with a shiver. He put the receiver down.

"Who was it?" Benny asked, suspicious. He'd stood up to listen on the extension, but there was no extension.

"My grief counselor," was all he could think to answer.

"Thing is," Marco was saying, staring moodily at the laptop, "they got our Pop for putting the squeeze on this ring of horse juicers, but that was just a cover. What it really was was payback."

"For what?" Cosmo asked.

"Read it in his book," Benny interrupted. "Come on," he said to Marco. "She's not here. Let's dust." But Marco had his eye fixed on Cosmo.

"There's bad blood out there," he said. "Why do you think we've been escorting Ann her whole life? Benny practically got a college education sitting in at UNLV with her."

"*Amo, amas, amat,*" Benny said. "Now let's blow."

"This Candi business," Marco went on, "it might just be the tip of the iceberg."

"What iceberg?"

"Any questions?"

"What iceberg? That's a question."

"There's no iceberg," Benny said. He closed the laptop, picked it up. "It's a metaphor."

"For what?"

"You already had your question." He took a step toward the door. On the coffee table were half a dozen twisted forks.

"If you see her, if she tries to get in touch with you," Marco was saying, "call us. We're telling everyone who knows her."

"Who knows her?"

"No one."

"Fine," said Cosmo. He folded his arms across his chest. "And the baby?"

"What baby?"

"You know what baby." He gave Benny a look like he was nobody's fool.

"Don't get smart. If what we think has happened *has* happened, there's people gonna get hurt. And we don't want some Michelangelo getting in the way."

"If she gets in touch with you," Marco put in, "tell her we can make the game for real."

"What game?"

"Tell her she can come in out of the cold. She'll understand."

And Benny shovel-passed the laptop to Marco, and they were both out the door.

Chapter 14

The Lie Detector

Half an hour later he was standing in line at a convenience store. The security camera recorded him: some new father sent out by his wife for a box of Pampers, Sweet Cheeks baby wipes, some other stuff. In the back of the van he lay the baby on a pile of painter's rags, took off his old diaper—strange, it was still dry; did this baby not engage in ordinary bodily functions?—changed him into a clean one anyway. When he stood up he gazed around the parking lot, the intersection, looking for meaning in a green Jaguar, in a blue van, in the general look of things. The whole time the baby eyed him with a black-eyed grimace like he couldn't quite believe that this, *this*, was the fellow he'd been sent to save.

Fifteen minutes later Cosmo was riding the elevator up to the twenty-eighth floor of the Carousel, the baby asleep in the van in the parking garage with a bottle of Similac in his little hands, the passenger window cracked half an inch.

He didn't recognize her at first. She was sitting at one of the window tables and she was wearing—no, it wasn't a wig. She'd dyed her hair, blonde, and she had sunglasses on. She looked nervous. Not the femme fatale he had expected. He stood over her table, expecting he didn't know what, and then sat down.

"I've got a gun," was the first thing she said. She nosed the barrel out of her purse. "So don't try anything."

He looked away, out over the sprawling glitter of the city, referenced his eye to the Golden Calf in the distance and watched as it moved away from him. An eighth of an inch, a quarter, three-eighths. In thirty minutes the bar would make one full revolution.

"Benny and Marco are looking for you."

She nodded, as if okay, that registered.

"And the police," he ventured. Behind her sunglasses her eyes narrowed.

"You weren't followed?" she asked.

"By whom?"

"By anyone." And she looked around the room, eyeing the other tables, the entrance, then him again. She seemed to poise herself on some mental precipice.

"I'm going to ask you once," she said. "And I want the truth." She stared him straight in the face. "Did you kill her?"

He stared at her in return. Was this legit? Or was it just part of the masquerade, something to throw him off, to toy with him?

"I won't tell," she added. "It doesn't matter to me. Not in the ordinary way. But I have to know."

"Why?"

"Because if you killed her, then it wasn't me you were trying to kill. And I can trust you."

She wet her lips, kept her eyes on him as if his expression might betray him.

"What does it matter if you can trust me or not?"

She leaned toward him across the table. "You," she said. "You either stumbled innocently into all this, or you've been planted. I need to know which."

Jesus, she sounded like him.

"I didn't kill her."

"How can I know that?"

"The police," he said. "I spent Christmas in an interrogation room."

"And then were let go."

"Only after your father intervened."

"Exactly," she said.

"Exactly what?"

"You're with them. You're his. Everything's his," she said bitterly.

"I"—he found himself pronouncing—"am with no one." And the sound of the words depressed him. "You, on the other hand . . . You were the only other person in the room."

"That we know of."

And, not for the first time, he felt the sensation of reliving those few minutes with the creepy thought of someone stealing into the room while he and Ann were in the bedroom, slipping into the bathroom, killing Candi, leaving the gun, snorting the cocaine, and going out the door with a tah-tah, good-bye.

"If I could know that it was me and not the cocktail waitress who was supposed to be killed," she whispered, "then I would know that you didn't do it."

Again he wanted to ask, so what? So what if she knew it wasn't him?

"Why can't it have been the cocktail waitress who was supposed to be killed?" he said instead, as if he were sticking up for Candi's right to be murdered. "Why's it have to be you?"

"It doesn't have to be me," she snapped. "That's the *point*."

"Listen, *Contessa*—"

"Don't call me that."

"Okay, *Ann*," he said, exaggerating the single syllable as if *it* were the phony name, "I didn't kill Candi. And the only thing your father's employing me to do is to square him with the afterlife. If the world's out to get anyone, it's me, not you. I'm the one under suspicion of murder. I'm the one with the dead wife. I'm the one who's got a gun pointed at him."

"Incidental," she said. "All three instances. You just get in the way, is the problem."

He leaned back in his chair. At what point should he mention the Gnostics in the newspaper? That might be good for a spike of paranoia.

"My safety's always been an illusion," she murmured, almost to herself. Outside, the MGM was coming into view; soon it would be the Luxor, where Cosmo had spent three months of his life immured in King Tut's tomb.

"Look," he said as gently as he could, "if you want me to help you"—he wasn't going to, of course—"then I need some straight answers."

She fidgeted, took her sunglasses off, put them back on.

"I would tell you everything if I knew who you were," she said, "if I could trust you."

He spread his hands before him. "I will *tell* you who I am," he said in as honest a voice as he could manage. "I'm a painter. I'm five foot five. Brown eyes. Sandy blond hair. My wife, before she was inexplicably murdered, used to tease me about looking like one of the Beach Boys. I loved her. I'm not in league with any cabal or conspiracy that I know of. This is who I am."

He looked her square in the face. How easy it was!

"Now you tell me who you are."

She crossed and uncrossed her legs under the table. "I don't know who I am."

"Stop talking like a movie."

She pressed her fingers to her temples. The gun was there, in her purse, on top of the table. He could reach out and take it if he wanted to.

"I don't know who I am," she repeated. She stared down at the tabletop. "Angelo D'Angelo is not my father. But I can't say who my father is. Or where I come from. There are stories—"

"Sure," he said, "the *Libro d'oro.*"

"Don't," she said, and behind her sunglasses her eyes had a beseeching look, as if his sarcasm, his disbelief, had genuinely stung her. Not to be suckered, he looked away. Out the window the Venetian was coming into view.

"Did you kill her?" he asked bluntly.

"No."

"Did you take her baby?"

She cocked her head. "What?"

He took a deep breath, decided to gamble. "Did you kill her, take the baby, and then leave him in my apartment?"

He didn't know what he expected—some sign, some look that betrayed her. But her brow furrowed and her eyes snapped at him.

"What are you talking about?"

"Somebody left Candi's baby in my apartment. When I wasn't there."

"That's impossible."

"Yes, it is. But I've got him all the same. Right now he's down in my van. Asleep."

"I don't believe you."

He stood up. It was so abrupt that she reached for her purse, for the gun. He made an I-dare-you gesture with his head, toward the elevator.

"What game are you playing?" she whispered. She took her sunglasses off, as if to see him better. Strange that her eyes were green, he could have sworn they were gray that first day, up on the scaffolding.

"What game are *you* playing?"

They stayed like that for a good half minute. The waitress came, apologized for taking so long. Neither of them answered her. Then Ann clutched her purse, pushed her chair back, and stood up.

"Okay," she said. "Show me."

And they left the waitress standing there, crossed the room, and got into the elevator. They were silent all the way down, the Pope's daughter with her hand in her purse, Cosmo trying to look cool, calm, in control. They got off at the third floor, entered the gray air of the parking garage, found the Amalgamated Illusion van where Cosmo had

parked it. Ann stood off a ways, behind him. Cosmo unlocked the passenger door, swung it open with a magician's
élan, swept his hand at the car seat. At the sight of the
sleeping baby, Ann's face registered something like shock,
as if the world's treachery had finally matched some
equivalent in her head.

"You *did* do it," she said. She fumbled in her purse, took
out the gun, and pointed it at him.

"What?"

"You killed her," she said. "It was *you.*" And she jabbed
the barrel of the gun at him. He tried to take a placating
step toward her, but the gun told him to stop.

"Let's have a little consistency," he tried. "You said if I
was the murderer, then I was okay, I wasn't trying to kill
you. So what's with the gun?"

"I get nervous around murderers."

"I'm *not* a murderer. I *didn't* kill her." Then, one last try:
"*You* killed her."

"Boy," she said and laughed a bitter laugh. "You are really
something."

"You were the only other person in the suite. Somebody
killed Candi, kidnapped her baby, and a couple of hours
ago dropped him off in my apartment. You are the most
likely candidate."

"The police are going to love this."

"That's my other option."

She narrowed her eyes. "You don't have any options, mis-
ter. I'm the one with the gun."

And they stood faced off against one another. A car was
approaching, slowly, looking for a place to park. The driver
saw them, saw the gun, nodded politely, and kept going.

"Get the baby," Ann said, and then, when Cosmo didn't move: "Get him, get the car seat," this time with a nudge of the gun.

"Why?"

"You're coming with me."

He balked and then shrugged, leaned over, and unharnassed the car seat. He picked the baby up and like a good father remembered the bag of stuff from the Jack-B-Nimble, and then walked where Ann told him to, down the incline of the parking garage to a stairway, up a flight, up an incline, to a Cadillac with CALF-3 for a license plate. She zapped the car with a remote, opened a back door for him to put the car seat in, and handed him the keys.

"You drive," she said.

"Where?"

"I'll tell you where."

So he got in, adjusted the seat, backed out, and with that Cadillac smoothness slipped down and out of the parking garage, the gun on him the whole time.

"Go south on the Strip."

So he did. In the misaligned rearview mirror he could see the baby with his bottle in the backseat. This, by Cosmo's count, was the third time the poor thing had been kidnapped in forty-eight hours.

"Benny and Marco," he said after a while, just to say something, to try to get under her skin, "they say you can come in out of the cold."

He could feel her eyes on him.

"They say they're ready to make the game real. If you want."

"Shut up."

He shrugged. In the backseat the messiah was blowing milk bubbles. They drove in silence until they reached the Golden Calf.

"Okay, turn in."

He turned at a break in the traffic and headed for the parking garage.

"Don't let anyone see me."

She scrunched down in her seat, the gun still trained on him. The baby turned his gaze to the space where there'd been a head a moment before.

They parked and walked through the parking garage toward the casino, Ann with her jacket draped over her gun hand, Cosmo carrying the baby. He tried to ask a couple of times just what it was they were doing, but she told him to shut up. She had her sunglasses on again.

Inside the casino, she steered him toward the blackjack pit instead of the elevators. Overhead, God and Adam and Eve were still where he'd painted them. Looking up he couldn't help feeling a sort of pride in the job he'd done, unfinished now. Who would step in? Betty? Veronica? Neither of them could draw to save her life.

"Sammy," Ann said to one of the men who patrolled the pit behind the blackjack tables. A wiry, dark man looked up, then stepped between two tables.

"Miss D'Angelo," he said. "You went and dyed your hair again!"

"It's a wig," she said. "Sammy, can you come with me a moment?"

"They been looking for you upstairs," the pit boss said. "I should call and let them know."

"It'll have to wait," Ann said and, sure enough, she

showed him the barrel of her gun. For the first time the pit boss seemed to notice Cosmo.

"He can't have a baby in here. It's underage."

"Just let's go to Security," she said and stepped back a bit to make room. "I'll tell you all about it there."

So they headed across the casino floor, Sammy in the lead, then Cosmo with the baby, then Ann. They went through a doorway next to the cashier's cage, past a trio of security guards eating take-out, into an office. Sammy switched the light on and closed the door. Ann put her jacket on a table, let the gun fall to her side.

"Sammy," she said in a voice full of Mafia bonhomie, "you gotta help me find out if this creep is telling the truth."

"Miss D'Angelo," he answered, smiling to excuse himself, "that's not in my line."

"I don't mean that," she said. "I mean the lie detector."

"You want I should hook him up to the machine?"

"Pretend he's applying for a job."

Sammy looked Cosmo up and down as if evaluating him as a potential employee. "Cripes, it's the painter," he said finally.

"Yeah. Come on. Hook him up."

So it was through another door, into an antiseptic room where there was an antique-looking lie-detector set on an old blackjack table. Cosmo stood in the middle of the linoleum, babe in arms, waiting for directions. The messiah was making faces for the surveillance camera.

"Sit down, maestro," the Pope's daughter told him. He held out the baby to her, then sat down in the applicant's chair, facing the blackjack table. Sammy told him to undo his shirt, then got to work putting a blood-pressure cuff on him, a tube around his chest, conducting jelly on his fingers. The whole time Ann stood off to the side, gun arm under the baby's rear, barrel pointing toward the floor.

"Okay," Sammy said when he was done and the machine was on. "You gotta ask him some easy questions first, so we can calibrate his response."

"What's your name?" the Pope's daughter said.

"No," said Sammy. "They gotta be yes or no questions."

She pursed her lips. "Is your name Cosmo Dust?"

"Yes."

"Are you married?"

"Yes."

She let a little pause go by. "Are you painting the Sistine ceiling?"

"Yes."

She crossed to Sammy, looked down at the graph paper the machine was scribbling on.

"Was he lying on any of those?"

"It looks okay."

"Well, Jesus," she said. The baby looked up at her. "He's *not* married, and he's *not* painting the Sistine ceiling."

"It's ambiguous, is why," said Sammy. "He's *sort* of painting the Sistine ceiling. Married, I don't know about. But we need questions that don't have ambiguity."

"No such thing," said Cosmo.

"Also, he might be a pathological liar. The machine don't work so well with them."

"Okay," said the Pope's daughter. She did an about-face, walked a step or two, played footsie with a cable that ran across the floor. "Did you shoot the cocktail waitress?" she asked.

"No."

"Were you her lover?"

"No."

"Did you burn her hair at that party?"

"Yes." How did she know about that?

She looked back at Sammy, but he maintained an impassive expression. She regrouped.

"Was the baby left in your apartment this afternoon?"

"Yes."

"Do you know who left it?"

"No."

She paused again. The baby was playing with the buttons on her blouse. "Do you know of any plots against me?"

"Plots?" he couldn't help saying.

"Just yes or no, please."

"No."

"Have you been involved in anything that might result in harm to me?"

Did Love Assassin count? "Yes," he said.

That seemed to take her aback, as if for the second time that day the phantoms in her head had found correspondence in the real world. "And what were these things?"

Cosmo and Sammy exchanged looks.

"Forget the yes and no," Ann said, pointing the gun out from under the baby's bottom. "Who've you been talking about me with?"

Should he tell her about the 6.8 Degree of Difficulty? What about the newspaper article with its weird insinuations? "With your father," he said. "With Benny and Marco and my lawyer, whatever his name is."

"With Joey Sorvillo?"

"Yes. And with the police. Listen," he said wearily, as though he might spare them all a lot of effort, "maybe it's just that the old paradigms don't work anymore."

At which Sammy looked up. The Pope's daughter said, "What?"

He gestured with one wire-encrusted hand at her standing there with the baby. "Mother and Child. The iconography of it. It ought to give you substance, purity. But the gun, and this machine"—and he shook his head.

"Jesus," she whispered. "Forget the iconography. I want to know did they refer to any organizations, groups, other families."

"I gotta get back to work," Sammy put in.

"We're not done here. I've got questions."

"Ask away," Cosmo said. "Ask me if I'm part of the world by free will or by coercion."

"What?"

"Coercion," he answered. "Ask me if I believe in the saving power of art. No, I don't. Ask me if I believe in the saving power of love. No, I don't. Ask me—"

"Shut up!"

"—if this messiah or any other is going to save me."

"Okay," she said, and she started unbuttoning her blouse.

"I gotta go," said Sammy.

"Okay, it's your turn." And she handed Cosmo the gun, yanked him out of the chair so his wires came off, pressed the baby on him, and sat down in the applicant's seat herself. "Sammy, hook me up."

"Miss D'Angelo—"

"Hook me up!" she said and grabbed the gun back from Cosmo, who was peering down at the baby, who was peering up at him. "Do it," she said with the gun pointed at Sammy.

"Listen," Sammy said. He turned to Cosmo. "Why don't you just ask her questions, and you"—he turned to Ann—"answer them truthfully. Who needs the machine?"

"Because nobody believes anybody, that's why."

"If nobody believes anybody, it's because you act like a crazy person, Miss D'Angelo. No offense."

"What's your point of reference?" she cried. Whoever was watching on the surveillance camera—the whole joint was watched, after all—why didn't they come with guns and Benny and Marco and everything?

"You're the boss," Sammy said with a sigh. He got out the conducting jelly, the electrodes, took the blood-pressure cuff off of Cosmo, bit his lip while he put the respiration tube just under Ann's bra.

"Okay," she said when he was done. "Ask me questions."

Cosmo looked to Sammy for help, but the pit boss just shrugged.

"Are you crazy or what?" was his first question.

"Serious questions," she said, and pointed the gun at him. What could be more serious? he thought.

"Is your name Ann D'Angelo?"

"Yes," she answered; then: "No."

"Is it Ann del Cancelliere?"

"Skip the name," she said.

She didn't *look* Italian; not her skin, anyway. It was very fair.

"Do you believe in the saving power of love?" he asked.

"Cut it out," she said. "Ask real questions."

He stepped back to look at the stylus scribbling on the graph paper. Well, what the heck, as long as he had her hooked up.

"Did you kill the cocktail waitress?"

"No."

"Is Angelo D'Angelo your father?"

"No."

"Did you leave a baby in my apartment?"

"No."

"Can I trust you?"

"Yes."

The stylus was calm. He gazed first at the quantified evidence of her blood pressure, her respiration, her heartbeat, and then at the real thing, the woman in the chair, her blouse undone, color in her cheeks.

"Are you in league with the dark gods?"

At which she gave him a look strange in its understanding. "Are you?" she asked in return. For a moment they seemed poised in sympathy. And then Cosmo was leaning over, baby on his hip, plucking the electrodes off.

"Let's get out of here."

Chapter 15

Comrades in Arms

Back on the Strip he made random cuts, in and out of the A&W, around and under cloverleaves, trying to lose whatever green Jaguars or blue vans or CALF-4 Cadillacs might be following them. They talked, compared notes, tried trusting one another. They'd get anonymous, ditch the Cadillac, keep away from his apartment, from Amalgamated Illusion. Did she have a place they could stay, anywhere that was beyond the reach of whomever it was who was reaching? She gazed at him from the island of her aloneness and shook her head.

In the end they decided on a car rental—Hertz, Avis, Budget: not telling, Reader, in case you're in with the dark gods—left the CALF-3 Cadillac outside the Liberace Museum, and headed for one of the casino hotels, let's say New York New York, where they strolled through SoHo and the Village, took the baby up to the arcade at Coney Island for a Nathan's Famous. Or maybe it was a crêpe in Montmartre. Or Monte Carlo, where they purchased pajamas and some toothpaste.

When the cell phone rang they were sitting in a Mandalay Bay café.

"What's it to you?" was the first thing Ann said. Then: "Paris, Rome, Timbuktu."

He watched her face, hardened, suspicious.

"It's *not* a game," she said. "At least not to me."

The phone itself was some first-generation thing. Big, clumsy, double-A batteries or something. Didn't the Pope's daughter rate something sleeker?

"He wants to talk to you."

"Who?"

"Marco," she said and held the phone out to him. "Only you shouldn't believe anything he says."

He took the phone, said an uncertain hello.

"Had a baby since we saw you last, maestro?"

So it *had* been them. Candi, the baby, the lock on Cosmo's apartment.

"Saw you on the TV," Marco said, as if he could follow Cosmo's reasoning. "The surveillance cameras. Just didn't get to the elevators fast enough."

"What do you want?"

"It's Mr. D'Angelo. He took a turn for the worse last night. We got the priest here. If you got any influence over his so-called daughter, get her back here."

"Sure."

"Listen, screwball. You're in way over your head. She's not who you think she is." And then, when Cosmo let his doubt hang heavy on the line: "She's unstable, in case you haven't noticed."

"She's stable enough to want to get away from you."

A silence came over the line, then: "Just drive the Caddy back here. And bring the baby with you."

"Can't," he said. "We ditched it. The Caddy, I mean. Now we're ditching the phone, too." And he hung up, switched the phone off, and handed it to Ann with a that's-that smile. "Anonymous," he said.

Back in the car he tried to keep up the feeling—that wan happiness at having a comrade in arms—while they looked for a hotel to chance. And yet once they'd gotten a room, once Ann had set down their packages with a mock-embarrassed look at the king-sized bed and the mirror on the ceiling, once she'd gotten out her new pajamas and had brushed past him into the bathroom, the first thing he did was snoop through her purse. But he found nothing except the ordinary. Well, okay, a gun, but otherwise just girl stuff: the cell phone; credit cards; her driver's license photo, showing a woman a few years younger and with a flapper perm, height 5'6", weight 120, eyes gray, corrective lenses needed, her choice apparently being color contacts since her eyes were green, not gray, right?

So if she was stable, maybe it was he, Cosmo, who was unstable. He took out his own wallet, his own credit cards, his driver's license, spread them out on the bed to show her if she wanted to see. There he was in all his Cosmo-ness. Height: 5'5". Weight: 140. Hair: blond. Eyes: brown.

In among his bills he caught sight of the Gnostic newspaper article. He took it out, sat next to the baby on the bed, and read it again to the background sound of Ann in the bathroom. Again, he found himself struck by the weird confluence: Gnostic messiahs, Popes' daughters, a suggestion of the real hidden below the parodic. Ten minutes went by. When Ann came out, her hair done up in a turbaned towel, he held the clipping out to her.

And watched her face for a sign as she read it. She let out a low whistle, scrunched up her nose, bit her lip. When she was done, she held the clipping between thumb and forefinger like a stinking fish.

"This could not be more weird."

And she let it flutter to the bed. She shook her head slowly as if contemplating the info, or maybe how far she'd let him in on it. "I told you there were stories," she said finally. He lifted a brow. "I told you I was born in Italy. About my mother."

"What's she got to do with it?"

"She was a friend of the Archbishop of Venice. Before he was Pope. There are stories, rumors." She picked up the baby, set him on her knee, let her eyes return to the clipping. "Boy," she murmured after a minute, "they're in trouble if they're awaiting *my* enlightenment."

Him, too, he figured, and gazed from baby to babe with frank skepticism. What, after all, was the likelihood that a fellow would wind up in a Las Vegas hotel with not one, but two—count 'em, *two*—messiahs?

"This is not a question of off-the-shelf Christianity," he found himself announcing in case there were off-the-shelf Christians listening in. "It's a question of the need to be saved. The sneaky feeling that you—Moshe, Mohammed, Marianne—are doomed, doomed, doomed."

Over on the bed the larger of the two messiahs blinked and stared at him. "Look," she said, "there's sufficient weirdness here without your adding your bit. If we're going to be a team, we need calm heads, mental competence. Understood?"

That was the pot calling the kettle black, he wanted to say, but instead he merely assented. "Understood."

"These people," she went on, gesturing at the clipping on the bedspread, "have gotten hold of an old rumor and are running with it for all it's worth."

"What rumor?"

She gazed at him, trying to figure one last time if he was trustworthy.

"It's a real Italian opera," she warned, and she straightened out the slumping messiah on her knee. "Order a bottle of wine and I'll do my best."

gregory blake smith

Chapter 16

The Pope's Daughter,
Sung in Italian,
with English Supertitles

Let's say, while the orchestra tunes and Ann and a confused Cosmo start on a bottle of Chianti, that according to the program notes she really *is* the Pope's daughter, and not the Pope of Las Vegas but a real Pope—the thirty-four day Pope, John Paul I—from when he was Cardinal Albino Luciani, patriarch of Venice. And let's say that her mezzo mother died when Ann was four, a troubled woman who had married the Conte del Cancelliere when she was a too-young seventeen. That there had followed a disastrous honeymoon in San Remo (*pizzicati* rain, says operatic Ann), an all-out assault on her virginity in a roadside pensione that ended in a duet of tears, miles of silence on the road to Rapallo, and, when finally they returned to Vittorio Veneto, the *conte* motoring off the next morning for an open-ended stay with his friends in gay Trieste even before the cook could give his usual egg its full four minutes.

"Plot outline courtesy of my mother's maid," Ann says to a not-so-sure-about-all-this Cosmo. "Deaf and senile now in a convent in Ravenna, but filled-to-bursting with the story three years ago when I was doing the bloodhound thing. Just ask Marco."

"No need," Cosmo says. "Trust, calm heads, mental competence. Right?"

The first time the *contessa* tries to slit her wrists she does it the wrong way, across the vein. ("There's a wrong way?" Cosmo wonders). The second time it's lengthwise, but the maid enters stage left and gets her to the hospital in time. In the morning she wakes to the sight of the future Pope at her bedside, sings an aria on forbidden love, and goes home with bandages like corsages on her wrists.

And for the rest of the first act she plots her own damnation. Her husband comes and goes, poets and lovers and hangers-on trailing sometimes for days. Her own first adultery is with an out-of-work actor who cries afterward. The second is with a marchese who travels in a battered Alfa with a Weimaraner and a bottle of grappa in the passenger seat, and who thinks it a rare thing to boff the *contessa* after buffing the *conte*. After each sin, she goes off to the diocese mansion and in the sumptuous parlor or the side garden confesses everything to the Archbishop.

"Right," says Cosmo, who is taking notes for Orel Sloan in case new allegiances should prove unstable.

She keeps trying to make the Archbishop—and later, Cardinal—admit that she's damned, that there is no penance, no purgatorial fire that can burn her clean. Cardinal Luciani listens to her with that smiling pastoral patience that will later get him elected Pope, even when she begins to kneel before him, resting her head in his lap, running her hands under his soutane and sotto voce: *Now? Am*

I damned yet? He gazes down at the black mass of hair in his lap and lets her do what she wants, as if to prove by the imperilment of his own soul that the Church accepts her, that there is no perversity in her spirit that the Church cannot endure and still welcome her.

When she gets pregnant the first time she has an abortion. The second time she has the baby, names her Annunciata, and announces to everyone who comes near that the *conte* is not the father. For the baptism she wears a demure suit with three-quarter sleeves so that the two raised crucifixes on her wrists will show. When the ceremony is over she stage-whispers how wonderful a thing it is to have her baby christened by a great and holy man, and also the child's father. At which the Cardinal falls to his knees in prayer, whether for the *contessa*'s soul, or the child's, or his own, the maid can't say.

When we return after the intermission, there are choral numbers celebrating the election of John Paul I, followed by selections from the Pope's thirty-four day reign.

"Here, perhaps," intones on-a-roll Ann, "a glance at the program notes might clarify the miasma of conspiracy that cloaks the death of my maybe-dad. This consumed me for two years, you understand. I've got boxes and boxes of stuff on it. Let's see . . ."

First (and this while a ghost-chorus of murdered Popes and Antipopes high-kicks it across the stage), first there are all the heads that are going to roll when the new Pope cleans house, particularly the banker-priests who for some years have been laundering money for the American Mafia. ("True," says Ann when our Cosmo looks doubtful. "I've got *New York Times* clippings. Indexed.") Second, there's the list of Freemasons published in *L'Osservatore Politico* and reading like a *Who's Who in the Vatican*. Third, there's within this cabal of Vatican Freemasons a shadow lodge called P2—

"Maybe we could just listen to a highlights album," Cosmo suggests.

—a kind of secret society within a secret society, with connections to the Milan Mafia, the right-wing Fiancés of Death, all of whom are threatened by the new Pope's dream of a poor Church, one of whom gets suicided in London, hanging from Blackfriars Bridge with a brick in his pocket—

"What's this got—"

—Blackfriars being another name for Freemasons.

"What's this got to do with—"

"What this has to do with me—" she shouts, twisting apart an Oreo she's nicked from the minibar—"is this. After Papa Luciani is found dead in his bedroom in nineteen seventy-eight, and with rumors of murder and conspiracy swirling about Rome, my poor mother becomes convinced the two of us are in danger, packs up me and my nurse and her maid, and hits the road. I'm three years old now, you know. No real memory of it."

"*If* it happened," Cosmo interjects.

"*If* it happened," she agrees.

For the last act the plush drapes and floor-to-ceiling windows of the Vatican get struck, and in their place when the curtain rises are the crooked windows of out-of-the-way pensiones, rooftops with the right operatic geometry to force perspective. Little Annunciata is onstage for the first time, dark hair and pale skin and almost wordless in her part. For a year she travels with her mother and her maid from town to town, hotel to hotel, Mondolfo to Vieste to Metaponto. To hear the maid tell it, it's the weirdest year of her life. First there's the *nihil obstat* on the underwear. ("The what?" asks Cosmo. " 'Nothing objectionable,' " Ann translates. "The Vatican's imprimatur.") *Nihil obstat* embroidered per the *contessa*'s order on all of little Annunciata's underclothes. And there are the black Fiats and the white Lancias that seem always to be behind them when they're on the road, parked across the street when they're in a hotel.

"A leitmotif," Cosmo says.

In the end, this is how the *contessa* gets it: in a pensione just off the Via Sistina, the maid sleeping in an unheated room on the floor above, the *contessa* and Annunciata taking a bedroom with an old-fashioned *stufa a gas* ("A whatta what?") in one corner. How the gas gets turned on, who knows, though the *polizia*—even after they hear the maid's stories of black Fiats and white Lancias—record suicide because, after all, there weren't any signs of forced entry, were there? And didn't the deceased have a history? But what a miracle that little Annunciata was sleeping next to a cracked windowpane, fresh air seeping in like the breath of God! None of which does the suspicious maid buy, and after berating a priest parked in a white Lancia outside the hospital, she takes Annunciata to Milano, where she dumps the confused girl with the maid's own father—who, it turns out, has connections with the Milanese Mafia—and, no kidding, in a final aria that brings down the curtain, enters a convent.

"Where," Ann finished up, draining the Chianti bottle, "she lives to this day. Senile, like I said." With a shrug.

Out the window the Strip was still there, lights burning, traffic flow performing its inscrutable ornament. On the bed the baby was concentrating on growing its fingers and toes. Ann blew a note or two on the empty wine bottle, then tossed it aside.

"I ended up here because someone owed someone a favor. Las Vegas as a way of putting me out of the reach of whoever was reaching."

"And who was reaching?" Cosmo asked.

"Maybe no one," she answered.

Someone was reaching. There was Candi, after all. Blue vans and green Jaguars. Even if it was just rumor, a self-destructive woman, and whatever stories lingered after her death—if it was enough for the New Gnostic Church to know about, it was enough for others.

"So all this investigation I did," she was saying, "there was this swirl of suspicion because of the Pope, you know, had he been murdered and stuff. Not just the Freemasons and the banking scandal but all kinds of theories about why he might have been killed. My mother was just one of them."

He tried to make an encouraging expression but it didn't come off.

"I know what you're thinking," she said. She smoothed the bedspread around her. "Delusions, megalomania. I know."

"No."

"I would be thinking it, too."

He bit his lip. "It *is* a bit unnerving," he said by way of excuse.

And they were silent for a good minute. Finally she lay

back on the bed, stretched herself out next to the sleeping baby, backstroked one hand behind her, and turned the nightstand lamp off. The room filled with trapezoids of light from the Strip—red, green, lavender. They blinked like doors opening and closing to improbable worlds.

"Thing is," she said in the dark, "I *do* have a memory of my mother. Some fountain I'm standing in with the water falling on my head and a laughing woman holding a towel out to me." She stroked her hair off her forehead. "That's all. There's a green lawn, glittering light—I can't even describe it."

He looked at her, stretched out on the bed, her arm a pale crescent across the pillow.

"Everything else," she said, raising her hand in the dark, letting it fall in dismissal to the mattress, "I can't tell the real from the unreal."

He didn't answer, just stretched out on the bed himself, the baby like a bundling board between them. He still had his clothes on. Above them their mirrored selves lay looking dimly down at them. Five minutes went by.

"The bridal chamber," she said out of nowhere.

"What?" he whispered. He had been wondering at what point he should tell her about his life of celibacy.

"One of the Gnostic sacraments," she said. "It celebrated the reunion of the lost spirit with its heavenly counterpart." And she seemed to nod at their heavenly counterparts in the mirror above them.

"A lovely idea," she whispered in the colored dark. "Union with your lost self."

He looked at her reflection hovering above him, then at his own. But it wasn't his own self he wanted to be united with—as if a supersized Cosmo would have any better clue as to what it was all about! No, it was her. The woman above him in the mirror, beside him on the bed. If only his heavenly counterpart could turn to her heavenly counterpart and kiss her, whisper to her, do something, anyway, that would cause their arms and legs to interweave, their ribs to cleave. He found himself reaching upward in the dark, not in entreaty or supplication but because—oh! he had lain on his back too long painting Adam and Eve!—because he wanted to dispel the dark pools where her eyes should have been and repaint them lighter, brighter, maybe looking at him with hope and love. He let his arm drop. Silly Michelangelo!

He lay where he was. She lay where she was. The baby breathed in and out. Sirens sounded up and down the Strip.

Chapter 17

The Possibility Cloud

The next morning while Ann fed the baby pieces of toast and jelly, Cosmo called Crazy Herman with the idea of getting someone out on the Web to do some cyber-sleuthing, track down the ontologically weird. But before he could finish his list of weirdness, Crazy Herman started congratulating him.

"Lack of cause and effect, baby disappearing, baby reappearing: These are all what we might call non-Cartesian counterfactuals. Which would indicate that your life has gone nonlinear."

Cosmo blinked into telemetric space.

"Dig it," Crazy Herman explained. "The problem with trying to live your life in Cartesian space is that every point has to signify something meaningful. But life!" He laughed like the word itself was QED. "That old insistence on logic, on x, y, z. You've gone beyond it. I love you for that."

On the television the morning news was just coming on. Would there be anything, Cosmo wondered, about Candi, about himself?

"What I need," he tried again—no, just footage of a burned-out automobile in a parking lot—"is for you to get on the Web and find out whether there was ever an Italian Countess del Cancelliere—"

"Countess del whatta what?"

He spelled it for him, shrugged an apology at Ann for his apparent doubt. "And whether she's dead. And if she is, how she died. And if there's any linkage between her and Pope John Paul the first."

"Linkage?" Crazy Herman repeated, like that was uncomfortably close to cause and effect.

"Anything. Rumor. Paranoia. Conspiracy."

"Right. Connect the non-Cartesian dots from the countess to the cocktail waitress." He sounded pleased.

"Exactly," said Cosmo.

"Search words: *Pope, countess, Cosmo, murder.* I'll get Munjoy on it. Give us an hour." And he hung up.

On the television, as if Cartesian space really had grown a sixth finger, there were photos of the Golden Calf, then—cripes!—the H. Litsky Cream & Eggs photo! Then a youngish Angelo D'Angelo in black and white, a fifties Golden Calf sign behind him. Cosmo wondered what the heck, zapped the remote so the sound burst on.

"Hey!" he said to Ann. She had gone into the bathroom.

"*—long reputed to have mob connections—*"

"Hey!"

It was the Cadillac, the Liberace Museum.

"What?"

"It's our car."

"*—a throwback to the gang wars of the fifties—*"

"What?" she said again, coming into the room.

And then she seemed to understand, listened as the voice-over salted the scene with mob insinuations, reified the stagy nostalgia for the Mafia in the burned-out torso of the Cadillac: close-up of the CALF-3 license plate, tie-in to the recent murder of the cocktail waitress. They watched, dumbfounded.

"—not releasing identities pending notification of the families."

They exchanged stunned looks.

"That was meant for us," Ann whispered finally. "For me."

His head tumbled with combinations. They had gone into the Liberace Museum to call a taxi. How long had they been in there? How much time did you need to plant a bomb, to wire it to the starter? He had been so assiduous in making sure they weren't being followed—who, other than Benny and Marco, could have known the car was there?

"I have to call home," Ann said, reaching across Cosmo for the phone. He got out of her way, crossed to where the baby was sticking empty jelly packets on his fingers. She started to dial, then stopped, bit her lip in indecision, and held the receiver out to Cosmo.

"*You* call," she said. "Ask for Benny and Marco. If they're there"—she let a look heavy with implication pass between them—"tell them you know where I am. That you need to set up a meeting. You need"—and she searched for something—"you need to know how they plan to make the game real."

"And if they're not there?"

"Then we'll know something."

So he let her dial the number for him, put the receiver to his ear, listened into virtual space. After a couple of rings a voice answered.

"Who's this?" Cosmo asked. Who was *this*? the voice wanted to know. He decided to give Cartesian logic a chance: "Cosmo Dust," he said. "Now, who's this?"

He was Father Michael, from the Nevada diocese. How pleased he was to meet the famous painter. Alas, Mr. D'Angelo was unconscious, but he had been asking for his daughter. Had Cosmo seen her?

"Is Benny or Marco there?"

Benny and Marco were . . . indisposed. Had Cosmo seen Mr. D'Angelo's daughter? There was someone here from Rome, from the Vatican. They were so concerned; they would like to speak with her. Was that a baby he heard?

At which Cosmo hung up.

"What?" Ann asked, all ears.

"I don't like it."

"What?"

On the TV the news had moved on to the Kenotic Messiah.

"Let's get out of here."

So it was back into the pinball of the streets, Ann with the baby in her lap, Cosmo watching the rearview mirror so much he nearly rear-ended a Toyota. They got coffee at a drive-thru, drank it while zigzagging through the suburbs. They were at a loss for where to go, what to do. Cosmo had the thought that they could call Orel Sloan for the inside dope on the Cadillac; he put the idea to Ann, who didn't much like bringing the police in, but okay: They were out there on the streets, in between Cartesian loci, so go ahead.

"We been expecting you," came Orel Sloan's voice over the cell phone. "How about you drop by the station?"

"No, thanks."

"Then let me treat you to a lunchtime Campari and soda at the Venetian. You can bring the nonexistent Pope's daughter along with you. Also the nonexistent baby. Are we getting a trace on this call?" he said in a stagy aside. "Just kidding. Ha-ha."

Cosmo thought he heard a *click*, *flick*, relays being closed, opened, who knew?

"I'm just trying to be a solid citizen," he said. "The hit this morning, it was meant for us."

"Us?"

"Me and the nonexistent. That was our car."

"Like we don't know this already?"

At which Cosmo halted, nonplussed.

"You wanna know who it was?" the detective intuited. "Why don't you ask the Pope's daughter? She's right there with you, isn't she?"

He looked hurriedly around for police cars, upward through the windshield for a helicopter.

"And while you're at it ask her about the Antipope and the Antipope's daughter."

"What?"

"And Benny and Marco's father."

"Dead," said quick Cosmo. "Rayovac flashlight, fedoras, H. Litsky Cream and Eggs."

Orel Sloan let out an oh-my whistle. "You're good, Dust."

"But that was forty years ago."

"Nobody keeps bad blood bad like the Jews," was all he

said; then: "Now, how else can we help? What can we arrest you for today?"

"Tell me straight," said Cosmo. "Who was in the Cadillac?"

"Nothing's straight, Dust. Haven't you learned that yet?"

"Tell me crooked, then."

"I already did. You gotta pay attention, son." And he hung up.

Up on Highway 15 Ann wrinkled her nose: "The Antipope?" she repeated. "Who's the Antipope?"

They were headed north. Let speed for the moment be their hideout.

"That's all he said. Ask her about the Antipope. Ask her about the Antipope's daughter. Ask her about Benny and Marco's father."

What he imagined was this: an anti–Golden Calf, an anti-Cosmo painting the anti–Sistine ceiling (Armageddon, perdition, souls evaporating in terror and darkness), and up on the penthouse floor, the Antipope and his even-keeled daughter.

"He's got to be talking about the Englestein family. They're the ones who hit Benny and Marco's dad. It was all part of the Jewish Mafia thing back in the fifties, sixties. The Italians and Jews, they didn't get along so well."

"But the Antipope?"

"Izzy Englestein. He used to be D'Angelo's partner, back in Brooklyn, then out here—look, this is all written about. Ancient history. Part of the lore. Cripes, they teach it in Las Vegas civics classes. Where you going?"

He was pulling a U-ey, crossing the median strip illegally, looking for copycats. Now they were headed south, toward Amalgamated Illusion. After a few minutes, the old drive-in screen loomed to the east. They exited the highway, turned down this street, that street, circled back, and stopped at the gates to AI and waited. Were their haunts—the Golden Calf, Cosmo's apartment, AI—staked out? They looked around for suspicious cars, blinds from behind which murderous eyes peeped out.

"Do we go in?" Cosmo asked.

Ann bit her lip, looked around at the industrial Quonset huts and staging loggias, and then, as if for answer, opened the car door, swung the baby onto her hip, and got out.

"Whoa, dude!" Tim Munjoy said when they entered Crazy Herman's lab. He was eyeing the Pope's daughter. "Six-point-eight Degree of Difficulty." And he whistled a low whistle and gazed at Cosmo with awe, then at the baby like, dude, fast work!

"The Contessa del Cancelliere," Crazy Herman said from his desk.

"Here," said Ann.

"No, here." And he pointed at his computer monitor.

"And here," said Tim Munjoy, jabbing a remote at a TV screen on which there jerked to life video of somebody—a priest? a bishop?—walking in what looked like a private garden.

"First things first," Crazy Herman said. Tim Munjoy paused the video so that the priest got stuck between steps.

Cosmo made introductions.

"Coffee?" Crazy Herman offered. "Tea? Tour? Care to jump off the Golden Gate Bridge?"

Ann looked at Cosmo like, these are your friends?

"Maybe later," she answered. From down the hall Betty and Veronica sirened Cosmo's name in unison.

"Ooh-la—" said Betty.

"—la," finished Veronica at the sight of the Pope's daughter, then the baby. Crazy Herman made a gesture of grand welcome.

"This is your One-Stop Contessa del Cancelliere Information Center," he said. "Gather 'round."

"We want the baby," said Betty.

"We'll take him out to the swing set."

And they snatched the baby from Ann with motherly coos. Ann looked at Cosmo to see if this was all right or what.

"What we found," Crazy Herman was saying, "might surprise you."

And, keeping up a running commentary, he clicked them through dozens of conspiracy sites devoted to the death of John Paul I: political intrigue about the liberalization of the Church, the financial doings of the Vatican bank, a society of married priests, the *fratelli neri*, the P2 consortium— there it was in black and white—*and*, Crazy Herman said, like he'd trumped them, the Pope's wife—

"Wife!" cried Ann.

"—and daughter, caught on video here—roll it, Munjoy— this being circa nineteen seventy-eight, strolling through the gardens at the papal retreat in Castel Gandolfo, the woman, there, see her? And the little girl—"

At which Ann closed in on the video monitor, peering at the downloaded footage, the maybe-Pope in his robes, an indistinct woman glimpsed between the arthritic branches of olive trees, and—holding a toy telescope to her eye, looking first toward the sky, then the distant hills, then straight down at her shoes—a girl of three in a starchy pinafore.

"That's me," Ann said, first to the screen, then with eyes wide and strangely moved, to Cosmo.

"We don't want to know," Tim Munjoy said. He put hands to eyes, to ears, to mouth.

Depending on what site they looked at, the Pope had been murdered because he had intended to embark upon the abolition of a celibate clergy, the ordination of women, the bringing to light of a Gnostic cabal within the Vatican; because he had fathered a daughter, secretly taken—or intended to take—a wife, said wife murdered as well, by whom depended on whose ontological motel you steered your virtual car into. The whereabouts of the daughter was a big question: rumored to be dead, Rapunzeled in some Vatican tower, rusticated to America, bodyguarded, a Hollywood starlet whose name you would recognize. In addition to the videotape—which might or might not be Ann, thought careful Cosmo, might or might not be her mother—there were photographs on one of the sites of a girl, a woman, a kind of anti-Ann, and tantalizing hints of DNA tests being performed, already performed, to be performed in the very near future.

"This all reminds me," Tim Munjoy said out of nowhere, "of the Pythagoreans inventing the counter-Earth as a way of balancing the universe." And he looked tellingly from Ann to Cosmo, then back to Ann. Crazy Herman clicked them to some new site.

Where it was reported that the Vatican was trying to buy back all supposed relics of John Paul I—his hair, mostly, a side business got up by the former papal barber—buy them back because, according to the Vatican, such things were idolatrous, but according to the conspiracy sites, because they were trying to prevent someone from pulling a Sally Hemmings on the Catholic Church.

Crazy Herman leaned back in his chair, swept his dreadlocks aside, studied Ann, studied his monitor.

"The recursion," he said finally, "by which an ersatz Pope's daughter"—pointing at Ann—"becomes the *real* Pope's daughter"—pointing at the computer monitor—"deserves some comment." And he paused, swiveled in his chair, looked at them as if waiting for their explanation.

"It's the counter-Earth," Tim Munjoy chimed in. "Roll the metaphysical tape, please. Here on the Earth the usual process of iteration is to move from the genuine to the fake, e.g., Sean Connery to Pierce Brosnan. But on the counter-Earth the movement is from fake to genuine." And when they only stared blankly at him: "Let me illustrate with the following. *The Ten Commandments*," he said. "The nineteen twenty-three silent version, not the Charlton Heston remake." And he aimed a remote at his TV like the film might come up. "When they were done with the set—Egyptian temples, sphinxes—they bulldozed it into the sand dunes where they'd done the filming. And now this team of archaeologists from UCLA is digging it up. They're out there in the California desert with their little brushes brushing off Egyptian statuary, labeling and preserving everything. It's become authentic."

"But that's on *this* planet," said Cosmo. "The Earth."

"Exactly," said Munjoy.

"And so is she," Cosmo said, pointing at Ann.

"Exactly. The Earth is in the act of *becoming* the counter-Earth. It *was* the Earth, it *was* genuine, but since the movement on the Earth is from the genuine to the fake—dig this—the Earth moves irrevocably toward the counter-Earth, where, paradoxically, the fake moves toward becoming the real. Hence"—he made a gesture toward Ann—"the fake Pope's daughter becomes the real Pope's daughter."

"By which recursion," Crazy Herman put in, thoughtfully, "Polly Sensoria, on the counter-Earth, would be a real woman."

"She *is* a real woman," Tim Munjoy whispered, and he cast his eyes down, his ears coloring.

And by which recursion, Cosmo muttered in his head, counter-people would flock to see the counter–Sistine ceiling, stand under it in awe and adoration.

"Give me a break," said Ann with a disgusted look at the three of them. "Real and degenerate worlds. In the meantime, people are trying to kill me." And she put miffed hand on miffed hip.

"You've got to be annihilated," Munjoy said. He shrugged his shoulders like, hey, it's mathematics.

"Why?"

"Because you're real. It's a question of symmetry."

She grimaced, glared at Cosmo, looked back at Tim Munjoy. "We're all real."

"Nuh-uh." Munjoy shook his head. "Not me." And then, with an ipso facto stare: "No one's trying to kill me, are they?"

At which Ann mouthed *ay-yi-yi* at Cosmo.

"If I understand the problem," Crazy Herman said, clicking back to the site with photos of the anti-Ann, "biomass distantly related to you both, in the forms of wife, cocktail waitress, the bodyguards, are getting killed. Is that right?"

"Annihilated," Munjoy corrected.

"And this is making you feel"—he searched for the word—"insecure."

"They need to find an inauthentic existence," Munjoy put in. "Or possibly an *authentic* existence." And when they stared at him: "Don't you see? You're caught in the turbulence of the Earth changing into the counter-Earth. You can't tell whether you're genuine or fake. You may be both."

"I'm fake," said Cosmo. "Michelangelo. The Sistine ceiling."

Munjoy pointed a finger-pistol at him. "Bingo!" he said. "And you?" he quizzed Ann. She pursed her lips, shot Cosmo a look like, was he with her or not?

"Turbulence," Crazy Herman mused. He tied one dreadlock to another under his chin like a hat string. "Cathy, the cocktail waitress, the Pope's daughter, the real Pope's daughter—it may be that these are all terms of a nonlinear equation with you, Cosmo Dust, as the strange attractor on the brink of a catastrophe fold."

"Metaphorically speaking," Ann put in.

"Metaphor?" Crazy Herman wondered at her.

"The pancreas replaces its cells every twenty-four hours," Munjoy said. "The brain replaces its protein every month. Can you even be sure there's anything of the original you left?"

Crazy Herman untied his dreadlocks.

"If we follow out this line of reasoning—"

Ann snorted. "Reasoning?"

"—then the suspects in each of these iterations form what we call a possibility cloud, a place where mutually exclusive solutions coexist. Dig: Each suspect is a mutation of original information, and in a possibility cloud the mutations engage in a kind of Darwinian fight for survival. Cosmo"—here he touched Cosmo on the arm—"this is what I'd look out for. Whoever killed Cathy, whoever killed the cocktail waitress, whoever's suspected of killing them, whoever's potentially the killer—they're each threatened by the others. Fake and genuine, real and unreal, killer and suspect: Each iteration, in order to survive, in order to become or remain real, must kill the other."

"*I'm* a suspect," Cosmo said.

"There you go."

"Where?"

"It's either you or them."

Cosmo looked at the computer monitor, at the photo of anti-Ann, at the paused video of maybe-Ann and her mother. Could one simply back out of this? Leave Tim Munjoy and his pancreas, Crazy Herman, Polly Sensoria in her pod, Ann and the Pope's daughter, simply back out the door into the bright sun of rationality? Or had he become a kind of postmodern Calamity Jane, about whose person chaos had Velcroed itself, perverse, recursive, intractable?

"Let me see if I understand you," he said in what he hoped was a calm and rational voice.

"Shoot," said Crazy Herman.

"My life has become a mystery novel gone haywire."

"*Haywire* being a citizen's term for *nonlinear.* Check."

"A mystery novel where the red herrings, instead of trying to prove innocence, fight one another for the status of killer, because to do otherwise . . . ?"

"Shut up, shut up, shut up!"

They turned to Ann.

"They weren't red herrings!" she said. "Benny and Marco. They bought me A and W hot dogs when I was little. If it was them in the car, then somebody killed them."

"Him," said Tim Munjoy, pointing at Cosmo like he was trying to beef up Cosmo's ontological status.

"Somebody killed them," Ann repeated, and then counted on her fingers: "Not me. Not Cosmo. Not the maniac who killed Cosmo's wife. Or the cocktail waitress. Somebody else."

"But if you want to continue existing in the possibility cloud," Crazy Herman said patiently, "it's got to be you who did the killing. Otherwise the equation goes on without you."

Ann pressed her fingertips to her temples. "It's not an equation," she said with her own brand of patience. "It's life."

At which Crazy Herman and Tim Munjoy exchanged indulgent smiles. Ann closed her eyes as if to make them go away.

"You're a suspect, too," Cosmo found himself saying to her.

"Right," she said, opening her eyes and turning to him. "And we're not trying to kill one another, are we?"

"Not yet," said Tim Munjoy.

"Not yet," said Cosmo.

She glared at him. "Sympathy," she said; then: "Whose side are you on?"

"He's got to be on his own side," Crazy Herman put in. "Otherwise it's blinko, the void. Though"—he paused with a new thought—"you could look for an intermittency."

"I'm not listening anymore," Ann said. She stuck her fingertips in her ears.

"A what?" said Cosmo.

"An intermittency," Crazy Herman repeated. "A strange attractor has a memory of order. Somewhere inside the turbulence of its nonlinear feedback is the original equation. An intermittency is a moment when the old order is discovered again, discovered in the very iterations that are producing the turbulence."

"La-la-la," singing to herself now, eyes closed, fingers still in her ears.

"It's a window of order in chaos."

"On the counter-Earth," corrected Tim Munjoy. "On the Earth, it's a window of chaos in order. Like Charles Manson auditioning to be one of the Monkees. Which he did, you know. Did you know that?"

Cosmo turned back to the computer screen. Did the dark gods have a Web site? he wondered. Did Cathy's killer? Suppose you typed in *cyanide* and, say, *messiah;* what electronic grid would fire with meaning, with layered connection?

"Hey!" came the sound of Betty and Veronica from down the hall. "Hey, is this baby okay?"

They came into the room, the messiah between them.

"Yeah, like, we dropped him, and he didn't even cry."

"You did what?" Ann said, pulling her fingertips out of her ears and reaching for the baby. Tim Munjoy threw Cosmo a look like, where'd you get the uptight chick?

"He's very resilient," Betty offered.

"If one were so inclined," Cosmo wondered to Crazy Herman, "how would one go about finding one of these intermittencies?"

"I need some fresh air," Ann said.

"It's got to be in whatever the original equation was," Crazy Herman said. "Your life, the thing as it was before it went nonlinear."

"But that," Cosmo objected, a sudden lump in his throat because he'd almost said *she*, "is never coming back."

"I know, man," said Crazy Herman, a meaningful, friendly look on his face. "But you're still here. It's a question of the equation finding in itself the old terms, the old order. A miracle window."

"The baby and me," Ann said, "we need some fresh air."

On the computer monitor the screen saver had kicked in: red and yellow fractals wheeling against the cosmic black.

"Fresh air is toxic," said Tim Munjoy as Cosmo backed up, helped Ann with the baby. A miracle window? he was wondering. "Massive microbial death occurred in the Pliocene when bacteria began releasing oxygen as a waste product."

"Okay," Cosmo said.

"It's called the oxygen holocaust."

"Okay," he said again. "Thanks." He guided Ann into the hall.

"Shoot to kill!" Crazy Herman called.

Chapter 18

The Inquisitor

It may be that on the Earth—after a nervous lunch, a nervous try at various plans—Cosmo Dust and Ann D'Angelo and the messiah placed a phone call to Joey Sorvillo, Cosmo's sometime lawyer, looking for a way for the three of them to get safely into the Golden Calf; could he meet them at New York New York? But on the counter-Earth they managed on their own, sneaked onto one of the Golden Calf's elevators (a quick look into the main casino: anti-Betty and anti-Veronica up on the scaffolding working on the face of the deep), got off at the fourteenth floor, coldcocked the sentry, got a suitcase for Ann, and a stash of cash. Out at McCarren they bought first-class tickets and, after a tense, three-hour wait, where every suitcase held a ticking bomb, every draped trench coat a gun muzzle, boarded a 727 for Dallas, a 747 for Rome, then by train to Venice, where they registered in an out-of-the-way pensione and later hired a gondolier to pole them under the Bridge of Sighs, authentic selves achieved at last, authentic world, not this counter-, anti-, pseudo-, quasi-, would-be, so-called—

"Miss D'Angelo," Joey Sorvillo said politely when he found them seated at an outdoor café in New York New York's Little Italy. "It's been a couple of years."

"Yes," she said coolly, again with—why? Cosmo wondered—the femme fatale act in gear: sunglasses, silk scarf about her hair. As for Sorvillo, he had the diamond stud in his right earlobe still, the thousand-dollar suit, the cuff links, the to-die-for tan.

"Now you," he said, seating himself at their table and holding out a pinkie for the baby to grasp, "I've never met you before, have I?"

To their questions he said, no, no, it hadn't been Benny and Marco who'd gone to get the car. He'd just been talking to them. It was a regular soldier—at least that's what Marco had said. And her father? No, he hadn't seen him since that day on the rooftop with Cosmo. He'd taken a turn for the worse, he understood.

"But Benny and Marco," Ann said. "You're sure they're alive?"

"Unless someone was imitating Marco on the phone!" And he laughed, the good fellow. But sure, if they insisted, he could get them safely into the Golden Calf.

When the waitress came he ordered—and this spooked Cosmo—a Campari and soda, settled back, looked around at New York. "Makes me homesick," he said, then laughed. "Never even been to New York, but this"—he gestured at the red bricks, the espresso machines, the steam rising out of the manhole covers—"it's ancestral, or something."

Ann was eyeing him with something like suspicion. He seemed to sense it and turned to her. "Miss D'Angelo?"

"What do you know about me?" she asked.

"Something."

"What?"

He held his hands up in a don't-shoot posture. "Before my time. I only been around, what, eight years? But there's a file."

"What file?"

He shook his head, went lawyerly on them. "Not my place to disclose this. Your father," he said and made a gesture of sorrow at the inevitable, "there's going to be big changes. But it should be Benny and Marco telling you. Not me."

"Benny and Marco," she repeated, doubtful. "They said they wanted to make the game real. What do you know about that?"

Again, he made a hands-off gesture. "Let's go. We can *ask* them. Me, I don't want to do anything beyond what I'm paid to do. It's not in my interest." Then, as if it were an excuse: "I'm a *lawyer*. And a good one, eh, maestro? Still running around free?" He smiled, raised his eyebrows in invitation. "Shall we go?"

They stayed seated, exchanged looks, edgy, unsure.

"You're father's dying," he said in a voice solicitous and calm; and then, as if hinting at momentous discovery: "It's time."

So out on the Strip they followed Sorvillo's Caddy in their rental, no evasive maneuvering, the green Jaguars and blue vans in the rearview of paranoia strung out behind them for blocks. At the Golden Calf they avoided the company spots, spiraled up to the third level of the parking garage, and inside at the concierge's desk picked up a couple of guys from security.

Up on the penthouse floor, when they stepped out of the elevator, instead of the usual guard in the foyer there was a priest. He was seated at the guard's table, a bag of CheezTwists on his lap, his fingers stained yellow. He smiled dimly at them, at Ann, nodded to Joey Sorvillo. Cosmo thought he looked like Benny—Benny with a priest's collar. The security guards stepped back into the elevator.

"Hey!" Ann said, spinning around, but the doors were closing.

"Hello, Miss D'Angelo," the priest said in a Jersey accent. He pulled a goo-goo face at the messiah in Cosmo's arms.

"Who're you? Where's Benny?"

The priest made an acquiescent gesture with his hands. "The diocese sent me over. For your father."

She shot a look back at Sorvillo. "Where's Benny? Where's Marco?" And Jesus—maybe this could have waited, Cosmo was thinking—she scrambled the gun out of her purse, held it at tummy height like Ingrid Bergman in *Casablanca.*

"I have one of those, too," the priest said and smiled. Licking the dust from the CheezTwists off his fingertips, he opened the drawer of the table, took out a gun, barrel-first, and held it out to them with both hands like a Communion wafer.

"Put it back," Ann said to the priest, urging with her gun. The priest shrugged.

"Okay."

But instead he turned the gun around, pointed it at her. He smiled at the stalemate. "Thing is," he said, sounding like Benny, "there's someone here who'd like to see you. All the way from Rome."

At which Cosmo kept himself from glancing at Ann.

"Who?" she asked.

"He's down in the big room. C'mon."

And the priest stepped gallantly back and made way for Ann to pass, but she wiggled the gun at him like a movie moll, got the priest to shrug and start down ahead of them; Sorvillo, too.

"Let's get out of here," Cosmo whispered to her, but she shook her head no and made a gesture with her chin at whatever it was down the hall, like she needed to find out. Cosmo fell in behind her.

The big room was indeed big, with a view of the Strip south, a semicircle of plate glass looking down to the corner of Tropicana: the Statue of Liberty outside New York New York, fireboats spraying water, and beyond, the Disney towers of Excalibur, the black pyramid of the Luxor. The room itself had a plush eighties feel, upholstery everywhere, and at its center some steps leading down to a sunken seating area filled with throw pillows. Stretched out there on a kind of chaise lounge was another priest, this one watching the Apocalypse on the huge projection TV. He wore a purple skullcap, a gold cross slipping off to one side of his chest. He muted the TV at the sight of them but stayed stretched out where he was.

"*Contessa*," he said, and then something Cosmo's Italian couldn't catch.

"What do you prefer?" he asked in accented English: "Countess? Miss del Cancelliere? Miss D'Angelo? Annunciata? Ann?"

He said each one like it was an accusation, though he smiled the whole time.

"It depends on who's asking."

"Let me introduce you, Miss D'Angelo," Sorvillo said, stepping forward. "This is Monsignor Alberti. From the Vatican. From the Congregation for the—um, what was it again?"

"The Congregation for the Doctrine of the Faith," the monsignor replied evenly; and then, like a good host: "Can I have them get you a drink?" And he raised his own glass in something like a salute.

"This is *my* house," Ann said.

"Soon to be very *much* your house," the monsignor intoned meaningfully, and he smiled to himself, as if he were poised on the question of whether to give the whole game away or not. "Too bad for the Catholic Church," he said. "We only get to dance with all this"—he made a gesture at the room around him, at the sundae supreme of Vegas out the window—"should you no longer be alive at the time of your father's death. Do I have that correct, *consiliere*?" And he turned to Sorvillo, who nodded, tugged at the diamond earring in his right ear, threw a sheepish look at Ann.

But Ann was stepping forward, gun still at the ready. "The Congregation for the Doctrine of the Faith," she said. "Isn't that the Inquisitor's Office?"

"*Ai!*" the monsignor said, and pretended to crumple where he sat.

"The Office of the Holy Inquisition."

"*Ai, ai!*" Then a smile: What a kidder! "Old terms, ancient names, *Contessa*," he said and stood up. "Water under the bridge. We apologized for all that." He trotted up the carpeted steps until he was level with them, his drink still in hand. "Nowadays it's just arguments over life *in utero*, American divorces, South American Marxists, the occasional Freemason, the occasional Gnostic." And there came again the sly, inward smile.

"What do you want?" Ann asked.

He tapped his lips, considering, gazed at the baby. "So this is him, eh?" he said, avoiding the question. He sighed, regretful. "More DNA. A pity."

And he turned away, crossed to the bank of floor-to-ceiling windows, where he stood with his back to them, looking out at the scene below. They watched him—eyes accustomed to Palladian vistas, Bernini's columns—watched him take in the riot of the Strip, the desert beyond.

"You have a good view here," the monsignor said when finally he spoke. "An excellent vantage on the ruin of Man as an end in himself." He put his hands on his hips like Yul Brynner in *The King and I*. "*This* is where the Renaissance ends," he said with a laugh. "The self declined into the selfish. Eh, maestro?" And he turned to Cosmo, who felt himself flinch.

"It's not my fault," was all he could think to say; then, by way of clarification: "The Renaissance, I mean."

"*Bene, bene*, okay . . . ," the monsignor allowed, turning back to the window. "After all, we live in—*il paradossale?*—ah! paradox! Yes! It's what I love about your Las Vegas.

There is nowhere else that is so completely without the sacred. It brings one back to God. Don't you feel that?" And he turned to Ann. "*Contessa*, don't you feel that?"

Ann eyed him warily.

"At the Venetian casino they've made a replica of the San Marco Madonna and Child. The one on the Torre dell'Orologio. You've seen it, of course? Marvelous!" he cried, and his eyes shone. "The Madonna used for purely pictorial effect. The infant Jesus as stage business, as . . . what? The music you hear in—yes! elevator music!" He was laughing outright now.

Ann took a step forward. "What are you doing here?" she asked again.

"Looking for the sacred," the monsignor answered. "Isn't everyone?" And when they didn't respond: "Forget the incense and the stained glass. It's here where we can feel God. Here where we feel His presence by His absence." And he paused as if to let them take that in, dug his fingers into a nut bowl on the table next to him, popped some cashews in his mouth. "Gambling, cars, sex, money. At the end of it all, when you are still hungry, eh? . . . That hole inside is God." He looked at the CheezTwists priest as if for a reaction; the priest had his gun in hand still, but it was pointed not at Ann or Cosmo, but, oddly, at the Inquisitor himself. "This," he went on, again indicating the Strip, "is Christ's best hope. This is what I argue for when my fellow Inquisitors meet over an espresso. Let us have *more* of a world that denies Him. If faith is nothing but brain chemicals? *Evviva!* I say. The human mind made into ones and zeros? The universe expanding into a final nothingness?

Evviva! Hurrah! Hurrah for a world where every icon of the sacred is trivialized! *Novus ordo seclorum.* And oh! the Sistine ceiling, maestro!" He put his hand over his heart as if he were awed. "You," he said to Ann, moving his hand from his heart up to his lips as if overcome, "*cara*, you are dear to me for these very reasons."

"Me?" Ann said, startled. "What have I got to do with it?"

"You are a throwback, *Contessa*. The Borgias, *il papa terribile*, the intrigue, murders, concubines, bastard children. You, the daughter of the Smiling Pope. How valuable you could be!"

"We have to be going," Cosmo said.

"The files we have on you! The reports of miracles while you and your mother were running from us. Your own files," he said with a gesture down the hall, "which we took the liberty of looking through." He smiled apologetically. "The Vatican Gnostics, the Sophia cults, the Fiancés of Death. You have uncovered your own mystery. All this is why it makes me sad"—here he paused as if on the shore of an unfortunate duty—"sad to have been sent here to oversee your liquidation."

And once again Cosmo felt the raw clutch of the real. The world was not just dream, construction, paranoia. Nor was she. Her, the woman over there. Someone had just said he was there to kill her.

"My colleagues," the monsignor said, again with the apologetic show of his palms, "my fellow Inquisitors. They take direction from the old paradigms. Christ, the cross, salvation." And he shrugged as if at the quaintness of it all. "They see you as a threat, *Contessa*. Oh, the attempts on your life those first few years! And your poor mother!" He crossed himself, fixed his eyes expectantly on the Cheez-Twists priest until he had done likewise—clumsily, Cosmo would later remember thinking—then smiled wryly at the piety. "Now your protector is dying. There's this DNA business. Benny and Marco Merula—no longer dependable. In *my* view, all things that magnify the Lord, but in the view of my brothers, a threat to the Church. Believe me"—here, a palm to the sincere heart—"I have tried to convince them. You cannot restore an old world, I tell them. I have tried to show them the beauty of *il Cristo postmoderno*—absence, indeterminacy—but they insist. Alas, they insist." And here he took his skullcap off, rotated it in his hands. "It's at this point," he said, turning to the CheezTwists priest, "that you should be pointing the gun at *her*." He indicated Ann with an index finger. But the CheezTwists priest kept the gun where it was, pointed at the Inquisitor.

"*Her*," the Inquisitor repeated. The priest cocked the gun.

"You wops," the priest said with a laugh and a wave of the gun that took in Ann, Sorvillo, the Inquisitor. "You're all such big shots."

And he stepped forward, took Ann's gun from her, stuck it in his waistband. The baby looked around like, what's going on? Ditto Cosmo.

"The Mardi Gras Store," the priest said, as if to help them out, "for all your impersonating needs. I figured you, at least," he said to Sorvillo, "would blow wise. But the collar, whatta disguise!"

"Benny Englestein," Sorvillo muttered, shaking his head like, how had he not seen? The priest made a curlicue doff of an imaginary cap.

"What's a Jew like me doing in a place like this, hey?" And he laughed, took out a cell phone, and flipped it open. Speed-dialed a number. "It's okay," he said into the mouthpiece. "I got her."

"Benny?" Cosmo repeated. He threw a wondering look at Ann.

"What's your game, Englestein?" Sorvillo was asking.

The priest slipped the phone back into his pants pocket. "Same game as always. Getting even is fun. You ready to go?" he said to Ann.

"*Scusi,*" said the Inquisitor, stepping forward before she could answer. "You Americans. You move too fast. What is going on?"

"I'm taking the shiksa off your hands. Restoring a proper balance. Questions?"

"Why? What is she to you?"

"Long story," the priest answered with affable menace. Cosmo took a step forward. The gun told him to stop.

"You've got the wrong Pope's daughter," he said. The priest grimaced like, who was this guy? "You want the one on the counter-Earth," Cosmo said, because he couldn't think of anything else to say.

"Meshuga city," the Jewish priest said, making cuckoo circles around the side of his head.

"The Jewish Mafia, the Italian Mafia," Cosmo stalled. What else? "Fedoras," he said. "You're writing a book about it."

The priest gave Cosmo the stink-eye. "That's my brother," he said. "He's the one writing the book. How'd you know about that?"

At which Cosmo thought he could hear the hum of turbines, the dynamos of the dark gods—but he had enough bluff left in him to say it again: "You've got the wrong Pope's daughter. You want the real one. The one with the Web site."

"No," said the Jewish Benny. "This is the one. We been watching her for twenty years. Biding our time. This is the one."

And as if it were all choreographed, the door to the Pope's bedroom opened, and in walked another priest, a touch older, a touch more handsome, with Marco's graying temples, his assured manner. He made a heartfelt gesture at the interior of the sickroom he'd just left, crossed himself—left to right, then right to left, with a quizzing look like, could he get expert instruction on this?—then winked at his little performance.

"Ready?" he said. "Set? Symmetry reestablished?" And he smiled at Ann, at Cosmo, chucked the baby on the chin. "Then let's go."

Chapter 19

The Babylonian Captivity

Okay, there it was again. You could look around and see for yourself: the 2+2 reality of the world, in this instance the interior of the CALF-4 Cadillac and, out the windows, the right-angled grid of streets, the assurance of traffic lights in patterns, order—see for yourself; when Cosmo and Ann have green the others have red, never fails—and the sun going down in accord with the clock on the dash. So maybe it was colder than it ought to be, dipping into the thirties, but that was still within the bell curve of the possible. Look, there was Ann in the driver's seat. She did not metamorphose into Betty Grable or Cathy Dust. The Cadillac itself did not turn into a Toyota or a turnip. These things could be relied upon. Over and over—Cosmo watched; he was good at this—over and over the Cadillac did not turn into a Toyota. See, there it went again, not turning into a Toyota.

And yet he could not shake the feeling that these two—the one in the front seat with his gun trained on Ann, the other in the backseat with Cosmo and the baby—that these two had been constructed only minutes before, had been issued their identities—size-ten shoes, sixteen-inch necks—out of the prolific womb of contingency, Crazy Herman's possibility cloud. Which in painterly Cosmo's mind had become a kind of sci-fi roiling of metastasizing color inside which swam the mannequins of the potentially real, all fighting for the right to be Candi's killer.

"Meyer Lansky," anti-Marco murmured. He'd been doing this all down the Strip, reciting the arcana of the Jewish Mafia—names, phrases—as if the words themselves helped establish him, gave him body, authenticity.

"Hester Street," answered anti-Benny.

Thing was, Cosmo didn't feel any less himself. And he ought to. If these two had only just now come into being, if they had sprung fully formed from the brow of the possibility cloud—complete with the instinct to take Ann's cell phone from her, empty it of its double-A batteries like they were bullets—then shouldn't he be proportionately less? As rival for the prestige of being Candi's killer? Cosmo Dust evaporating in the backseat of a Caddy on the Las Vegas Strip as Benny and Meyer Englestein solidified?

"The Lower East Side," Meyer murmured. Then, after another couple of blocks: *"Aquiline nose."* The neon lights slid up the windshield, across their laps, out the back window.

They were moving toward downtown, the big casinos behind them, December sun failing in the west. Strange how the world was still beautiful after all this. Not just the postcard sunset and the cataracts of neon, but as they moved into the low-rent streets where the dogs slept outside the bail-bond bungalows, the stray vista, the glimpse of a dry wash that hadn't been backfilled, a relic of another world hanging on by the skin of its teeth.

"The Stork Club."

So, okay, what were they? Passwords, phylacteries, a kind of verbal fraternal handshake? Or the argot of the newborn? The scent by which they imprinted and then recognized one another? Just to see if he could intersect one dead world with another, Cosmo gave it a try, said "Yenta," in that road-hypnotized murmur; then: "Shtetl." But there was no response, not from Meyer or Benny, anyway; Ann turned briefly in her seat, shot him a look.

"Watch the road, dollface."

She looked back at the goon beside her. "Don't call me dollface."

"Cutie," Meyer said.

"A looker," said Benny.

It turned out that where they were going was one of the old downtown casinos, what used to be called a sawdust joint, as opposed to the carpet joints out on the Strip. The Babylon. Cosmo wasn't sure he'd ever even noticed it before. Definitely low rollers, reconditioned slots, two-dollar blackjack tables. They pulled up under a rundown carport, got out, gave the car keys to a valet with stains on his red valet suit. It was cold and there was nothing warm to wrap the baby in, so Cosmo tried to keep him cradled in his arms as they headed into the casino.

Inside, with the slots screaming, Ann stopped a man in horrible corduroy, told him she was being kidnapped, maybe murdered, but Benny ha-haed her along, on through the blackjack and gai pow tables, over to the elevators that ran up to the hotel rooms above. They got in, ascended, waited for the doors to open, got out. At least there was no little desk in the foyer, no rabbi eating CheezTwists.

They ended up inside a hotel room. Standard issue: queen-sized bed with molded headboard, bolted-down television. They were told to wait. They waited. Opened the door once to discover that, of course, Benny was posted outside, Meyer gone on what errand, to whom, and why, who could say?

"You'll find out," Benny said.

"Latkes," Cosmo tried. Benny winced like it was amateur hour.

Five minutes later Meyer was back. The two of them came into the room, sat on the bed, put their feet up on the mattress, Benny still in his collar and black suit, Meyer with a manila envelope in hand. They looked around expectantly like, when was the entertainment gonna begin?

"How is my father?" Ann said finally. "You saw him. How is he?"

"Dead," said Meyer.

"Dead?"

"Dying. Not feeling too well."

"*Com vos er lebt,*" Benny said, and he crossed himself like he couldn't get enough of that joke.

"What do you want with us?" Cosmo asked.

"You," Meyer said, "we don't want nothin' with. You're strictly a passenger. But you," he said to Ann, "you we want to show to someone."

"So why *don't* you already?"

They got a kick out of this, pointed at her, pointed at

each other, like, this was good, just what the doctor ordered. "Can't right now," Benny said. "The someone is sleeping."

"Dying," Meyer put in.

"Almost dead."

"Symmetry," Cosmo whispered.

"Bingo!" said Meyer. "We knew you'd understand! These things've got to be done right." He sat up on the bed, gave a pleased look all around. "They got to follow the archetypes. Just like you been doing with the Holy Family," he said with a knowing nod, an appreciative gesture at the three of them. "Mother, Father, Infant: nice!"

"Again with the Holy Family," Benny muttered, shaking his head like, give me a break.

"It's a beautiful image, is why," Meyer said, a bit miffed. "You got your Virgin, your innocent child. These things have value. It's all in my book." And he tapped the manila envelope on the mattress beside him, then put his hands behind his head, kicked back, relaxed. "Take Benny and me," he said. "We got a certain history, a certain place in the American fabric. There's a pattern that's gotta be followed. Like killing you," he said with an apologetic smile at Ann. "It's part of the mythopoeic structure. The Jews. The Gentiles. The Sanhedrin. Benny and Marco, if they were here, I'm sure they'd understand."

"Benny and Marco!" Benny howled. "Don't make me laugh! A coupla *pisk-malokhehs*. Even the grease wasn't real. They never whacked nobody."

"We ought to be charitable," Meyer weighed in. "They died so that we might live."

"Strictly Brylcreem!"

Meyer made a gesture maybe-yes maybe-no. "Now, what *you're* trying to do," he went on, giving Cosmo and Ann an appraising look, "is master level." He cocked his head like he was considering the odds. "You're trying to *transcend*, is what you're trying to do. The Holy Family," he said with mixed parts admiration and boy-you're-gonna-get-yours. "It beats being a Mafia doll, a nobody painter, but . . ." He let his voice trail off into misgiving, doubt, a touch of derision.

Benny spat in a wastebasket, threw Cosmo a dirty look. "He's nothin' but a little *pisher*!"

At which Ann rolled her eyes. "Will you quit with the Yiddish already?"

They sat up, turned to her. "Quit with the Yiddish?" Meyer said. "You want we should evaporate? You want we should cease to exist? The dollface," he said to Cosmo, "she don't understand. She don't understand about the fabric, about the patterns." He shook his head. "Listen, we haven't even gotten started. The garment sweatshops, the tenements, memories of the shtetl. We're tapped in, filled out. We got heft. We don't need you comin' in here with your sorry Blessed Virgin shtick and tellin' us enough with the Yiddish already."

They stood up. Interview over.

"Here," Meyer said and scooted the manila envelope across the bed. "You might learn something."

They headed for the door. Benny made a sidestep, yanked the telephone cord out of the wall.

"You can't just keep us here," Ann said.

"Sure we can," Meyer said, turning at the door. "You got your amenities. It's all downscale from what you're used to, I know, but hey! The Italians got the Golden Calf, the Jews got this dump." He shrugged, opened the door. "Try to get some sleep. We can kill you tomorrow."

And they each, the two of them, made a pistol of thumb and forefinger, shot Ann, shot Cosmo for good measure, and went out the door.

Chapter 20

The Annunciation

So began their night of Babylonian captivity, Benny sitting sentry in the hall, Cosmo and Ann in the room paging through unlikely escapes. They still had the cell phone, but no batteries. And an SOS on an adjoining wall had only brought a nix, nix from Benny at the door. After a couple of hours a dinner tray arrived, along with a bottle of wine and a deck of cards. There was nothing to do but eat, drink, and play gin rummy. Afterward Ann took a shower. Cosmo watched the ten o'clock news; the weatherman was forecasting a 40 percent chance of snow. Cut to file footage of the last time it snowed in Las Vegas: swirling spirals in the lights from the Sands, snow-covered donkeys in the crèche outside St. Mark's.

On CNN the Apocalypse continued apace. They were running a retrospective of millennialism through the ages, had gotten as far as the Millerites in the 1840s and the First Disappointment. When the end came—not *the* end, there was no *the* end—but when the Kenotic Messiah's compound was stormed by the FBI, or when the whole thing just petered out after the first of the year and the Kenotic Messiah went off to appear on *Larry King Live*, would there be a Collective Disappointment? Or just Cosmo's? Not disappointment that the world hadn't ended, but that it was still going on, with its parodic shadows, its empty appetites.

On KLVS it was a 50 percent chance of snow.

"I would like," he found himself saying when Ann came out of the bathroom, towel turbaned about her head; he soft-muted the TV, took a deep breath. "I would like to fall in love with you."

She stopped in her tracks. The towel about her midsection threatened to unwind.

"That's a heck of a thing to say."

"If we *were* to fall in love," he went on, precise, careful of her feelings, "it would have to be real. Human. No imitations."

"Boy," she said. "You sure know how to woo a girl." And she took the towel from around her head, began shimmying her hair dry.

"It's going to snow," he said lamely.

"Go back to the part about falling in love with me," came her voice from under the towel. "I liked that."

He meditated a moment. Under the circumstances, how did one prosecute love?

"Maybe it's impossible," he sighed. "Maybe all you can do nowadays is imitate love. We've seen the forms. We know how it's supposed to be."

"Did you talk to your wife this way?"

"No."

"Talk to me like you talked to her," she said. And then,

realizing what she'd said, she straightened up, came out from under the towel. "I didn't mean that." Her face went teenagey-boy-am-I-dumb. "I know you can't do that."

She crossed and sat beside him on the bed. She had no makeup on. Beside them, the baby was watching the shadows from the TV leap across the ceiling.

"The poor thing," Ann said. She kissed him on the temple, then lay beside him, her hip in the air, head on her hand.

Mother dead, father unknown. Kidnapped by Benny and Marco, or anti-Benny and anti-Marco, or the Inquisitor, and let's not forget the donkey in the desert: some irresponsible murderer or other who'd turned him over to Cosmo for safekeeping. Cosmo Dust, hopelessly out of the loop, yet irrevocably drawn in by the need for a puzzled father.

"I'm keeping him," he found himself saying. "No matter what happens, I'm keeping him."

And as if his body still had an intuition of how to be human, he moved next to the woman provided, kissed her on the lips.

"Oh, my."

He let his arms stretch out alongside her, felt for her hands, found himself delicately touching her fingernails, tracing the tips, the cuticles, feeling the little corrugations in the nails themselves. He wondered if lovemaking had changed during his absence. If so much else had deconstructed—identity, meaning, reality—could one rely on the matériel of love having remained constant?

"Decuit, potuit, ergo fecit," he heard whispered in his ear. But he was concentrating on what came next—first base, second base—because in this, of all things, one wanted the straightforward: sperm swimming toward egg,

cells splitting into legs, toes, eyes, spinal cord; everything in the right place at the right time, coalescing in an organism who would trot off to school with a Mickey Mouse lunch box in his/her hand, milk money ringing in his/her pocket. *Ergo* what?

"The motto of my Catholic grade school," she whispered. "Latin. A turn on, don't you think?"

"No talking," Cosmo muttered.

"It refers to Jesus being present during his mother's conception."

He unwrapped her towel. Jesus present during his mother's conception? "No talking," he said again.

But she launched into it anyway, letting him kiss her up and down her neck and instructing him on how the Catholic Church had ruined everything with the Immaculate Conception. That the beauty of it—*the beauty!* she gasped when he kissed her collarbone—the beauty was in *needing* to be saved. And they had stolen that from Mary. Pope Pius IX had, by claiming Jesus had been present at his mother's conception, and therefore Mary had never known original sin. She was stainless, immaculate. But how much lovelier *conceptio carnis* was! Wasn't it? And she pulled Cosmo on top of her.

"Say something," she whispered in his ear.

What?

"In Latin."

But he didn't know any Latin, just things like: *"In nomine patris—"*

"Yes."

"—et filii—"

"Oh."

"—*et spiritus sancti.*"

"Oh!"

What kind of lovemaking was this, anyway? He reached out, as if to orient himself, felt on the bed beside him Candi's baby. And out of nowhere he remembered a pro-life van that had been parked outside the clinic that terrible day, its panels plastered with the usual signs and bumper stickers. But among them had been a hand-lettered placard: EVERY CHILD COMES WITH THE MESSAGE THAT GOD IS NOT DIS-COURAGED. It had sung out to him in the midst of all the abortion cant, stayed with him for days afterward. He let his hand rest on the baby beside him, ran the other along the flank of the woman under him. These two, with their mothers murdered, fathers unknown. If you couldn't get saved by the immortal, the infinite, could you be saved by a wounded woman and an unlucky baby? And they, in turn, by a Cosmo Dust?

"What are you doing?" she asked under him.

He had stopped moving—in protest, surprise, dismay, he couldn't have said—but he had lifted himself up on his knuckles, lifted his knees off the mattress so that he was only touching her in the one spot.

"Resisting," he said.

Her eyes were on him, moist, Madonna-soft.

"Resisting what?"

"Life," he said; then: "Illusion."

"Don't," she whispered. She closed her eyes, put her hands behind him, and tried to coax him back.

"Deception, delusion, false dawns, false horizons . . ."

"Cosmo . . ."

"Can you promise me you won't get shot?" One of his legs was beginning to shake from the strain. "Strangled, knifed, poisoned?"

"We're making a new baby," she said. "It's an act of faith."

"Drowned, suicided . . ."

"Faith, belief, hope."

Oh! the fraud! The trickery! He collapsed back onto her, buried his face in her hair. Let the destruction come! If the dark gods needed the kick of his own complicity, so be it. Oh, there was her skin, her clavicle, the cradle of her hips, the corpus delecti in all its constituent parts. He reached out and, as if to overwhelm himself with the purely physical, touched the baby again, ran his hand from tiny toe to fat knee to double chin. But his fingers no sooner reached the open eyes than he was lit with a thought—more than a thought, a grace, an *annunciation*, for Chrissakes!—that it was not a new baby they were making but the very one beside them. Inside the crèche of Cosmo Dust's head some bewinged angel kneeling with the news—*Ave, Cosmo!*—filling out the motif of Messiah and manger, all to the accompaniment of the riot of *Annunciation*s that used to be Scotch-taped to the walls of his wife's office!

No wonder the baby seemed retarded. He was in a holding pattern. He was awaiting his soul, Cosmo's seed, somebody's cry of love to animate him and oh! didn't Cosmo know the thousand and one paintings of the moment: the Holy Ghost flying in at the window with the news of his own conception. Botticelli's *Annunciation*, Argenti's rainbow-winged angel, Vasari's glittering dove, and Leonardo's! The Renaissance ringlets of Mary's hair so beautiful that it had once made Cosmo weep with jealousy that there was someone who could paint like that, once a world where such a painting could be made.

"What am I doing?" he said out loud. He looked up. On the television, the Kenotic Messiah was talking, live or on tape, he couldn't have said.

"You're making love to me," came the answer from below.

He looked down at her, looked at the flesh and blood of her. The last woman he had made love to had been Polly Sensoria. Polly Sensoria kissed on her divan of diodes, felt up in the electronic twilight of her pod. Before that it had been his wife. Before that, the usual string of girls, leading back to hipless, breastless Patty Gensch, whom he had tremblingly kissed in the rain out behind the Pawtucket YMCA. Now, it was the Pope's daughter. Six-point-eight Degree of Difficulty. Who was it, what Pope or saint or church father had said the best way to save your soul was to save someone else's body? Well, damn his soul: If he could stave off the onslaught of doubt, the effusions of the possibility cloud, he would save this baby's body, give it a father, a mother if he could, do his best to help the ecstasy outweigh the agony, if only by an ounce or two.

"*Consumatum est!*" the woman under him cried.

He closed his eyes, ground his face into her hair, opened his eyes, and saw her shoes on the floor where she'd left them, spilled like a schoolgirl's. And over by the bathroom door the pool of her undressing. This was it, then. The quiddity of the real. The sound of her—that throaty cry of pleasure, something Polly Sensoria just could never get right—her voice mixed with the rumble of the heating unit, the blood in his ears . . .

He buried his face in her hair again, looked out again, and this time saw Candi's baby, *his* baby, staring back at him like the child half of one of Cathy's Mother and Childs: the spooky adult awareness, the look like he knows more than you do, knows ultimate things, the hand already raising in benediction as though he had, at last, recognized Cosmo.

"Oh!"

The female orgasm, he remembered Cathy once drunkenly declaring, was a curious thing. Not needed for procreation, was it? Not like the male's. Aquinas or somebody had maintained it was necessary for the full forming of a child's soul. Well, how far he had come! From not wanting a baby to kidnapping Candi's to impregnating the Pope's daughter so that she could give birth to it (small matter of being out of sequence), and now, like a good father, making sure that he'd have a soul. Adding his own release for good measure, its lower reaches starting just as Ann's was subsiding. And with it came the bizarre feeling that there was someone else in the room with them. He looked over toward the door like maybe Benny and Meyer had come in, but as soon as he did, he felt it, the presence, at the other end of the room, turned his head, half-expected to see his burro standing there, munching, its own look of recognition in its burro eyes. And then there was some other sound, maybe the whisper of angels' wings, the sifting drift of a feather falling in the blue TV light—and still, over there on the floor, Ann's scuffed shoes—and then his eyes were closed and he was gone, lost, in love.

Chapter 21

The Kenotic Messiah

She fell asleep, her head on his shoulder, her hand palm-down on his chest. On the TV the Kenotic Messiah was seated with two interviewers, cigarette in hand, Uzi on his lap like a briefcase. Cosmo watched out of the corner of his eye, not daring to move, as if this new beauty, this new harmony would dissolve if any one note were changed. Mary, Joseph, Messiah, three wise men on the TV, burro lurking in the room somewhere: This was the honest-to-God world. If it resolved into myth, archetype, patterns of prefabricated salvation, who was Cosmo to complain?

"*—as maintaining that you do not believe in Christ,*" one of the interviewers on the TV was saying. The sound was still soft-muted, but in the quiet when the heating fan took a break Cosmo could hear. "*Yet you claim to be Christ.*"

"*Yes,*" the Kenotic Messiah answered, thoughtful, professorial. Cosmo tried reaching for the remote without moving the shoulder upon which his love's head—let's repeat that—upon which his love's head lay, but he couldn't quite make it. *"I do not believe in Christ. Yet that one needs to be saved, how can one doubt?"*

He was dressed in a sweater, chinos; behind him there was a fire in the fireplace, real or gas-flame Cosmo couldn't tell. He looked like any other celebrity caught at home, informal, wearing his fame with ease. He took a drag on his cigarette.

"Christ is an emptiness." He picked a piece of tobacco off his tongue. *"An emptiness whose very absence proves his presence."*

This was a rerun. He'd seen this before, in the early days of the siege. Only the sports scores crawling at the bottom of the scene were different.

"When Paul uses the word kenosis *his idea is that in taking human form, God emptied himself of his divinity, entered the world abject—"*

"You agreed to this interview—"

He picked up the Uzi, aimed it at one of the interviewers, then at the other, then straight out at the camera. But it didn't matter. It was on tape. It had already happened. Cosmo moved his shoulder an inch, managed to grab the remote without waking any of the messiahs present.

"The kenotic Christ is a divine void," the Kenotic Messiah said; the Uzi went back onto his lap. *"When He enters you, He enters as emptiness. He is paradoxically there and not there. The idea of Christ, of salvation, remains. But it is simultaneously absent. You cannot fill yourself with Him, but neither can you empty yourself. He is that emptiness, and as such, is always part of you."*

And he smiled, took a drink of bourbon, was about to go on, but Cosmo crucified him with the remote.

And bethought himself: Don't TV remotes take double-A's?

He looked down at it, looked over to where Ann's bag lay with her antique cell phone stuffed in one of the pockets. In a matter of minutes he'd moved Ann's hand off his chest, slipped his shoulder out from under her head, got the cell phone out of her bag, opened up the back, put the remote's batteries in, turned it on . . . and was just on the verge of dialing 911 when the phone chirped at him. It made him jump. He looked over at the bed to see if Ann had awakened. The phone chirped again. He lifted it to his mouth, said a wary hello. Whoever was on the other end didn't seem to be expecting him. There was a pause, a void on the line. He said it again: "Hello?" Over on the bed, Ann lifted her head, caught sight of him, said "Darling!" then turned over and fell back to sleep.

"That you, soldier?"

It was Orel Sloan.

"No," said Cosmo.

"So you're in on this, too," came the detective's voice. "I shoulda known."

"In on what?"

"It's Michelangelo," Cosmo heard him call to someone— Carlotta Valdez?—and then he came back on the line. "How'd you get this phone? Is she there?"

"Listen," whispered Cosmo. "Try not to act crazy, and listen. We've been kidnapped. We need your help."

"The 'we' being?"

"Me and the Pope's daughter. Ann D'Angelo. Who do you think?"

"We might be stupid, Dust. Sure, it might take us a few days to catch on to your scam. But didja think we'd never blow wise? Ann D'Angelo!" He laughed. "We got Ann D'Angelo right here!"

At which one of the shadow-demons dancing on the walls took the shape of his burro, brayed, honked, laughed, dissolved into a siren outside. Cosmo looked at Ann on the bed, her hip turned up, hair scribbled about her head, and knew, at least, that she was real, alive, part of the world.

"Ann D'Angelo," he whispered into the phone, backing into the bathroom, "is here with me. Asleep. Kidnapped. Held hostage. But here. I'm looking at her right now. Would you like to change your story?"

"She's cold meat, Dust. The short order cooks have got her. We're gonna put her in a wooden kimono, a Chicago overcoat, we're gonna—"

"Look," said Cosmo, closing the bathroom door as quietly as he could and standing naked in the dark, "forget Richard Widmark for a minute. We need your help in the form of a squad car descending on the Babylon Casino and Hotel, two uniformed police officers coming up to room six-eighteen, knocking on the door, rescuing us. Do you think that properly falls in the purview of the police?"

"Your dialogue coach," Orel Sloan said, "I'd give him the gate if I was you."

Cosmo closed his eyes, swallowed, said in an even, patient voice: "Come get us and . . . and we'll spill."

"Better."

"We'll sing."

"Not bad. But the thing is," the detective said and paused, "the piece of information you seem not to be hearing, is that the dead body in the bathtub, the one you filled with daylight, checks out in the direction of Annunciata D'Angelo. The so-called Pope's daughter."

"You said she didn't exist."

"Repeat after me: Ann D'Angelo is the twist what I gave a case of lead poisoning to."

"You said you'd never heard of her."

"That's what we call a ploy, Dust. At the time we thought we only had a cocktail waitress on our hands."

"I've got news for you—you've still only got a cocktail waitress on your hands."

"And I've got news for you, pal. The twist you shot is Angelo D'Angelo's only daughter. What kinda flowers you want on your grave?"

"Look, if they've been telling you stuff over at the Golden Calf—"

"Fingerprints. Dental records. What're we, amateurs?"

He stared at the motes of darkness floating in front of his eyes, then backed up, sat down on the toilet. "I don't believe you."

"And we don't believe you," a woman's voice broke in. It was Carlotta Valdez. He closed his eyes, tried to concentrate on the darkness inside his head. The motes were still there.

"Let us say," he said after a silent minute had passed, "for the sake of argument—"

"That you're a fruitcake."

"—that the body in the . . . that the woman in the bathtub was Ann D'Angelo, the daughter of Angelo D'Angelo. Why was she working as a cocktail waitress? Why was she *dressed* as a cocktail waitress? Why did she come up to see me? And who"—was he really going to say this?—"is the woman I just made love to?"

"Hoo, boy!"

"Can you describe her to us?"

He hung his head between his knees. "She's Ann D'Angelo, I tell you. She's the Pope's daughter."

They stopped laughing. "Don't you get it, Dust? She's the cocktail waitress. She pulled the switcheroo on you."

The universe was at it again. But this time he was prepared. He had stability, order, harmony. These were the gifts of love. He pulled a towel off the towel rack, draped it over his head like a wimple, dug himself in.

"To what purpose?" is what he said next.

"Purpose?" Carlotta Valdez wondered. Orel Sloan snorted.

"You expecting plausible motivation, Dust? You expecting your dialectical ducks to line up?"

He breathed deeply. Now was not the time to panic. "To what purpose?" he asked again.

"She was twisted. It was a kick for her. She liked to go slumming."

" 'She' being?"

"Ann D'Angelo. The Pope's daughter. You gotta pay attention, son."

"And why would *she* do it? The cocktail waitress, I mean. Candi." Candi? he thought. Was it possible?

"She was a pro skirt. She was getting paid. Why *wouldn't* she do it?"

"Not much of a pro skirt," Carlotta Valdez said, "if we can believe the other *putas* at the Calf. But she and D'Angelo's daughter began trading places. The bored daddy's girl; you get the picture. Are you telling us you didn't know anything about this?"

"*I'm* asking the questions." And when they didn't object: "You say you know she's—"

"Which 'she,' Mr. Dust?"

He started over again. "You say you know the dead body is Annunciata D'Angelo because of her fingerprints, is that right?"

"Yes."

"Why would you even *have* her fingerprints? Ann D'Angelo's. On record, I mean."

"The Clark County Police Department had previously made her acquaintance."

"She was a hophead, Dust. She shot the heavy artillery. Smack, nose candy, you name it. Hell, she was even gowed up the night you squirted metal into her. You didn't notice?"

"The baby . . . ," he found himself saying.

"Seven pounds, thirteen ounces. Delivered at a private hospital in Beverly Hills. Good color, reflexes, mostly nines for Apgar scores."

He stared through the dark, x-rayed the bathroom door out to where he supposed she lay on the bed still, loved, sated, dreaming of him.

"She knows Latin," he said weakly.

"*E pluribus unum,*" Carlotta Valdez answered.

He gritted his teeth, nursed his head in his hands. Somewhere on the street below a car alarm was having a nervous breakdown.

"You ain't dizzy on this dame, are you, Dust?"

The motes were dive-bombing his eyes. "Why . . . ?" he started to say, but couldn't settle on what question followed. "Benny and Marco—" he grasped.

"—couldn't stand her," Carlotta answered. "She was a pain in the ass, real spoiled. Turning tricks for the kick of it! Mainlining everything she could get her hands on. We had to talk Benny out of staging a hit on her. Remember?"

"Do I!" Orel Sloan cried. He sighed a those-were-the-days sigh. "They was fed up."

"Marco asked for a little legal leeway."

"We had to take Benny out for a Big Mac, to get his mind off things." And they paused in the shimmer of reminiscence.

"How do you know they *didn't* whack her?" wily Cosmo asked.

Orel Sloan made a giddyup cluck with his tongue. "Hypothesis *número uno*, Dust."

"Dos," Carlotta corrected.

"Right. *Dos.*"

"Uno being?" Cosmo queried. There came a silence and a grin across the line. Of course—who else but Cosmo Dust?

"But the reason we called this number is not to bump gums with you, Dust. We wanna talk to the cocktail waitress. Candi."

"Susan," Carlotta said.

"Yeah, whatever. Put her on."

"She's sleeping," he said.

"So wake her up."

He opened his eyes, looked at his naked legs in the dimness. They seemed to oscillate: white, weak, not quite there. He put his hand in front of his face. It was fingerless.

"You still there, soldier?"

"Yeah," he said; then, standing up as if some action were called for: "If you want to talk to her, you'll have to come get her. The Babylon, like I said. Room six-eighteen." And he flipped the phone shut, turned it off so they couldn't call back, and shoved it into his pocket.

He stood there alone in the dark. Neither the real Pope's daughter, nor the phony Pope's daughter. No Pope's daughter at all. A cocktail waitress, maybe a prostitute. He shook his head from side to side as if to rid it of stray hallucinations. The motes began spiraling in the air, then, by some animator's trick, formed themselves into dancing burros. He opened the door to the bedroom.

She was still sleeping, the light from the window like a shroud. He went and stood at the foot of the bed, staring down at her. There had been a time when he had been capable of reasoning through a problem, but now, what was there to think? Where could he stand with any certitude? He knelt on the floor like he was going to say his prayers, put his head down at mattress level, peered at her—really *peered*—careful not to let his breath awaken her. She looked like a sleeping child, her mouth open, the drizzle of hair at her temple lovely, a moist glint of teeth, her expression faintly wondering.

A liar, a cheat; at best, mentally ill.

Yes, they could have been lying—Carlotta Valdez and Orel Sloan—planting some elaborate ploy whose secret richness would reveal itself in time. But somehow—by what residual faith in the rational, he couldn't have said— he didn't think so. And yet, how could she have been so thorough in her impersonation? Her suicidal mother, Vatican conspiracies, *nihil obstat* on her underwear.

For Pete's sake, he almost whispered aloud.

His head tumbled with questions. He hadn't ever—had he?—been in her presence with Benny and Marco. With anyone, for that matter, who really knew her. Sorvillo hadn't seen her in two years. Maybe the pit boss—what was his name, the lie-detector guy? How much could two people look alike, anyway? Outside of fairy tales, the prince and the pauper sort of thing. Well, really, how much did they *need* to look alike, what with the Golden Calf's protocol for cocktail waitresses: the Cleopatra wig, eyelids heavy with kohl, push-up bra, chiton, heels, Nefertiti fire-stripes at the wicks of the eyes? He tried to page back through the different Candis. The girl whose hair he'd set on fire—Candi or the Pope's daughter? The next day, up on his scaffold, that lost, hurt—sort of charming, he realized now, looking at her, *her*, the woman he'd just made love to—that lost soul asking him for politeness, consideration, because wouldn't the world be better off? But the Jacuzzi? It'd been the same woman, hadn't it? Or had it? He tried to remember. Tried to picture, forgive him, her breasts in the water. They, at least, hadn't been made up, bewigged. He had just been—by gosh— kissing a similar pair. Were they the same? Different?

He wondered what was in it for her. Okay, sure, at first, not having to be a cocktail waitress, inept prostitute, ankles hurting from those heels, money presumably. But what about later, *after* the murder? Why keep up the masquer- ade? Why not run to the cops, Benny and Marco, this or that pit boss, anybody, really, if she was just the innocent citizen? Unless they—*they?*—unless whoever was after her hadn't been after her at all, the Pope's daughter, he meant, but after *her*, the cocktail waitress. And this was her way of hiding out, *find*ing out. Which was, more or less, what she had been saying all along, trying to discover who was killing whom, small matter of pretending to be the alive body instead of the dead body. And you couldn't very well blame a girl for that, could you?

He stood up, walked in an impossible circle, knelt back down again.

Fact number one: Somebody was dead, somebody else was alive. There the alive somebody was, a foot or two away from him. Breathing.

Fact two . . .

Fact two: There *was* no fact two. There was just the breathing woman; the baby beside her, also breathing; Cosmo Dust, ditto. Just life and its obvious corollary: the lunar xeriscape of St. Mark's Cemetery out along Maryland Parkway, waterless, treeless, a patch of kenotic earth.

He stood up again, fished a cigarette from his shirt pocket, crossed to the window, and looked out onto the spasm of downtown Vegas. No sign of snow yet. No sign of anything except the concrete spoor of humanity, the parking garage across the way, the rotating horseshoe atop Benny Binion's. From the hotel towers there rose great plumes of vapor, as if the buildings themselves breathed. And yet he could not see a single human being. Not in the streets below. Not in the hotel rooms across the way. Just the lighted buildings, the blinking traffic lights, the strobe-lit ellipse of an airplane, siren, sound, exhaust: the husk of presence. He backed up, sat down in an armchair. Across the way a crane climbed the side of a new hotel tower like a giant insect.

He smoked his cigarette, swiveled in the chair so that he could see her, lying on her side, her hip a bell curve under the covers. He smoked and thought, resisted the urge to wake her, to confront her. What was it, anyway, that he had let himself fall in love with? How much of it was the physical her—say, the way she had of peering into her lap when she was about to reveal something (lies, lies, lies!)—and how much of it was the intangibles of identity? If it was the one, then it didn't matter that she was not who she said she was: She was her body, her gestures, her perfumes. And if it was the other? What *was* the other, after all? A congeries of mists, memory, longing . . .

He stubbed out his cigarette, pulled his legs up under him in the chair, closed his eyes. With luck, the police would be there soon. He might try to sleep until then. Save any confrontation until then. And yet he couldn't keep himself from opening his eyes, from looking over at her, couldn't quite rid himself of the thought that she was the dead woman—cocktail waitress, Pope's daughter, it didn't matter which, but the dead woman, her identity mistakenly kept alive in the wrong body.

And it was something like that that he dreamed when finally he fell asleep. A dream of Venice—oh! there had been dozens of them in the last year—but this time a Venice empty of anything living, in which he wandered through impossibly wide streets, along black, motionless canals until he found himself in a piazza, dream-empty and yet paradoxically filled, a presence that was somehow the Pope's daughter half-hidden under a shadowy loggia, and an absence that might or might not have been Candi, might or might not have been Cathy, lurking in an embrasure across the way, and in the stillness of midnight the soul of each leaping like non-Cartesian points from one body to the other and back again, without crossing the space between.

Chapter 22

The Antipope

When he woke it was to someone kicking him in the shin. The world shuddered back. But instead of Orel Sloan standing over him it was anti-Benny, anti-Marco back by the door, anti-Ann sitting up on the bed in a *Playboy* pose, sheet clutched to her breast. The baby was levitating an inch or two off the mattress. He lowered himself courteously when Cosmo refocused.

"Sheesh!" said Benny.

"We'll wait in the hall," Meyer added with a polite wave of his gun. They left the door ajar.

There passed between them a look—cold on Cosmo's part; warm, searching on anti-Ann's—until she realized the look of *his* look, whereupon she cast her eyes down in confusion. She kept the sheet clutched about her when she stood to dress.

Five minutes later, they were being marched down the hall, past the look-alike doors, the recessed ceiling lights dropping pools of dingy light on the carpet. Anti-Ann kept darting wondering looks at him, hurt, lost, damaged. *Darling!*

"So," Meyer said as they stepped into the elevator, "did you read my book?" And he hefted the manuscript he'd given Cosmo. *"Memoir of a Parody."*

The elevator doors closed. They moved even farther away from the Earth's crust.

"Sorry," Cosmo answered, "didn't have time."

"Too busy *shtuping* the Pope's daughter? Eh? One last *zetz* before—" and he made a finger-pistol, shot a spectral Pope's daughter who happened to be standing beside the real Pope's daughter; that is, the fake Pope's daughter.

"Too busy calling the police," Cosmo countered. He patted the cell phone, which was still in his pocket. "They should be here any minute."

"They shoulda been here hours ago," Meyer counter-countered: "In fact, they *were* here. But we worked something out with them. If you'd read my book—"

"They were *here*?" Cosmo couldn't help saying.

"Nobody's interested in your book," Benny muttered as the elevator came to a stop.

"Top of the bestseller list," Meyer said. "Just wait. Parody is big. People are interested in the marginalized, the disenfranchised. Who's more unempowered than the mirage, the spoof, the doppelgänger? After you."

They stepped out of the elevator. Benny gave Cosmo's arm a confidential tug.

"Don't mistake the real thing for the parody," he warned, gun in his suit-coat pocket like an accompanying illustration.

"Or the parody for the real thing," Cosmo countered with

a shotgun blast at anti-Ann. She hiked the baby higher on her hip, stared bewildered at the stained carpet.

They went down a hall identical to the one they'd just left, the same water spots blooming on the same false ceiling. No penthouse this, none of that expensive shiver of concealed lighting like at the Golden Calf, the curved sweep of tinted glass where the hall opened out like the bridge of the *Enterprise*, with or without Vatican Inquisitor. They stopped outside an ordinary door. Benny gave a courtesy knock, tried to stifle a yawn with a whispered "Cripes!" and unlocked the door.

"The dying," Meyer said, as if by way of explanation, apology, "don't keep regular hours." And with a gracious smile, he ushered them in.

It was the same sort of room they'd just come out of, same window, same door to the bathroom. Only it had its own furnishings, not standard hotel fare, but stuff from who knew what old domicile: sitcom sofa, Copacabana fern tree, sad prints of no apparent relation hanging on the walls. At its center were a hospital bed and an IV-hookup, and under the covers—little head peeping out with fevered eyes, stricken expression—was the Antipope.

"At last," he whispered.

He was looking at Ann, not Cosmo. Over in the corner a nurse with orange hair sat reading a fat novel. There was the smell of ointment, medication, death.

"We got her, Pop," Benny said, his voice warm, solicitous, maybe even loving. He crossed to the side of the bed, brushed with his third and fourth fingers a strand of white hair off the Antipope's forehead. "Ann D'Angelo, Pop. It's payback time."

The old man's eyes blackened. He made a gesture, weak, to be lifted up, pillows propped behind him. Then he pointed at Cosmo.

"The painter," Benny answered.

His brow darkened.

"You remember, Pop. The Sistine ceiling. We encourage him to quit with the painting. It's a bonus."

The Antipope closed his eyes. A hand, bony and spotted, came out from under the sheets. It tried to reach toward something, something vaguely in the air, and at the same time the old man tried to speak, but the words only fluttered about in the cavity of his mouth. The hand fell back to the bed.

"Okay," Meyer said, opening his manuscript, leafing past the title page, resemblance to persons living or dead, table of contents. "We gotta set the scene. The shtetl, pogroms, let's see, dum-di-dum, all day long I'd biddy biddy bum. . . ."

"Oy vey!" said the pseudo-Pope's daughter.

Meyer looked up, smiled. "That's the spirit." Half-glasses had somehow appeared on the end of his nose. He let himself peer over the tops of the lenses, then went back to his manuscript.

"We gotta get the proper coloration and mood: the sound of pushcarts on the Lower East Side, awnings on the storefronts, fire escapes, the smell of cabbage. . . ."

A smile for the moment, soothed, reminiscent, appeared on the old man's lips.

"Hester Street. H. Litsky Cream and Eggs. Street urchins. Among whom . . ." and his voice trailed off in fond memory.

"Give me a break," said the pseudo-PD. "What do you know about the Lower East Side?"

Meyer fixed her with a look. "You're not listening right," he said. "You gotta listen with your imagination. You gotta listen with your ethnic sorrow."

"I don't have any ethnic sorrow. All my sorrow is personal."

He painted her with a look of pity. And then, like an offer to share: "Dumbbell tenements, shirtwaists. It's the nineteen-twenties. It's the garment sweatshops. Steam from the pressers, the whir of sewing machines. Benny and me are runners for Berman Brothers, just a coupla tykes in button shoes and knickers, hoofing it through the streets with a load of shirts or waistcoats or what-have-you on our shoulders, see the photo opposite page forty-eight. The cloaks they hung all the way down to the ground, front and back, we was so short. Remember, Benny?"

At which Benny scowled.

"We had to walk on tiptoe to keep them from dragging in the dirt."

"And this was when?" Cosmo—always the stickler for details—had to say.

"Nineteen twenty. Twenty-one."

"Oh, sure."

Again, with the pitying look. "You still ain't listening right." Across the room, the nurse looked up. Cosmo wanted to ask her what was her deal, was she in on this, just a bystander, what? She gave him a tired look—*pfft!* you're all meshuga—and went back to her book.

"Fanny Brice on the sound track, calendar leaves falling away, now here's me and Benny older—not a bad job on the casting—we got the tough-guy look. We got the Semitic hair, the mythopoeic noses. Eh, Benny?"

"I wouldn't know," said Benny.

"And we got a score to settle. Our Pop," and he made a loving gesture at the old man under the sheets. "*Your* Pop," he said to Ann, "and your son-of-a-bitch grandfather," he said to the baby. "We got a long history. The Jews. The Italians. Little Italy right alongside the Lower East Side. The ginnies movin' in on us. You got time for the whole story?"

"No," said Cosmo.

"Sure," said pseudo-Ann.

"Forget the whole story," said Benny. "We got business to do."

But Meyer waved him away, sat down on the bed next to the Antipope, caressed the old man's hair. "The Italian boys, they'd come over from Little Italy." He was saying this to the old man now. "Her father, the Pope, before he was the Pope. You remember that time—it was the Day of Atonement—when him and his ginny brother showed up at B'nai David dressed as Hasidic Jews, checking us out, seeing who's there, who's not, and in between morning and afternoon services we're all outside, beautiful fall day, and these two they light up a cigarette."

He started laughing. Even Benny cracked a smile.

"A cigarette, with matches!"

He was about to bust a gut.

"Fire!" he cried. The Antipope was leaking laughter himself. "Some Hasidim they were." He wiped away stage tears, smiled down at his father, then looked at Ann. "Out here, our guys, they was the first Popes. Siegel, Lansky, Davie Berman, our Pop. But the ginnies they move in, they steal everything. Christ, they stole Jesus, didn't they? Whose Messiah was he, anyway?"

And he gazed around at them. Point taken?

"I want to go home," was all Cosmo could say.

"Not without paying reparations," Meyer said.

"For what?"

"For killing the Jews."

Cosmo grimaced at the menorah on the bureau. "Mythopoeically speaking, you mean?" he said.

"Myth," Meyer answered, taking out his gun, bringing the barrel up to his cheek in a pose at once thoughtful and threatening, "is as close to reality as we ever get." Over on the bed, the Antipope closed his eyes like this, at last, was it.

Cosmo shifted his weight. "I didn't kill any Jews."

"Everybody's killed a Jew."

"Not me."

"You're implicated," Benny put in. Cosmo shot him a look. "By virtue of what?"

"By virtue of *shtuping* the Pope's daughter."

"I didn't *shtup* any Pope's daughter."

They let out a laugh.

"I didn't." Then, with a jab of his thumb and a stagey oh-you-mean-*her* look, "*She*'s not the Pope's daughter."

And he let a look, frank and—strange to feel it on his face—bitter, assault Ann where she stood. She returned it with wonder: What's wrong? What have I done?

"So tell us something we don't know," Benny was saying. He turned to the old man, shrugged his shoulders like, what are these two, amateurs? "You think we don't know the whole story? You think we don't know about the real Pope, the Countess del Cancellieri? About the rumors, the factions, the threats? Only thing that matters to us is she's *his* daughter. *He* brought her up. The Pope. *Our* Pope, the dying son of a bitch."

"No . . . ," Cosmo began.

"Although," philosophical Meyer interrupted, "the fact that she carries with her a connection to the Vatican, the whole mysteries of the Virgin shtick, is a plus. Seeing as how we're Jews and all."

He kept his voice playful, like this was all part of the script, but the look he shot Cosmo was one of warning, threat, back off now.

"We gotta do it before he dies," Benny put in with his own look of nix, nix, "is the motivation. In case you're wondering."

"You don't understand. She isn't *any* Pope's daughter." And at that the Antipope opened his eyes. Again, from Meyer, came the dark look, like, quit it, understand? But Cosmo was having none of it. "She isn't the real Pope's daughter, and she isn't the Pope of Las Vegas's daughter. She's a cocktail waitress."

"You're pissing us off," said Benny.

"A cocktail waitress. Who knows what else."

Meyer let his manuscript fall onto the bed, took his reading glasses off. "What're you, the slow kid in the class?"

Cosmo shook his head.

"A real dumkop. Of course she's the Pope's daughter." And then to Ann: "Aren't you?"

"Who else would I be?"

"Candi," said Cosmo, looking at her finally. Their eyes locked, and he didn't know what it was he saw in her— hurt, anger, contempt? "Or Susan. Who knows, but not the Pope's daughter."

"Don't listen to this guy," Benny said, turning to the old man, who had been watching the four of them out of the hollows of his eyes. "He's a big nothing."

"A real *nukhshlepper.*"

"The real Pope's daughter," Cosmo continued, undeterred, "is dead." He turned to Benny and Meyer. "You killed her."

"You're having trouble with your tenses," Meyer said. "We're *going* to kill her." He let his gun level on Ann. "Future. Not past."

"You killed her in the bathtub. Or Benny and Marco did. Or the Inquisitor. Or some as yet unknown iteration of the possibility cloud. Whoever, but she's dead."

"You think this is gonna work? You think you're gonna stroll out of here because you tell us she's not who we think she is?"

Cosmo pulled the cell phone out of his pants pocket and held it out to Meyer. "You say the police came by? Orel Sloan? Carlotta Valdez? Give them a call. They'll tell you."

Ann was looking at the cell phone like, what was wrong with him?

"No batteries," Benny put in, smug.

Cosmo snapped the back off, showed the batteries, snapped it back on. "Give them a call."

"This guy," said Benny, thumb over his shoulder to indicate Cosmo. "What a hero. What a Lochinvar. He's trying to save her. Sweet, nice."

"There's no logic here," put in Meyer. "Is there logic here?" he said to Ann. "If we already killed you, would we engineer this whole thing? Bring you here?"

Cosmo hitched up his pants. "You killed her in the bathtub. But then you found out it wasn't her, and you tried to kill her in the Cadillac. That didn't work, so you came and kidnapped her. Only it *was* her. In the bathtub, I mean. It was the Pope's daughter pretending she was Candi. Don't ask me why."

"Why?"

"So let's just quit it. She's dead." He turned to the Antipope, who had the whole time been staring at Cosmo. "She's dead already. Ann D'Angelo. You can't kill her a second time. It's one of the rules," he found himself adding. "You can't be killed twice."

And he planted himself there, on the carpet, like this, *this* he was sure of.

"You gotta picture it," Meyer began after a moment had passed. He tried a let's-just-ease-off smile. "You gotta picture the Vegas of the seventies. We're just holding on by the skin of our teeth. Everywhere there's assaults on us. On who we are. On where we came from. Meyer Lansky is down in Florida in his retirement home watching *The Gangster Chronicles* on television. Joey Stacher's in Israel with a twenty-three-year-old Tel Aviv college-student girlfriend. Everybody's gone. Everybody's lost who they were." He sounded, suddenly, breathless, a little panicked. "We're the only ones left. H. Litsky Cream and Eggs. And then *she* shows up." And he gestured at Ann. "She's four years old. Capable of being killed. It gives us something to live for."

And he looked at them, at anti-Ann, at Cosmo, with something like pleading in his eyes.

"It's a question of identity," Benny helped out. "It's a question of—"

"Survival," anti-Ann said. They all turned to her.

"You understand?" Meyer wondered.

But she kept her eyes on Cosmo. "It's a question of what world you're going to live in. And whose world."

"Exactly," Meyer sighed, relieved.

"The girl is smart."

"If you kill me," the girl said, "then both our worlds are legitimized."

"Whew!" said Meyer, like he was in the presence of a prodigy.

The three of them had moved closer together, in a kind of ontological solidarity in which Cosmo was the odd man out. Whose world, indeed! He shoved his hands in his pockets, decided to insist on the real.

"You."

They all turned to where the voice had come from, to the Antipope lifting himself up on one elbow and motioning for Ann to come toward him. He waved Benny and Meyer away when they stepped forward to help, motioned again for the Pope's daughter to come. With an arch, to-hell-with-you look, she handed the baby to Cosmo. The old man lay a palm on the bed for her to sit down, and when she did, peered up into her face.

"Who are you?" he croaked.

"Ann D'Angelo," she said without missing a beat; then: "Born Annunciata del Cancelliere. Adopted nineteen eighty-one by Angelo D'Angelo. Renamed. Reworked. Retooled." And she spread her hands as if to indicate veracity in her very being.

"See?" said Benny.

The old man waved him off, eyed Ann with a diseased look. "Prove it," he said.

"I don't have to prove it."

"Pride, arrogance, general smart-assness," said Meyer. "What more proof do we need?"

"I don't have to prove it," she repeated. "But just to help out . . ." And as if she took pity on them all, Cosmo included, she reached around to her back pocket and pulled out a passport. "Here," she said and handed it to the old man. He took it, a little nonplussed, and with shaky hands thumbed through it, brought it up close to his face.

"My eyes," he muttered, and held the passport out to Meyer. Meyer took it, looked at the photo inside, turned it this way, that way, then held it out to Benny, who went through the same drill.

"It's her," Meyer said. "It's got the seal and everything."

"Signed, too."

"Signed, sealed, and delivered. It's her." And Benny held the passport out, wagged it in the air at Cosmo like, okay, you give? Cosmo stepped forward and with the hand that wasn't holding the baby reached for the passport, but Benny pulled it away. He reached again, and this time Benny frisbeed the little booklet to Meyer.

"Name," Meyer said, stiff-arming Cosmo and holding the passport away from him, "Annunciata D'Angelo. Date of birth. Place of birth. Says 'secretary of state' here. You calling the secretary of state a liar?"

"Let me see it," Cosmo said.

"Go ahead," Ann put in from over on the bed. "Let him see it."

There was a reckless edge to her voice, like she meant to brave it through to the end. Cosmo took the passport from Meyer, opened it to the photo. Maybe it was just the absence of exaggerated features—big nose, say, or curly hair, freckles, squinty eyes—but they *did* look alike. And yet it was clear—he could see it; never mind instability— they were not the same person. He looked across at anti-Ann and felt for the first time something like sorrow for her. Whoever she was, whatever had led her into this, she was even more lost than Cosmo Dust.

"It's not her," he said, looking straight at the Antipope, tossing the passport onto the bed beside him. Ann picked it up, fingered it thoughtfully. Off to the side Benny and Meyer seemed caught in between the need for belligerence and the urge to avert their eyes.

"Listen," Ann said, and she lay her hand gently on the Antipope's chest, fingered the piping on his pajama top. "I'm her." She smiled down at him, kindly, daughterly. "I'm her if you want me to be." And she opened the passport, held the photo out to the old man as if to encourage him. "This is me," she went on. "This is me the way you are you. Mr. Englestein, look where you came from. You traded in the Lower East Side for Las Vegas. You traded in being a schmuck for being somebody. Can't I have done the same thing? Traded in where I came from. Italy? Or Darlington, Wisconsin? The first floor of the Golden Calf for the fourteenth floor?" And she raised her brows, smiled a broken smile.

"You're her," the Antipope managed.

"I'm her," she said, and with a little meditative smile she unbuttoned and rebuttoned a button on the Antipope's pajamas, patted his chest, safe, secure.

"Benny," she mused, and when Benny took a solicitous step toward her: "*My* Benny, I mean. Benny Merula. He used to take me for A and W on the Strip. Root beer. A hot dog. Then we'd go out in the desert and he'd let me sit in his lap, steer the car. He'd gun the engine. We'd make donuts in the desert. I was nine, maybe ten years old."

At which the old man smiled, as if he could picture it. An old Vegas memory.

"I was brought up like a princess. Everybody in the casino knew me. I didn't have to use money. I could get gum, Hostess Cup Cakes, whatever I wanted from the concierge's shop on the mezzanine. Get Marco to come outside with me and see how many makes of cars we could count going by on the Strip. Packards, a Nash, a Studebaker."

"No Studebakers in the nineteen-eighties," Cosmo said, but they all ignored him. "No Studebakers in the nineteen-eighties," he whispered in the baby's ear, like it was important that the baby know what was real and what wasn't.

"Backstage with the showgirls. Playing with their makeup. The costumes. Sometimes a TV personality would show up. Imogene Coca, William Bendix, Broderick Crawford—"

"Broderick Crawford," Cosmo whispered to the baby, "would've been dead by then. William Bendix, too. These are facts."

"I was part of it," Ann whispered to the dying man. "What you saw, I saw. What you felt, I felt. Your life. I was there." She reached up, and with the flank of her little finger swept aside a bit of hair, tenderly.

"*Sophie Tucker*," Benny intoned from where he stood.

"*My Yiddishe Mama*," said Meyer as if he were in a trance.

"You're her," the old man murmured after a moment. He tried to lift his head, but fell back. "D'Angelo's daughter."

She smiled, regally, accepting the designation.

"The princess . . . the *contessa* . . ."

Still, she smiled. The old man closed his eyes. Outside, on the street, a car alarm went off.

"Roll up your sleeve," he said.

And there it was, an intrusion in the atmosphere, the insertion of the no-nonsense guy he must once have been. He opened his eyes again, fixed them on Ann, waited.

"My sleeve?" she managed to get out.

With a nod of his head, the Antipope indicated to Benny that he was to come forward, perform what needed to be performed. But before Benny could acquiesce, Ann tossed her head back, and with a look of defiance unbuttoned the cuff of her sleeve and bared her forearm. And then, as if she understood what was wanted, she pulled the sleeve even farther up so that the inside hollow was exposed.

"My eyes," the Antipope said, again excusing himself. He indicated for Benny to come forward and look. "Needle tracks," the Antipope said, as if to forestall any confusion. Benny stepped forward, made a show of looking, then gave way to Meyer, who did the same.

"There's nothing there," Cosmo said from across the room.

"Who asked you?" Benny said.

The old man lifted an arm, took hold of Ann's bicep, felt with his fingertips up and down her arm. When he was done he closed his eyes—pained, betrayed—and turned his head from them. "You're not her," he muttered to the wall. Outside the car alarm stopped in mid-sentence.

"What the hey!" Benny began to say, trying to get some belligerence going, but Meyer signaled ix-nay, it was too late. A minute passed in silence. A world seemed to have collapsed in the room. Ann reached out a hand, laid it on the old man's shoulder.

"I would've done it right," she said quietly, almost dutifully. "I would've fulfilled my obligations. Me, you could've killed and felt like it meant something." She patted his shoulder again. "I'm sorry," she said, and shifted her weight off the bed.

They stood there, the three of them, hands hanging at their sides, rubble all around. Benny shot Cosmo a boy-whatta-jerk look. After a minute, with a shrug, Meyer opened the door into the hall.

"Wait," said Cosmo, nonplussed. He felt strangely bereft. He tried to catch Ann's eye but she stepped past him, went out into the hall.

"It's a delicate art, son," Meyer said, avuncular hand coming to rest on Cosmo's shoulder. "Reality, I mean. It requires a light touch." And he chucked the baby under the chin, showed them the hall. Benny stayed behind to comfort the old man.

"Hey!" Cosmo called after Ann, but she wouldn't acknowledge him. He turned back to Meyer. "Hey," he said again, for lack of anything else to say.

"Easy, you know, does it," was all Meyer would answer. He handed the parking claim to Cosmo.

Down the hall, the elevator doors opened as if they knew all about it.

Chapter 23

A Low-Impact Burial Space

They walked wordlessly through the casino, through the ringing and chinking of the slot machines, past the roulette wheels with their covers on, the craps and blackjack tables with their weary six-in-the-morning dealers. Outside in the surprising cold Cosmo handed the parking claim to a valet who disappeared and five minutes later—during which time Cosmo still didn't speak to, didn't even look at, the ersatz *contessa*—pulled up in front of them not in the CALF-4 Cadillac, but in a yellow, rusted-out Toyota. The appearance of which—and of the valet hopping out and holding the door open for madam—made them finally lock eyes.

"What's it prove?" said Cosmo. The ersatz *contessa* stepped forward, and with a look that could have been wounded, sad, sorry, but Cosmo wouldn't credit it as such, took the baby from him and slid into the passenger seat. The valet shut the door.

"It's not our car," Cosmo muttered, walking around the hood and climbing into the driver's seat. The valet came over to the door, whether to pursue that curious comment or to try for a tip, Cosmo didn't wait to find out. He peeled out from under the carport and headed for the Strip.

And anyway, why didn't *she* say something? Wasn't it supposed to be the person who had cheated and deceived who felt an obligation to explain? Or was that just more obsolescence? Well, he wasn't going to be the first one to speak. He wouldn't even give in enough to look across at her, though he could see out of the corner of his eye that she was herself looking straight ahead, her chin raised ever so slightly, as if *she* were the injured party.

So to hurt her, however cryptically, to show her what *really* mattered to him, he turned onto Maryland Parkway and headed for St. Mark's Cemetery. He thought he could feel her eyes slip over him, questioning. But he didn't turn, didn't speak. At the sight of the familiar mission-style bell tower he felt a little thrill of revenge. He pulled into the gravel parking lot, shut the engine off. Over the rim of the steering wheel were ranks of headstones set against the unlikely emerald of the grass. The early-morning sprinklers were up and slapping water in a dozen different directions.

"What?" Ann said, as if she couldn't keep quiet any longer.

But he didn't answer, got out of the car, made sure he took the keys with him, and entered the cemetery. It was cold, the spray from the sprinklers grazing his face, but he kept going. He made it through the older section to where the grass stopped and a xeriscape began. ("An ecologically low-impact burial space," the cemetery brochure had said.) He knew the way by heart, through the sage and the mimosa over to the Mexican bird of paradise that, in a foolish, broken moment, he had paid the cemetery to plant beside her headstone. He drew up to it now, its lacy branches and still-green leaves standing indifferent guard. At his feet was the headstone, set flush with the ground. He squatted and brushed the grit from the face of the stone, digging with a twig in the incised letters. And then he stood again. There had been the sound of footsteps behind him.

But when he turned she was moving away, as if she'd understood at the last moment and hadn't wanted to intrude. She had, somehow, a second jacket on, a big, plaid thing she must have found in the backseat of the Toyota, inside of which the baby was riding on her hip. He watched her go and then turned back to the grave.

"I tried," he whispered to the patch of desert that had become Cathy to him. He sat down, cross-legged, like a child. He *had* tried, hadn't he? Tried to overturn the world by a willed act of innocence. Sure, okay, there was the Latin and the odd hallucinogenic moment vis-à-vis the Annunciation, but on balance the act had been devoid of the inauthentic. He had extended himself in good faith. The world had said no, had killed his wife, and yet when the dark gods had deposited a baby in his apartment he had said yes. Had said yes again when they'd delivered a woman.

"Listen," he whispered to his listening wife.

He had said: It's going to snow and I'm going to fall in love. And he had said it, he knew, in some obscure way because of her, Cathy Dust, as if he had meant to allow her to influence him, even from the grave. Whether it was also the only way he could allow himself the betrayal, to sneak into bed with the Pope's daughter through the back door of Cathy's humanity, he didn't discount. But it wasn't the main thing. Kissing Ann D'Angelo had had its impulse in a genuine—a *genuine*—desire to embrace life again, to do what Cathy would have done had it been he who had died. He had tried. After all those months of coming out here, of sitting on her grave and talking to her, tears streaming down his cheeks, drinking himself into a stupor so that the groundskeeper had had to ask him to leave once, he had tried to fall in love with someone using Cathy's memory as a kind of matchmaker, and the dark gods could not even wait until morning to reveal it as a fake, a forgery, plagiarism.

"Hey," he heard softly behind him. He did a quick check for tears—no, he was all right—and turned his head. She was standing just off the grave, in deference to him. He hung fire a moment—what was there to say to her?—and then inclined his head slightly, as if giving her permission, and turned back to the stone. She came forward and knelt beside him. His anger, hurt, whatever it was, seemed to have drained out of him.

"I should have had her cremated," he said after a minute. She was silent, respectful. Overhead the sky was gray. "But it was just too awful."

Her poor body. Her face the mortician had handled with who knows what carelessness. To send her into the fire. It had been too much for him.

"But this—" he said with a limp gesture at what lay so horridly beneath them.

"You loved her," she said finally, half question, half statement. She reached out, touched his knee in a gesture of comfort. For a moment the intimacy of the night before awakened between them.

"Yes," he murmured.

The baby was draped languorously across her thigh, like—he couldn't help noticing—the Carpaccio Madonna and Child in the duomo at Rapallo. Like he was trying to tell Cosmo something.

"I'm sorry," she said.

Everyone was sorry. Except, presumably, the anonymous hand, the hideous joker who had killed her. He looked out across the low-impact landscape, the dried-up flora quivering in the desert wind. And he had, suddenly, a vision of that day in the Fenway, Cathy alive and amorous in the wet, humid, verdant fens. He felt an old swelling of disbelief. How could he have left her in this dead place?

The baby had lifted his head up, like the baby Jesus in the Bellini *Sacra Conversazione*. Like, get it?

"Who are you?" Cosmo said. Not to the baby, but to Ann.

Her face hardened ever so slightly and she glanced away. He waited a good minute.

"You owe me an explanation."

"Yes," she whispered.

But there was no explanation coming. She had bowed her head, sat tracing the weave on the plaid hunting jacket. "What do you want to know?" she said obscurely.

"I want to know who you are."

"I'm Ann D'Angelo," she said, and she tossed him a look that managed to be both defiant and entreating. He wondered if he pressed her, insisted on the arithmetic of identity, whether she might not just vanish, head backstage, have a cigarette with one of the dark gods.

"If you *weren't* Ann D'Angelo," he found himself trying, "who would you be?"

And to his surprise a softness came over her, almost a look of gratitude. "Susan," she said. "Susan Kane. From Darlington, Wisconsin. That's who I'd be."

It was strange, wasn't it? It was probably the truth—why not?—and yet it sounded like she was making it up.

"And I'd be one of the cocktail waitresses at the Calf. Candi would be the name I'd go under. I would have come here with my husband. Boyfriend." And she paused as if to get her ducks in order. "He would've known Mickey, the head bartender. He'd be the kind of guy to have big ideas. The boyfriend, I mean. They'd get into trouble. Because she was young and stupid and she loved him. And Benny and Marco would have to step in and straighten them both out. That's how she'd end up working, you know, extra."

Now it was the Child in the *Madonna of the Orange Tree*, the same look of intelligent appeal: hands spread, eyes up-lifted, leaning off Mary's thigh as if defying gravity by way of illustration.

"But not only that. She'd catch the eye of the daughter of Angelo D'Angelo because they looked alike. Because she got the idea that a double might come in handy. Like with czars and emperors." And she fixed him with her own look of appeal. "That's how it started."

A pair of butterflies who didn't know it was almost January staggered by, landed on the bird of paradise, took off again. Cosmo watched them go, continued looking off into the distance even when the woman beside him began speaking again.

"Or maybe it'd be that she was a dancer"—her voice quickened—"a dance major at Marquette, and her boyfriend who always had big ideas saw a flier for floor-show auditions at the dance school and she went just to please him, didn't even do her best, but got hired anyway. Only when they got to Las Vegas, the mean little shit of a choreographer fired her during the first rehearsal. And she was sitting out on the casino floor in her gold lamé breakaway bra crying when the head bartender saw her, comforted her, walked her over to the personnel office. And she wrote down Candi—Candi Kane, a nickname from high school—on the application. They dressed her in one of the waitress outfits, checked for cellulite, bad posture, good cleavage, and hired her. And that's how she began to hate being who she was."

He had looked back to see her green eyes fixed on him—what color had they been in the passport? what color had they been a day ago?—daring him to tell her she was lying. There was something nervous and fragile about her, as if she were telling the truth, or some version of the truth, and wanted to be believed, and yet couldn't tell it flat out, straight. For what reasons—guilt, shame, a predisposition to the underhanded, or because it *wasn't* in fact the truth?—he didn't know.

"And so when the Pope's daughter started getting weird on me, I got weird right back." He noted the switch back to first person. Not a slipup, judging by the challenging look she gave him. "At first it was just the prince and the pauper thing. Trading places, exchanging identities. I couldn't tell whether it was for real or not, the whole air of threat, I mean, the sense of danger. Maybe it was just a spoiled girl's twisted idea of self-importance. Though there *were* the bodyguards, plenty of rumors about her, not to mention her father. But I was getting paid; I didn't care."

"Where was your husband?"

She didn't correct the term. "He'd disappeared." She shrugged, brought her fingertips to her lips, kissed him good-bye. "At first, I just got paraded around by the bodyguards. For the benefit of whose eyes, I didn't know at the time. But then she really started getting into it. Changing identities. It was a kick for her. Everything she did was for the kick. Benny and Marco just humored her. You could tell they didn't like her. Heck, they liked *me* better. We used to have a pretty good time, traipsing about. I taught them ballroom steps. The bossa nova, the fox-trot. Benny was pretty good."

She took up the baby's hands, danced them a little dance, looked up with a smile for Cosmo. He felt a little stab of love. Oh, his stupid heart!

"We even came up to look at your painting once. You remember?"

He remembered. A good three, four months ago. He'd stayed out of the way, tried not to be attracted or intimidated or anything by the sudden appearance of the well-dressed woman.

"That was you?"

She nodded.

Did he believe her?

"Here's how we used to pull it off. I'd go up in the elevator or into a back room with my waitress tray, or to the kitchen, and she'd be inside, dressed as a cocktail waitress. The whole deal: eye shadow, wig, push-up bra, heels, my name tag. She'd go out with my order or whatever and I'd take my makeup off and change into her clothes, come out a moment later with Benny and Marco on either side of me.

I'd look around to see who was watching, see if I could figure out who it was they were trying to trick, but of course everyone was watching. I was the Pope's daughter."

And she tossed her hair in a gesture not of feigned pride alone.

"Sometimes I'd just stay up in the penthouse with the baby. You know this is *her* baby, right?" And she fixed him with a look meant to take stock of just how much he knew. "Sometimes they'd let me go up on the rooftop. It all had to do with the Pope, whether he was up and about or not. Mostly not. But they had to keep secret what they were doing, letting his daughter out on her own. He didn't even know about the baby. How they managed that, I don't know."

The baby turned his hand palm-up, like he didn't know, either.

"I swear, by the end, I was spending more time with the baby than she was."

"You know his name, then."

That seemed to take her by surprise. Could she, after all, just be making it up? Or making up parts of it, for some reason of her own?

"He doesn't have a name."

He gave her a skeptical look.

"He *doesn't*. She hated him. It was her way of getting back at him."

Which was what the Pope's daughter had said, more or less, that night in the Jacuzzi.

"Thing is," she said, thoughtful, "it wasn't enough for her to be me. I had to be *her*. It was like she wanted to pour herself into me. How much of it was the heroin I don't know, but she'd send for me, have me brought up to the penthouse, to her room, and show me things. All that stuff about the Pope—the real Pope, I mean. Freemasons, Gnostics. I didn't tell you the half of it. She had boxes of stuff. All about her. Or who she thought she was. You saw some of it on the Web. It wasn't friendship," she said with a shake of her head, pausing as if even now she was trying to figure it out. "It was something else. Like if she could make me into her, into who she thought she was, then she'd be real. *It* would be real. She wouldn't be the daughter of the Pope of Las Vegas, but the Pope's Daughter."

And she left herself poised on that thought for a good minute.

"She insisted I wear her perfume." She made an airy gesture just under her chin, wafting the scent his way. "She gave me jewelry, her exact same watch"—holding the expensive thing out to him—"and clothes. She wanted me to shoot, too. But I told her no, I wasn't there yet. She did my hair, showed me how she did her makeup. We stood in front of her mirror, made up, looking like copies of one another. It got kind of creepy at times. But also, I don't know . . ."

"You liked it, too?"

She lifted her chin in a gesture at once defiant and hurt. "I was unhappy. I needed money. I needed to get out of the mess I was in."

"And that mess was?"

She pursed her lips, wouldn't pursue it, threw him instead a look of appeal: Was he not going to understand her, forgive her? He closed his eyes and wondered by what alchemy he could just get in the car and leave, put Las

Vegas in his rearview mirror and drive up through Colorado, across the Midwest to Darlington, Wisconsin, look up the Kanes in the phone book, drive to their modest house on Summer Street, and find their daughter—the one everyone said would be a dancer—skipping down the worn wooden staircase from her room on the second floor, looking all Natalie Wood and a little shy to meet him, her identity without the slightest deformation of recursion, of her and the Pope's daughter having multiplied themselves in the mirrored bathroom on the penthouse floor of the Golden Calf.

When he opened his eyes again the baby had a look of disappointment about his mouth.

"Look," he said, and he reached out. She seemed to shrink from him, and he found himself instead touching the baby. "I need to understand this. I need to understand . . ." What was it he needed to understand? "The girl who's hair I burned, the cocktail waitress—was that you?"

She drew back a little, uncertain of allowing a version of herself without the loophole of reflection, surrogacy. "That was me *as* the cocktail waitress," she said finally.

"And the next day, up on the scaffolding? The Wild Turkey, the conversation about treating people politely? Was *that* you?"

She kept her head level, didn't tell him no.

"What about later, up on the platform? Sophia and the serpent? Was that the real Pope's daughter?"

She seemed to wince at the word *real*. "That was her *as* the Pope's daughter."

"And Christmas Eve, down on the casino floor—?"

"Me."

"And afterward in the hot tub? The cocktail waitress in the hot tub?"

At which she made a face like, how could it have been her? But he wanted her to say it, demanded it with his eyes. "Her," she murmured, "it was her dressed as Candi."

"And the woman who came in on us?"

"What do you want from me?"

"And who talked to me in the bedroom? Who kissed me? The Pope's daughter? Was that you?"

She looked away, hurt and at the same time seeming to see herself as he might see her: duplicitous, a little cruel.

"And when you left the room," he found himself saying, "why not kill her, take the baby, frame the painter, and start life for real as Ann D'Angelo?"

She shot him a look both pained and angry, and which— was it just his imagination?—seemed to have something of shame in it. What had she been thinking? That week on her own, the real Pope's daughter dead, Benny and Marco looking for her, the police looking for her, Cosmo Dust the suspect looking for her, who knew who else? *Make the game real.* She had said that the kick of changing identities had been the drive behind the Pope's daughter's behavior, but who, really, was the twisted one?

She said it again, whispered it: "What do you want from me?"

He reached out—she thought for an instant that it was to touch her, and her face softened, but it was her handbag he was after. He undraped it from her shoulder, opened it, and dumped the contents on the ground. He'd seen it all two nights ago, but who knew if in the meantime things hadn't changed. He opened the wallet and took out the credit cards, scrutinized the driver's license photo—it was different from the passport photo, but was it her, or the other one?

And for the first time since he'd talked to Orel Sloan and Carlotta Valdez it occurred to him that she might in fact *be* the Pope's daughter, that maybe there was yet another level of deceit, a more radical circle of uncertainty that included in its circumference the detectives, Benny and Meyer, the Inquisitor. He dropped the driver's license, looked up, startled, and stared out over the desert as if it, too, were an imposter, a counter-Earth got up by some god—what did the Gnostics call Him?—the Demiurge.

But for what purpose?

"We would switch wallets when we switched clothes," the Pope's daughter was saying. She'd reached out and was putting her things back in her handbag. "Marco got us false IDs, but we didn't use them."

But if it came to that, for what purpose was the *real* Earth got up?

"Cosmo . . ."

She reached out and touched him.

"I'm sorry."

Someone was saying his name. Someone was saying his name without the sarcasm of Betty and Veronica, without the insensitivity of Crazy Herman and all the others: Benny and Marco/Meyer, Orel Sloan. Someone was saying his name with care, like *she* used to say it.

"Who are you?"

She blanched, drew her hand back. "I'm Susan Kane." Then, with a little smile, the high-school girl: "Candi Kane."

He kept his face hard and ungiving.

"Ann D'Angelo," she said.

He closed his eyes.

"Who do you want me to be?"

And there was in her voice a battered appeal. The sound of it forced his eyes back open. He searched her face for some sign that it was not just more deceit.

"Are they paying you for *this*, too?" he asked.

The hurt in her eyes deepened.

"Or is it just you?"

"I don't know," she said, and there seemed in her saying it a world that was sadly parallel to his: lost, unsure, tricked. For a moment his distrust of her was absorbed by a felt awareness of how much she, too, had suffered. How much she had lost of her Darlington, Wisconsin, self. And yet it wasn't enough to win his faith, his forgiveness, whatever it was, and he found himself closing his eyes again, making the world disappear by the only means in his power. And he experienced—how strange!—an old trick of his childhood mind: the funny idea that the world changed when you had your eyes closed, danced about you in who knew what impossible ways, the flowers spinning, the birds doing acrobatic figures just for the fun of it. He had spent an afternoon—oh, how young had he been?—sitting on the back stoop, opening his eyes as fast as he could to catch the world resuming itself, but always it was too quick for him. The memory of it almost made him smile, sitting there in the desert, on his wife's grave, the world in some ways just too terrible to be believed. And for the thousandth time the image of what his dear wife's body must look like— even now! six feet below him!—stirred itself on the insides of his eyelids. All he could do was wait for the world to change. Wait for the right moment to open his eyes, for the moment when Cathy would be beside him, her skin fresh, her hair smelling of Prell, oh! whispering his name and leaning forward to kiss him, the tips of her breasts in that just-inches-away posture that he had always found so maddening. He heard her stir, heard his name. And then the light pressure of lips on his mouth. Fingertips at the back of his head. He waited, gave the world one last chance to not change back when he opened his eyes, took a deep breath. . . .

He heard it before he saw it. The falling sizzle in the dried leaves, so familiar from his New England boyhood. He opened his eyes. It was snowing. Not big, leafy flakes, but icy beads, dancing off the desiccated leaves and falling to the desert floor. Ann was just pulling back from having kissed him, the baby still on her lap. She was smiling. There were crystals of snow in her eyelashes.

"I'm Annunciata D'Angelo," she said. She took his hand in hers. "From this day forward. I've got the passport, the credit cards. The IDs. It doesn't matter who I was. From now on I'm her. You may call me Ann." She turned his hand over, placed her other hand on top and pressed. "My mother is dead. My father, too. I've never been married. Never had a real boyfriend. Never been in love with anyone. Never *made* love to anyone. This baby was the only child of a cocktail waitress who was murdered. I took him in. His name"—she got stuck for a moment—"is Giovanni. Giovanni D'Angelo. I'm his mother now."

He saw that she was offering him a choice: to accept this or not, to live by this as the foundation of their world or not.

"I used to live in Las Vegas," she continued. "I was brought up there. My adoptive father was the Pope of Las Vegas, but people say my real father was Pope John Paul I." She tossed her head magnificently. "There are those who believe I fulfill the Gnostic prophecy of the Messiah as the offspring of Peter. I let them believe what they want to believe. For myself, I am dedicated to life at the human level. To whomever loves me. This baby. My husband."

He lowered his eyes. What was it she was asking of him? That he legitimize her hallucination—not even *her* hallucination, but a dead woman's—by his belief? That he acquiesce to the inauthentic, *believe* in it, in her? He stared downward, through the dead earth, to his dead wife.

"Ann . . . ," he murmured.

"Cosmo," came the answer, strong and daring.

He raised his eyes to her. She was smiling at him still. The snow was ricocheting off the messiah's head, settling in the folds of his overalls. The baby looked at it with an infant's aplomb, like it was all just part of the miracle.

Chapter 24

Authorized Venetian Team Members Only

All the way down Maryland Parkway and onto the Strip he drove in a kind of daze. They were headed for the airport, just like that! All around, the world was celebrating, cars honking their horns, pedestrians dancing at the intersections. Because of the snow, Cosmo told himself modestly, though he wouldn't put it past the gods to throw a party for him.

They'd discovered upon starting up the Toyota that the windshield wipers didn't work, ditto the heater, and now heading down the Strip the car began to buck, surge, almost stall. Ann asked what was wrong. Cosmo threw her a look like, she should know better. Somewhere around the Frontier there was a minute when he thought it was going to be all right. The Toyota seemed to get a second wind. But when the Venetian came into view, the bucking began again. He pressed the gas pedal to the floor but it was no go. The lights on the dashboard glowed brightly and then died. The car huffed another block, then, as if by prearrangement, gave one last surge so that it rolled up even with the Campanile and quietly turned itself off.

They sat for a minute in the dead car, not speaking. A little ways down the boulevard the Eiffel Tower rose into the swirling snow; farther down they could see the filaments of the Brooklyn Bridge. Inside the car the air seemed filled with hypotheses.

"What do you say to some breakfast?" Ann said, turning her face to Cosmo as if she meant to show him, show the world, that normalcy was the norm. "A cup of coffee. Then a taxi to the airport."

It was like a dare. As though she were asking him to prove to her that he believed in this new world. (He did believe. He *did* believe.) So it was out of the car and across the Strip to the Venetian, up the stairway of the Palazzo Ducale, the gilded ovals and rectangles of Veronese's ceiling swimming over their heads. Cosmo had never seen it before—the imitation, he meant; the real one he'd studied with Cathy by his side.

At the top of the stairs they looked to the right, to the left. There was nothing but tourists.

They stopped first at a Starbucks, then strolled past the shops and cafés toward the Grand Canal, Ann with the baby on her hip, Cosmo with coffee, croissants, and napkins in hand. On either side of them were the Gothic porticoes and arcades of Venice, the salmon-colored marble, the greens and roses. The occasional bridge spanned the canal, and on its chlorinated waters gondolas were being poled by their handsome gondoliers, each sporting the white-and-black striped shirt, the red sash, the porkpie hat, and a mini-walkie-talkie attached to his belt.

Ah, but how strange that it brought back memories! Even our Cosmo with his firsthand knowledge of casino illusion found himself falling under the spell. Venice! With its quatrefoil loggias and serried ranks of windows. The crenellated façades, the stone spandrels, the carved palmettos. Never mind that the Grand Canal was a mere thirty feet at its widest point, that the mezzanines and top floors performed their illusion with the collapsed geometry of a theater set, that you could see the holes in the sky where the fire code demanded sprinklers. He was back in Venice! With his love and her child! Walking in the perpetual twilight, the violet sky overhead as magical as Magritte's. So, okay, there was the occasional out-of-the-way, utilitarian door with a sign saying AUTHORIZED VENETIAN TEAM MEMBERS ONLY, as if behind the pasteboard Venice there was yet another "Members Only" Venice, but that, Cosmo decided, was minor and should not be allowed to detract from the overall experience.

They passed a YOU ARE HERE map.

When they reached the Piazza San Marco they snagged an outdoor table in front of one of the restaurants, sat down, and ate their breakfast. The baby gummed bits of croissant and drank a couple of creamers. Cosmo and Ann barely spoke, merely smiled when a waiter came out of the restaurant and informed them that the tables were for patrons only. It was settled between them. Who they were, what they were, where they were going: somehow settled. They were in an intermittency. The old order—love!— discovered in the very world that had produced rapacious mutation. Their smiles lingered on their lips. The waiter shrugged and disappeared back behind the rich drapery that separated the interior of the restaurant from the out-door café. In a courtyard off to their left animatronic pigeons waddled and pecked and preened. A Pakistani family in shalwars and scarves tried to feed them popcorn.

And as if to authenticate the moment, the baby—little Giovanni!—who had not soiled his diapers since Cosmo had known him, accepted his humanity and did so. With a little smile (*The Madonna of the Pinks*) Ann stood, grabbed a Pampers from the plastic bag they'd been carrying around, and went in search of a restroom. Cosmo watched her go with an assortment of old emotion, then turned back to the piazza.

The world was beautiful viewed from the front porch of intermittency. Torus moldings, stone archivolts: the Renaissance in all its grace and grandeur. He let his eyes roam over the façade of the Doge's Palace, the windows of the second floor lit with apparent life, and up above, the tutelary statuary keeping an eye on things. Sure enough, there was the Torre dell'Orologio, missing its Moors with their hammers poised to ring the hour, but with the clock of the zodiac, phases of the moon and all, and the San Marco lion with his professorial paw on a book. In the aedicula between them—just like the Inquisitor had said—were the Virgin and her Child, the halo above the Madonna's head seeming to shimmer with special effects. She, too, was caught in all this. A bizarre fate! To have survived the centuries of adulation and tears, only to be trucked across the American desert and enthroned in a casino! And yet there she was, her head inclined slightly, the Child in her lap with his hand raised in benediction, behind them the beautiful field of blue enamel and the gilded pattern-work. He scanned the piazza, wondered what it all looked like from up there—the people in front of the shops, the bare midriffs, the pigeons, the fellow rolling a portable oxygen unit, the occasional epileptic. Did it look different from Venice? Did it look different from the fifteenth century?

So okay, what *was* it exactly? He was not a Christian. His conversion to Catholicism had been a gesture of love, not true belief. Even Cathy had known that. And yet he couldn't rid himself of the power in the image. Her, caught in all this. It was more than just his artist's love, the museums full of painted madonnas—which he *did* love, he would be the first to admit. But this was something more, something in the very heartbeat of the image. The inclined head, the soft face, the folds of her clothing, the compassion. *Caught in all this.* When she looked at that infant always in her lap— baby Jesus, baby Cosmo, baby you—and the people below in the piazza, did she see in the single face, in the single era and the solitary place, *every* place, every time, every generation doomed to the same struggling heart? And when she put on the knowledge that came with the Annunciation, did she understand that there was no recourse, no escape? And with all that could she still look upon the infant's face and joy in it?

He gazed out over the piazza, tried to look at the spectacle from the vantage point of love. There were caricature artists with their easels set up in front of the Palazzo Ducale, a white-faced mime in the costume of a Doge performing for spare change. From across the Bridge of Sighs a group of revelers in *Carnevale* costume came singing a madrigal. There was big-nosed Pulcinella and black-caped Scaramouche, a hunchback (fake) with a hand drum, and a dwarf (real) with a crocodile mask. They capered about, tweaking the tourists, passing the hat. Cosmo looked up to see what the Madonna thought of all this.

"May I?" he heard behind him.

He turned to see a well-dressed man standing over his table: the restaurant owner, Cosmo supposed, as the man had just come from behind the heavy drapery. Or maybe the maître d', since he was dressed to the nines: pearly gray suit, opal stickpin, tanning-salon tan, and with such a strong smell of cologne that it made the air around him almost have a taste. He pulled back a chair and sat down.

"There's a legend," he said, indicating with a glance the clock tower he'd caught Cosmo looking at, "that the Venetian Grand Council burned out the eyes of the clock maker to prevent any other city from hiring him." He fixed his eyes on Cosmo to see how he'd take this information. "Then murdered him for good measure. But after all"—a reasonable shrug—"the sun's rotation in relation to the zodiac, the calculation of favorable tides, these were important economic secrets for Venice."

"I'm just waiting for my wife," Cosmo said.

"Wife?" the man repeated with his brow raised in amusement.

"I'll leave as soon as she gets back."

He spread his hands, expansive, indifferent. "No hurry," he said.

Cosmo wondered at him.

"Burning out a clock maker's eyes," the man went on, meditative, "killing him, to keep his secrets, that would be a *purposeful* act of violence. Old-fashioned, don't you think?" He sniffed the air, as if sensing a word there. "Quaint," he said. "The kind of murder you'd put in a museum. If there were museums of murder."

And he inclined his head, pleased with his whimsy and expecting a response. Cosmo looked away, picked up his coffee cup, and drank from it. It tasted like cologne.

"Murder has its fashions," the man mused. "Like anything else."

He smiled, enjoying for the moment Cosmo's confusion. He put his thumb and middle finger on either side of his throat, smoothed his collar, and let his fingers come to rest on the thin knot of his tie. He seemed poised on some reflection. After a minute he let his hand drop and leaned forward with one of his elbows on the tabletop, keeping his other arm hidden below.

"I'm him."

Cosmo felt a deep unease lodge inside him. He looked out across the piazza in search of Ann and the baby. Where were they?

"I did it." A sheepish smile crept over his tanned, handsome face. He looked for some reaction, and when Cosmo still didn't understand, said, "I killed her."

He felt himself snapped back to the world. His first horrible thought was that the man meant Ann.

"Who are you?"

He let an upturned hand indicate the self-evident. "As you see," he said.

"You killed her?" Cosmo repeated stupidly, stalling.

He made a dismissive gesture, a gesture of modesty. "It was nothing," he said; he seemed even to blush.

The image of the body in the bathtub, the gun on the coffee table, spun in Cosmo's head. "Who are you?" was all he could say. The man fixed him with his eyes. They were a handsome blue.

"I am the one who is fatally linked to you."

It sent a chill down Cosmo's spine.

"I've been watching you."

The Jaguar!

"Ever since it happened. Ever since I saw you on the news. Ever since I learned who you were." He smiled, seemed on the verge of reaching across the table to touch Cosmo on the arm. "I've been with you. Beside you. Watching how it was I'd affected you. I've *affected* you," he said with a pleasure that seemed to move through him, through his torso into his limbs.

"I don't want to talk to you."

"You have no choice," the man answered. "Before, back then, you might have had a choice. We were unknown to one another, unaffected, unaffecting. But now"—and out from under the table nosed the barrel of a gun—"you have no choice."

He sipped air, felt his vision shudder. And then, out of the corner of his eye, there she was! With the baby, sidling along the store windows across the piazza. He turned before he could think not to. She caught sight of him looking at her, waved, made a funny little gesture as if to say, Who's that?

"Ah," the man said, following Cosmo's eyes and smiling. "Your wife."

"No . . . ," Cosmo answered, but he hardly knew what he was denying.

"The Pope's daughter," said the man.

Cosmo fixed him with a look. "Not the Pope's daughter," he said. "You *killed* the Pope's daughter."

"What?" said the man, and he blinked, wondered a moment. And then his face was smiling with insight. "Oh, I see, I see!" And he laughed outright. "No, no, not that business in the hotel room. Too messy. Too"—and he searched for the word—"too *straightforward*. No," he said and let his eyes linger on Cosmo's face with the expectation of a new pleasure. "Your wife, my dear boy. Your *real* wife. The Easter egg."

He felt frozen to the bone. What had he just heard?

"That's all I want credit for. That's the only signature I'd own to. The other, in the bathroom"—he made a dismissive gesture—"that might have been a parallel motif. Something to add texture, complexity. But the first. The purely random." He seemed to shiver at the exquisite taste of the word. "That's all I want to be remembered for."

What had just happened? This man, overdressed and with perfect fingernails, what had he just said?

"You couldn't have," he murmured. "How could you know? . . . You couldn't have known. . . ."

"That it would be *your* wife?" the man asked helpfully.

Cosmo nodded soundlessly.

"My dear boy, of course I *didn't* know. That was back when you and I . . ." He made a gesture of emptiness. "I was content to be supplied. Eh? The fates, the gods, whoever, delivered *you*."

He couldn't move, couldn't speak.

"Of course there was the child, too, the boy from the Mayflower Apartments. You should have seen his mother carrying on at his grave. Oh!" He gazed off, across the piazza, remembering. "But they moved away just after it all happened. And I had to make a choice whether to follow them or to stay with you." And he did it, reached out and touched Cosmo on the arm. *"I stayed with you."*

Above them, the clock tower began to ring the hour. A tourist took a photo of it, of the sound.

"Why?" Cosmo managed to get out. He felt—strangely, bizarrely!—as though his bones were crumbling—no, *melting*—as though his body were turning into a puddle.

"Why did I stay with you?"

"Why—?" and he couldn't finish the question.

"Why the cyanide in the first place?" And he laughed at the question. "Absurd! That you should ask such a thing!" He had gold molars. They shone when he laughed. "It was an act of perfect randomness." And he made a face, a sound—*pfft!*—at the utter chance of it. "But once the random has occurred, ah!"—and he whispered intensely— "*then* it becomes meaningful. Your wife is nothing to me. But you, my dear boy. *You* mean more to me than you could ever suppose." He looked at Cosmo with an exalted expression. "I have been so close to you without your knowing. I've taken the Sistine ceiling tour—oh, more than once!— come up on your platform while you worked, listened to the guide talk about you, watched your face. Watched you drink too much. Parked outside your apartment at night and imagined the pain inside. The hurt. The emptiness." He breathed in deeply, his nostrils folding and opening like wings. "I have authored you."

It was all he could do to turn, to look, like a drowning man, toward an impossible shore. She was there still, with the baby, window-shopping, waiting for whoever it was who was sitting with her husband to leave. The "help!" he wanted to cry died in his throat. He could feel, the whole time, like an insect crawling on the side of his face, Cathy's killer's eyes.

"Who you've become," he exulted, "what you feel, what you think: I made you that way. *I* did." He touched himself delicately, lovingly, on the breast. "There are times when it's all so radiant I wonder whether I act alone. Whether I'm not an agent of something larger. Eh? And that what I think is random is in fact a manifestation of a system. Do you see?" He wanted Cosmo to respond. "What different universes! In one, I'm your private torturer, your personal executioner. Conceived by chance. In the other, I only masquerade as chance, an unwitting agent of dedicated malevolence." He seemed to fairly tremble with the power of the idea. "Eh? What do you think?"

"Leave me alone," Cosmo managed to say.

"No," the man whispered back, again with the shimmer of exaltation. "I can never leave you alone."

She was coming back, threading her way through the café tables with a smile for whoever this was, this friend of Cosmo's. He wanted to leap up, to warn her to stay away, but his bones had melted. He watched as she drew up to the table, shifting the baby's weight on her hip. Cathy's killer—polite, the gentleman, hiding the gun—stood up.

"I think I know you," he said, kissing his forefinger in a gesture of thought. "Ann D'Angelo, yes?"

"Why, yes!" she said, pleased, and throwing silent Cosmo a look as if to say, See? Cosmo closed his eyes, swallowed, couldn't speak.

"Enchanté," Cathy's killer said, taking Ann's free hand. "I'm so very sorry to hear of your bereavement." The smile disappeared from her face. She looked at Cosmo, as if for explanation. "Oh, dear!" he continued, changing his tone at the sight of her expression. "Don't tell me you haven't heard?" She gave her head a little uncertain shake. "Now I feel positively like the Angel of Death"—this with a look at Cosmo before turning back to Ann—"I'm sorry . . . but your father . . . it was on the morning news. He's passed away."

"Oh!" she said, and for an instant she didn't quite handle her part; then: "I didn't know. I was away for the night."

"Yes, I know."

She let this pass. "My father," she said, turning to Cosmo.

"Yes," was all he could manage.

"It was on the news?"

"This morning," Cathy's killer said, still with the politeness, the funeral director's soft palms hovering in the air. "On the TV. A family spokesman," he said with a smile and italics in his voice for the phrase. "And also, a priest from the Vatican. He spoke of all his good works. The hospital, gifts to the Church"—he made a vague gesture, as if the good works were legion—"he was a great man."

They stood, silent. A family was seated for breakfast at the table next to them. Cathy's killer smiled a faraway, thoughtful smile.

"Odd," he said quizzically to Cosmo, "the number of deaths associated with the Golden Calf of late." Then, to Ann, the mask of civility slipping and something like menace coming into his voice: "Do you suppose there'll be many more?"

"What?" said Ann.

"Deaths."

She looked at Cosmo. Who was this? Why didn't Cosmo introduce him to her?

"We have to be going," Cosmo muttered. He managed to stand up.

"So soon?" The man appealed to Ann. "Just before you came up we were discussing moral equations. It's an old subject of ours. We used to talk about it 'til the wee hours, Cosmo and I. And his wife." He made an apologetic smile— a little *oh, dear* thing—as if he had misstepped by mentioning Cathy in the new wife's presence. "Cosmo here would argue for a symmetrical world. Good rewarded, evil punished. Everything adding up."

Ann had taken a half-step back, realizing something was wrong. This man, friend or not, something was wrong. She turned an anxious face to Cosmo.

"Whereas *my* idea," he went on, ignoring her expression, "was more geometric. That each of us is at the center of our own personal apocalypse. And that destruction moves in a geometric progression, beginning with one death—say, just as an illustration, Cosmo's wife's death—and then spiraling outward: the cocktail waitress, Benny and Marco Merula, Angelo D'Angelo, until we reach an infinitely dense death. What do you think?"

"What are you talking about?"

"I'm talking about a progression of death. I'm talking about whose death might be next."

She held the baby tight to her chest and her face hardened. "Go away," she said.

"An infinitely dense death," he repeated, and he made a gesture at the world around them, the piazza, the Doge's

Palace, Venice beyond. "The slow apocalypse. Don't you see?"

In a minute he would do it. He would lash out, push this man away. In a minute, when his breath returned, when his bones came back.

"It's a beautiful idea, no? Instead of the Kenotic Messiah's cataclysmic Apocalypse coming in"—he consulted his watch—"thirty-nine hours, it's been happening all along. A billion individual apocalypses. Yours, mine, the child's. Think of the complexity of the design. Everything ordered and patterned, an orchestration of infinitely interpenetrating deaths. All made to look random. It's proof of God," he exclaimed with a little laugh. "Such complexity! Everything pointless, meaningless, and yet conspiring and interdependent. All breathing together, moving together toward the extinguishing of life."

"I don't know who you are," Ann said. She had understood Cosmo's expression by now. "But I don't want you anywhere near me. I don't want you anywhere near my baby."

"Too late. I'm already near you." And he smiled, the gold molars glinting in the back of his mouth. "It might be years from now"—he smiled at Cosmo, at Ann—"it might be in the next minute." He backed up a step. "It was a pleasure meeting you," he said to Ann. He bowed his head slightly as if he were a Victorian gentleman. "We have had an effect on one another's lives. Don't you feel that?" And he placed a hand on his heart, a gesture of strange intimacy. "We penetrate. We depend." He took another step backward. "We can't help but see one another again." And with a smile, he turned and went back into the restaurant.

For a moment Cosmo couldn't look at her, turned his eyes instead upward to the clock tower, to the quaint Madonna, to the papier-mâché miracle on her lap. He had for so long, in such intense study, imagined Cathy's killer, paraded before his mind's eye a gallery of degenerate types—sallow-skinned, chinless stutterers with stringy hair who wouldn't look you in the eye—that to have the real thing bloom before him in such breathtaking contradiction had stunned him. He ran his fingers through his hair in panic and disarray. How to hide from it? "How?" he thought, and then realized he'd said it out loud.

"Cosmo?"

He turned to the woman beside him, saw the care on her face, the questioning. He tried to reassure her with a gentle look, but his body still wasn't working right. There was a strange swelling in the glands under his jaw, tinnitus in his ear. The man's cologne lingered in the air.

"I need to sit down," he managed to say. "Just for a minute."

She sat down with him, baby in her lap, her back to the restaurant. Out in the piazza Pulcinella was chasing Lucretia with a banana, Scaramouche drawing a bead on them with what looked like a starter's pistol. Ann reached out, touched him on his wrist.

"We have to get out of here," he said.

She nodded. "All right." Then, patient, solicitous: "Who was that?"

Could he tell her? He looked at her worried face, at her eyes. They were green now, had been green for some days past, hadn't they? He could trust her, couldn't he? He looked over her shoulder at the restaurant, at the curtain,

which furled slightly as though there were a presence behind it, and then away, out to the piazza, where Scaramouche was trying to poke his pistol up Lucretia's skirt.

"We have to get out of here," he said again.

But where to go? He had thought that they were in an
intermittency, that they had found in this playland of illu-
sory structures the old equation. But the old equation—he
realized now with an awareness that froze him—*included
Cathy's killer.* He had been present from the beginning,
would *always* be present, as original a factor as Cathy
had been.

He felt his jacket's inside pocket. There was his passport,
there was the baby's bottle.

"Cathy—" he began to say, but just as he uttered her
name he saw over Ann's shoulder, nosing out from between
the curtains in the slow motion of a dream, the black barrel
of a gun. For a second he had the bizarre thought that it was
mere stage play, like the quatrefoils and the palmettos, a
necessary prop. But in the next instant he gave a cry that
even to his own ears sounded crazed, and while Ann's face
registered shock, found himself knocking over the table in a
lunge that took her and the baby down onto the floor. There
were cries and a leaping up from the people around them.
Under him, Ann's eyes were wide with confusion. The baby,
as if this were the final installment of his humanity, let out a
terrific scream.

"What?" Ann cried.

There was a roaring in his ears as if his blood had
exploded.

"What?" she cried again, trying to sit up, trying to right
the baby on her lap. "What are you doing?"

He got to his knees, looked to the curtain, to where the gun had been, but there was nothing there. The curtain eddied, mute, malignant.

"Sir?" someone was saying.

"Shh," Ann whispered urgently to the baby. "Shh!"

The Doge had come forward, miming for all he was worth. Somewhere on the horizon, Pulcinella was knocking Lucretia to the ground, climbing on top of her.

"Shh."

He felt a wave of heat flood his cheeks, his forehead. "I'm sorry," he said. And then he found himself saying it over and over: "I'm sorry, I'm sorry!" And he was just in the act of reaching across to touch her when a shot rang out.

Chapter 25

The Counter-Earth

The animatronics on *these* pigeons are something else. They swoop across the backlit sky, full range of motion to their iridescent wings. And the sky itself: no sign of holes for the sprinkler system, no panel joints, no Sheetrock screws popping through. Exquisite! Even the color of the air is just as he remembers it, cerulean mixed with a little verditer blue. You can barely see the brushstrokes.

It's the last day of the millennium and Cosmo Dust is sitting in the Piazza San Marco in Venice. The real Piazza San Marco, he thinks, in the real Venice. The real Ann has gone to change the baby, and he is left as he had been left once before to marvel at the beauty of the place, the gold stars on the Torre dell'Orologio shimmering in the sun, the field of cobalt blue as intense as life. Any minute now Pulcinella will show up with Lucretia in tow. Any minute now Ann will come through the crowd from across the piazza, baby on her hip, love on her lips. There will be no maniac.

One of them—both of them, perhaps—is dead. Cosmo

isn't saying. Perhaps he doesn't know. Thinks, perhaps, that this is what the transition to the afterlife would be, a kind of cosmic sleight of hand: real pigeons, real Venice! This particular transition had necessitated the first flight out of Vegas that they could get tickets for (Boston, as fate would have it, leaving in twenty-two minutes, you'll have to hurry, sir), from Boston to JFK to Rome, then by midnight train into Santa Lucia Station in Venice where, after wandering through the northern streets, up and over the narrow canals, looking for a pensione with an insomniac concierge, they had come upon a crèche in an out-of-the-way court-yard. Dead tired, intoxicated by the authentic, Cosmo had evicted the plaster Jesus from his corncrib, put a real Jesus in his place, moved Balthasar out of the way—donkeys, too—spread some hay about as best he could, and lain down with his love in his arms. The cows lowed, the ox and ass kept time, and above their heads the Mediterranean sky sprinkled starlight on them, *pa rum pa pum pum.*

In the morning they had awakened to a toothless smile leaning over them with a plate of *panettone*, a bowl of warm milk for the baby. Somewhere, out of some open win-dow, someone was singing the Vivaldi *Gloria.*

Now, after having spent the morning, the dreamy after-noon, strolling about the Most Serene City, Cosmo sips his cappuccino and entertains options other than his being dead. In one of these he and the Pope's daughter have sim-ply morphed, à la Marco into Meyer. In another he marvels at his luck: He could have been, say, in Polly Sensoria's arms, or engaged in Love Assassin, or in the argumentative grip of one of his dark gods, when the counter-Earth com-pleted its one-eighty, but instead he had been in the act of being murdered. Or rather, he had been in the act of throwing himself over the woman being murdered. Let's try again: He had been in the inauthentic Venice about to be shot, maybe even *being* shot, when the world flipped from black to white, up to down, past to present, outside to in. And here he is. Alive. In love. Surrounded by the good and the beautiful.

He remembers a painting—it's somewhere in this very city; there will be plenty of time to find it—by the anonymous Master of the Roses, which depicts Mary and Joseph's flight into Egypt. In the foreground Mary is sitting on a burro, suckling Jesus. Beside her Joseph is standing, holding the reins in one hand and looking over a stone wall into the distance, where Herod's men are simultaneously Massacring the Innocents and being befuddled by the infant Jesus' Miracle of the Corn. It's painted with skill, but what Cosmo loved—even years ago, when he first saw the painting—was the way the unknown painter had posed Joseph's other hand—the one that wasn't holding the reins—in the act of reaching out toward Mary and the baby. The composition had placed it at the very center of the painting, a gesture that seemed at once fleeting and yet a pledge of protection and comfort. This, while in the distance Herod's men ran their swords through the bellies of babies, threw a little boy in a red hat out an upper-story window, stood laughing in a semicircle around the gaping mouth of a stone well. What, really, the Master of the Roses seemed to ask, could the merely human Joseph do in the face of that butchery? But still, there it was, the hand moving toward Mary, toward the baby at her breast.

When Ann comes back with Giovanni (see? no maniac),

they pick up their stroll, edge along the Palazzo Ducale. The whole day long he has seen bits and pieces of Cathy disappearing around a corner, vanishing in the crowd, a glimpse of her shoulder, her ashy hair in a sea of brown. He figures it's just part of the miracle, like the floating buildings. Memory reified. Why not? It's Heaven, after all (though why you can't talk to the dead, why they won't even look at you, ought to have given Cosmo pause, were he in a pausing mood). But oh, there's the café where he and Cathy used to meet, the jewelry shop where they'd once oohed over a gold bracelet. If he sees her there now, leaning on a display case—there! in that plaid retro skirt she'd worn that winter!—if he sees her now, it's just the machinery of Heaven, a miracle little Giovanni tosses off with a kick of his foot while studying his own miraculous fingernails.

Outside the basilica are vendors selling crucifixes, rosaries, pictures of the Smiling Pope. They pause at one and Cosmo looks for a family resemblance, looks from the Smiling Pope to his smiling love to the frowning baby. *Il papa*'s grandson. You can see it in the eyes.

Time to take stock. They have no clothes, no money except for what they changed into lira at Fiumicino. And just in case they're not actually in Heaven, they don't dare use Ann D'Angelo's Visa card for fear that someone somewhere will track them down. (Are there not still dark forces? Shadows leaping across the Atlantic in search of them?) The few concierges they had inquired of that morning had laughed themselves silly. (Rooms? On New Year's Eve? Get out with you!) Then there are the bodily necessities: Cosmo needs a shave; the baby needs a bath; Ann needs a feminine hygiene product. But it doesn't matter. When night falls they will find their way back to the crèche. And if not, no matter, another manger will materialize, another bowl of milk in the morning.

But not to take miracles for granted, Cosmo had earlier that day checked out the quick-draw artists in the piazza, then the copyists in the courtyard outside the Gallerie dell'Accademia, getting a feel for the competition. In a week or two he will get himself an easel, brushes, and paints, and he will set up shop on the ancient brick across the way from the Gallerie. He has a family to support. And anyway, he can paint circles around these Italians.

This will be the authentic Cosmo Dust; he will refuse to copy. But what he'll do is this: He'll replace the face of the virgin from Nazareth with the face of the virgin from Lawrence, Kansas; Titian's Joseph with the carpenter from Tennessee; the baby faces of various putti with the shortstop and center fielder of the Lexington Little League Angels. He will speak to the Americans in an English charmed with an Italian accent. *Eetsa no problem, signora!* And his specialty will be this, *this* will be what he becomes known for: When a young woman and a child come to him he will insist that they let him paint them in the pose of the seventeenth-century Dustini Madonna and Child. Never heard of Cosimo Dustini? *Si, si! He leeve over there!* with a wave at an ancient window across the courtyard. He will lift the red velvet curtain on the easel beside him and show how maestro Dustini caught his Madonna and Child just at the moment when the infant Jesus, bursting with life, has stood up in his mother's lap and is laughing. The Blessed Virgin has her hands around his waist, steadying him, scolding him with a smile of loving disapproval. There is something reckless in the infant's posture. His feet wobble on his mother's thigh. His arms are thrown open as if he means to embrace the world, everything, whatever is there just outside the canvas's frame. *Grazie, no, signora*—not for sale. *But prego*, and he will point to her own baby's fat calves, then to the Dustini Child's fat calves, to the ruddy skin, the hair, the pupils with tiny points of light at their centers. *Everyone a messiah!* he will cry out like a carnival barker, and he will take the woman by the shoulders and plant her on a chair, Jesus in her lap, wonder on her face, grace in the sunlight skipping off the building fronts. *Everyone a messiah*, he will say to himself over and over while he begins the pencil layout, smiling like a simpleton.

Now, the sun is beginning to set. The shops are closing. Around every corner comes a Lucretia, a Scaramouche on his way to the millennium celebration in the piazza. Against the current, Cosmo and Ann go up and over this little bridge, that little byway. There are still splashes of sunlight in the courtyards, patches of dusty gold on the brown canal water. Between the rooftops above the narrow *calli* the sky is turning violet. In a tiny grocery they purchase some food for the evening, some fontina cheese and prosciutto, a bottle of Valpolicello, some almond biscotti for little Giovanni to try his teeth on. On a news rack they catch sight of a headline in *La Repubblica*: the Kenotic Messiah has been taken into custody. Or taken captive by his own people. Cosmo's Italian isn't good enough to say which. There's something about crucifixion in the sub-headline, and there's a photo that shows him in the hands of the kenotically garbed, but they could be undercover agents. When

Ann starts to lift the paper to see what's below the fold, Cosmo places his hand over hers, shakes his head no, as if to prevent any communication from the Earth. Or maybe the counter-Earth. Wherever it is they're not. Agreed?

The grocer hand-slices a piece of *sopressata* salami for them to try. *"Signora,"* he says, and hands the meat to Ann. "Made een Veneto," he says and smiles. Everyone smiles.

Back outside there is a steady stream of people coming from the direction of the railway station. Cosmo and Ann try to continue against the current but finally turn and let themselves be swept along, back toward San Marco. There are signs and posters everywhere for the millennium celebration. A children's carnival. An Erotic Poetry Festival. Fireworks. A Passion Play. The Grand Zuppino is performing magic of Air, Fire, and Water! There's to be a Lover's Auction, a Circus Without Animals, the Doge's Ball with the Boomerang Orchestra! When the narrow street they have been going down opens out into a small *campo* they step out of the procession, find a stone stoop to sit on, and spread their picnic around them. The passersby laugh and smile as Cosmo uses his plastic knife and fork from the airplane to cut the meat and cheese. Alas! they have no corkscrew . . . but of course, it's only a few minutes before a tuxedoed waiter on his way to work sees Cosmo trying to dig out the cork with the point of a pen, and—*signore!*— whips out his waiter's corkscrew, pops the cork, spreads a handkerchief over his forearm, and with a professional flourish pours for them. He places the bottle on the stone step and begins to back away. *"Bene, bene!"* he says, laughing, winking at beautiful Ann. *"Felice nuovo anno!"* And he salutes, spins about, and disappears around a corner.

They sit for a long, long time, watching the people pass. The stone feels wonderfully cold under them. In addition to Lucretia and Pulcinella, there are Elvis and the Pope. There's Mussolini, and a squad of Blackshirts. The Fab Four in black suits, black boots. Cosmo, in an uprush of love, well-being, disbelief, kisses Ann, touches her breast when he thinks there's a break in the crowd. Someone applauds. Giovanni wiggles, wakes, falls back to sleep.

Sometime toward midnight—after they've watched a street-corner fire-eater, a pantomime horse singing Sinatra, *tableaux vivants* in the Campo San Luca—they find they have circled back to the Piazza San Marco. Even during *Carnavale* Cosmo has never seen so many people there. There's no place to sit so they just stand near the clock tower, trading Giovanni back and forth when their arms get tired. Above them the Madonna and Child sit in their niche, blue enamel and gold stars behind them. From amplified speakers somewhere in the piazza comes the sound of the archbishop celebrating midnight Mass in the basilica. There are troupes of jugglers, mimes, singers, but they've all quit performing. Everyone has quit—Cosmo and Ann, too. Madame Recamier has wandered over from her *tableau vivant*. They are all waiting. Out on one of the islands in the lagoon, fireworks go haphazardly aloft, explode, and fall back to Earth. They sound like gunshots.

Here's a fourth option: They are in an intermittency, after all. Inside the turbulence still, but on an island of order, beauty, restoration. Somehow—by what magic? what miracle?—the elements of the strange attractor, at the very instant in the Venetian when the gun was fired, found themselves—like schoolkids playing musical chairs—

absurdly back in their original positions. The world had cycled back, through some impossibly complex factoring of Earth and counter-Earth, Venetian and Venice, Cathy and Candi, and there was nothing to do but sit back down in your original chair. Sit back down and let Cosmo Dust remain standing in his old world of love, happiness, harmony.

And yet . . .

He looks uneasily at the carnival costumes, at the masks and mummery, and admits what he has been avoiding for the last hour or so: They are all here—the members of the possibility cloud, their agents and assigns, spies and stooges—strolling about the piazza, loitering under the blue enamel on the Torre dell'Orologio. They have either followed him here or they have always been here, have always been everywhere. Tucked away in an intermittency they are taking a breather, waiting for the clock to strike twelve, for the new millennium to begin, for the music to start up again. Even now, down in its lower frequencies, the equation is crunching numbers, cycling, recycling, moving toward the iteration that will bring them back to life.

A pantomime burro wanders past, gives Cosmo the stink-eye, and disappears into the crowd.

Someone somewhere has started the countdown—*ten, nine*—but it peters out. It's not time yet. From out on the lagoon comes the quack of an air horn. Cosmo tries to swallow, but the paralysis he'd felt a day ago in that other Piazza San Marco—the stung, voiceless feeling—is back. He wants to call out to Ann—whether for help or to warn her, he doesn't know—but he can't. In his arms, the baby feels like deadweight.

And then, from across the square like a wave moving

through the crowd, comes the real countdown. *Ten . . . nine . . . eight . . .* Through a break in the people he thinks he sees a mime dressed as the Doge. Thinks he sees the pearl-gray suit Cathy's killer wore. *Seven . . .* And he has the thought that when they get to *zero* he will be translated back to Las Vegas. That the whole intermittency—Madonna, manger, milk—has taken place in the time between when the gun went off and when the bullet reaches him. *Six . . .* That even now the bullet is speeding toward him, and it is only a matter of time—of seconds!—before the equation recombines and the bullet hits him. *Five . . . four . . .* For a full second his mind is frozen. *Three . . .* And it's then that Giovanni lets out a squeal of laughter, kicks himself upright, and throws himself toward the crowd. *Two . . .* Ann reaches out to catch him, presses him back into Cosmo's chest, and the two of them watch as the baby raises his hand in a gesture of benediction, forefinger to thumb, blessing the carnival before him—the grimacing faces, the misshapen, the empty, the parodic, the profane, as if he can see through it all to the sacred life beneath. *One . . .* Behind them there spreads a field of blue enamel, golden stars.

About the Author

GREGORY BLAKE SMITH is the author of two previous novels, *The Devil in the Dooryard* and *The Divine Comedy of John Venner*, which was selected by *The New York Times Book Review* as one of the year's Notable Books. He lives in Northfield, Minnesota, where he teaches American literature and creative writing at Carleton College.

a novel

THE Madonna OF Las Vegas

Gregory Blake Smith

Reading Group Guide

About the Book

It's the hair-raising countdown to a new millennium, and Cosmo Dust watches in dismay as the wreckage of his life comes into garish focus in the phantasmagoric glow of Las Vegas. Abandoned by his wife—whose death via a poisoned Easter egg has flummoxed Cosmo's sense of a moral universe—he is spending his days frescoing a faux–Sistine Chapel ceiling and flirting with the myriad opportunities Vegas offers for self-annihilation.

When a seductive femme fatale and a minxish, trick-turning cocktail waitress simultaneously barge into Cosmo's misery, he finds his world—and *the* world—turned inside out. Suddenly he's a murder suspect, a foster father, a fugitive hunted by both the Jewish and Italian mafiosi, and the unlikely partner of a woman whose identity becomes more inscrutable with each passing day. Is she Annunciata D'Angelo, daughter of the late Pope John Paul I? Ann D'Angelo, daughter of a dying mob despot? Or just Susan Kane, plain Jane from Darlington, Wisconsin? And does it matter? Cosmo and . . . let's call her Ann . . . must escape the clutches of the cops, the bad guys, the coming apocalypse, the tendency for all things Vegas to spiral toward entropy, and—most importantly of all—their own pasts if they are to have any hope of creating new lives in a new world.

It's safe to say that this metaphysical shimmy through Cosmo's cosmos, complete with anti-earths, multiple messiahs, and capricious dark forces playing with fate, is unlike anything you've read before. This guide is designed to enhance your reading group's discussion of *The Madonna of Las Vegas*.

Questions for Discussion

1. Packed with subterfuge, comic sleight of hand, and metaphysical subtexts, what challenges does this novel pose for discussion? What stable point of reference—Cosmo's love for Cathy? his horror at the degenerate culture of the Strip?—can you find to help anchor your response to the novel? Consider the first chapter: How does its polarities—Cosmo standing in line to commit suicide while remembering how he and Cathy met and married in Venice—lay the groundwork for the conflict in the book?

2. Cosmo is obsessed with the false, using words such as *inauthenticity*, *parody*, *caricature*, *plagiarism*, *mockery*, and *desecration* to describe not only Las Vegas but his life and the world at large. What trappings of the false does Cosmo purposely surround himself with? To what extent does Cosmo find comfort in the absurdity of his life? Does his relationship with Ann allow him to transcend this pattern by the end of the novel, or does their union represent a total surrender to "plagiarism"?

3. As Cosmo works on the faux–Sistine Chapel ceiling, he considers Dante Alighieri's concept of *contrapasso*, "the idea that the nature of one's punishment in the afterlife would be derived from the nature of one's sins in the earthly life" (p. 39). What specific "sin" from Cosmo's marriage haunts him? What does he perceive as his corresponding punishment? What about the narrator's suggestion: "Or was he just hopelessly in need of moral symmetry? Cosmo Dust jury-rigging a sin to match the suffering. All by way of preserving the security of moral cause and effect because guilt was an easier row to hoe than the blank of undeserved suffering" (p. 40)?

4. As one critic sees it, Smith's work is a "blend of comic buffoonery and subtle seriousness." And, indeed, at the heart of this layered, operatic, multidimensional story is the tale of one man's quest for salvation among the everyday. How do you rec-

oncile the more extravagant elements of the novel with its central longing for the ordinary: man, woman, and child?

5. One thing a reader of *The Madonna of Las Vegas* must come to terms with is the novel's use of Roman Catholic iconography. Is it blasphemous? Reverential? Or just another element of Western Civilization to be used for decorative purposes along the Strip? How does the religious imagery help carry the novel's meaning?

6. A recurring motif in the book is CNN and its continuing coverage of "the Apocalypse." How does the idea of apocalypse—the destruction of the world and the salvation of the few—work metaphorically in the novel?

7. At one point, Cosmo thinks the mafia should be put in the Smithsonian. The novel is filled with references to icons of American culture. What other ones can you identify? Do they exist in a pure state, or are they qualified or even debased in some way?

8. Kenotic theology is a controversial branch of Christology that emerged in the nineteenth century, rooted in St. Paul's letter to the Philippians. The gist of kenosis is the idea that Christ deliberately emptied himself of his divinity and all its privileges in order to live a fully human life. What role does the Kenotic Messiah play in the novel? How is the idea of kenosis—the emptiness out of which something comes—important to the novel?

9. How far does the author take the pervasive concept of "symbol and referent. The thing itself and its parody" (p. 18)? What characters, scenes, settings, actions can be seen as derivative of some more authentic original? What might the author be saying about the contemporary world?

10. Cosmo repeatedly refers to the baby as a "messiah" and describes him as performing miracles and having been "sent to save." When and why does he begin to refer to Ann as a messiah

as well? In what way can the novel be read as a parody of a nativity narrative?

11. As Cosmo waits for Ann and the baby in the piazza of the Venetian, he is mesmerized by the statue of the Madonna. "She, too, was caught in all this. A bizarre fate! . . . he couldn't rid himself of the power in the image. Her, caught in all this. . . . The inclined head, the soft face, the folds of her clothing, the compassion. *Caught in all this*" (p. 247). What does the author intend with the repeated phrase "caught in all this"? What epiphany about love does Cosmo attribute to this encounter with the statue? Why does it immediately precede Cosmo's ominous visit by the maitre d' (Cathy's apparent killer)?

12. Cosmo and Ann's refusal to be swayed by the maitre d' and his insistence on their cosmic codependence with him—"We penetrate. We depend" (p. 257)—represents the first time they have said no to fate. What gives them the strength to do so? What chain reaction does this act of self-determination set up?

13. A conventional murder mystery ends with the reader's learning who the murderer is, but in this book we never really learn who killed Candi. Indeed, suspects seem to multiply as the story progresses. Why? How does the book both fulfill and subvert the conventions of the murder mystery?

14. Venice occupies an important place in the novel. It is where Cathy and Cosmo first fall in love; its Las Vegas incarnation embodies the decadence of the Strip; and it is where Ann and Cosmo flee to make a new life. Discuss Venice as a symbol that carries some of the novel's thematic freight. How do you read the ending? Is it a conventionally happy ending? In what way does the millennium celebration with its masks and masquerade color the final scene?